When the Carny Comes to Town

ELAINE ORR

ISBN-13: 978-1-948070-68-3
Library of Congress Control Number: 2018902180

When the Carny Comes to Town is a work of fiction.

When the Carny Comes to Town
ELAINE ORR

When the Carny Comes to Town is licensed for your personal enjoyment and may not be duplicated in any form.

Discover all books in the Jolie Gentil Series

Appraisal for Murder
Rekindling Motives
When the Carny Comes to Town
Any Port in a Storm
Trouble on the Doorstep
Behind the Walls
Vague Images
Ground to a Halt
Holidays in Ocean Alley
The Unexpected Resolution
Underground in Ocean Alley
Sticky Fingered Books
New Lease on Death
The Twain Does Meet (novella)
Jolie and Scoobie High School Misadventures (prequel)

Look for the **Family History Mystery Series**,
set in the Maryland mountains.

❧

elaineorr.com

elaineorr.blogspot.com

Dedication

*To Aunt Tancy, who helped me win a plate
at my first carnival.*

Acknowledgements

Thanks to my husband, Jim Larkin, for insisting that I take the time to write what I want. I am grateful to my friend Lynn Gordon, whose comments on an early draft were especially helpful. And to her dogs Cheyenne and Legend, who taught Mr. Rogers and Miss Piggy a couple of tricks. The Iowa State Fair is the best in the nation. Thanks to the fair for providing several photos of the Midway. The cover of the first edition used one of those photos. Mrs. Leanora Kensil had many wonderful expressions. In her memory, one is used in When the Carny Comes to Town.

Chapter One

I SHOULD NEVER HAVE BET WITH SCOOBIE. I guess I could have bet about what color Aunt Madge's hair would be on St. Patrick's Day, but I should have insisted on a different wager. Whatever.

Here I am, sitting on the plank above the dunk tank at St. Anthony's spring carnival. OK, it's for a good cause. But at this point, it could be to save all the whales on the planet and I wouldn't...

Kerplash!

And who the hell said we shouldn't heat the dunk tank?

When my head came above the water line the loudest laugh was from Aunt Madge. Since she spent more than twenty dollars trying to dunk me, I wasn't surprised that she was so pleased. *I'll get her later.*

I swam the two strokes to the small ladder and George Winters reached down to give me a lift out of the tank. Honest, I didn't plan it. It was a natural reaction to all the stupid things he's said about me in the *Ocean Alley Press*. George kind of catapulted over me, somersault style, and there was a really loud splash.

I moved up the ladder as I heard George break the surface. "I'll get your ass Jolie Gentil! You owe me a new phone!"

If I had planned it I'd feel guilty about him ruining his mobile phone. But, I didn't plan it, so no pangs of remorse. Not now anyway. *Maybe when I read the paper tomorrow.*

"All right, Jolie!" Scoobie scrambled up from where he'd been sitting on the ground laughing his tail off and hurried to steady the small ladder that led down from the dunk tank. He knew I wouldn't pull him in. I wanted to get as far away from George Winters as I could in ten seconds or so.

I accepted the towel from Reverend Jamison and kept moving.

I made it to the ladies room before George could catch me. Since we were on church property he didn't follow me in. Just before I slammed the door I heard Father Teehan tell George to watch his language.

I was sitting on a toilet, bent over laughing, when the door to the restroom opened. I looked under the stall and saw Ramona's ankle-length skirt. Since I hadn't latched the booth door, she stuck her head in.

"I can't believe you did that." Her large eyes were wider than ever. "I mean, I can believe you'd want to, but at a church carnival..." Her voice trailed off and she grinned at me. "You know you'll pay for it."

"It was worth it." I wrapped the already wet towel around my hair and grinned back at her. Ramona is a lot taller than my five feet two inches, so from my sitting position I had to lean my head back to look at her. "If he hadn't written about the hospital giving me a donut cushion when I broke my tailbone I might ignore him."

The door to the restroom opened again. "Jolie." It was Scoobie. "It's safe. Winters went home to change."

Ramona moved back so I could stand and lean out of the stall to look at Scoobie, or rather Scoobie's head, complete with wet beard. He knew better than to walk all the way in. "You're setting me up. He's out there."

Scoobie had the decency not to look offended. "If I could get away with it, I'd help him throw you back in the tank, but he really did leave." He looked behind him and then back at Ramona and me. "I think Reverend Jamison wants to talk to you." Scoobie left.

Reverend Jamison is the main reason I'm sopping wet. He's the minister at First Presbyterian, where Aunt Madge has gone to church for forty years and I now chair the food pantry committee. OK, he's one of the reasons. Having a dunk tank fundraiser at St. Anthony's spring carnival was Scoobie's idea. All the churches in town contribute to the food pantry, so Father Teehan was glad to have us.

As fundraisers go, it was a good one. The last time I saw the list there were more than forty people who'd agreed to sit on the plank and have people try to hit the lever that would throw them into the four-foot deep, soft-side swimming pool.

I pulled the towel off my head and threw it over my shoulder. "I guess I better go face the music." I looked at Ramona. "And I don't believe you have a cold."

Ramona has a strong sense of style, which I do not. I'm perfectly happy in khakis or jeans. She makes a lot of her clothes because she favors the tie-dye skirts and loose-crocheted vests that were popular in the early 1970s, and she wears them well. I had known all along she'd find a reason not to get dunked.

She shrugged. "We make more money if I keep doing my caricatures."

She's right. She usually does them on the boardwalk in the summer, but the chair of the St. Anthony's carnival asked her to do her charcoal pencil drawings at the carnival, and she agreed if half the money could go to the food pantry.

The first person I saw when I walked out was Scoobie. He was still grinning. Instead of his usual jeans and t-shirt, today he was wearing a pair of 1900s-style swimming trunks with horizontal stripes, which hit him below the knees, and a top from the same era. Aunt Madge made them for him.

I looked around. "Where's Reverend Jamison?" I eyed Scoobie with suspicion.

"I lied. Come on, they got the cotton candy machine working again. I'll get some for both of you."

"Uh uh. My clothes are in my car. I'm changing first."

He shrugged. "OK. Come on, Ramona. Miss Party Pooper can find us when she dries off." He studied me for a couple seconds. "You might want to comb your hair while you're at it."

I threw the towel at him.

TWENTY MINUTES LATER my shoulder-length hair was as dry as it was going to get without a hair dryer and my wet clothes were in the trunk of my car in a plastic bag.

"Hey, Jolie."

I knew the person didn't know me too well, since he mispronounced my name. Jolie Gentil is a French name. The J and G are soft and the L at the end of Gentil is silent. Translated my name means "pretty nice." My French Canadian father is very proud of his novel naming idea. I am not, but it's my name so I live with it.

I looked closer and recognized the owner of our small beach town's in-town grocery store. He knows me, since I hit him up for donations to the food pantry, but I guess I've never clarified the pronunciation for him. "Hey, Mr. Markle. Glad you could get away."

"I'm on my way back to the store." He waved as he kept walking toward his car. "I heard you were going on the plank at one, and I was going to try to knock you off."

"How nice of you." I can't be rude, he does give us food.

My car was almost a block from the church parking lot, which houses the carnival, so I had a chance to take a good look at the entire carnival as I made my way back. The Ferris wheel is visible for blocks, but you can't see most of the other rides and booths until you get closer. A few years ago St. Anthony's built a new church on the edge of Ocean Alley, and there are a bunch of larger pine trees that surround three sides of the grounds. Aunt Madge said they used bingo money to buy the big lot.

There were more than a dozen colorful canopies along the edge of the carnival, each one housing a so-called game, such as throw-a-dart-to-pop-a balloon-and-you-win-a-plastic-snake or — if you win enough — a stuffed animal. I've played these games enough times that I know the darts or softballs are weighted oddly so you have a hard time winning.

I smiled to myself. When I was about five, I wanted to win a little doll by throwing a coin onto one of many small plates sitting on a low-level table a couple feet away. Every coin skidded off until Aunt Madge gave me a nickel. I won the doll and Aunt Madge told me years later that all the plates had a tiny bit of cooking oil rubbed on them, so the coins would skid off. She had slyly spit on a nickel and rubbed it in a bit of the sawdust we were standing on, so it didn't skid. My aunt, a pillar of propriety.

"Ladies and gents." The loud speaker carried the voice of the carnival's manager for blocks. He gets on the PA system about every five minutes. *I wish he'd get laryngitis.*

"Ladies and gents. You haven't eaten even half the foot-long hot dogs. You can't come to a carnival without eatin' a dog." His voice droned on.

I got to the edge of the carnival and carefully looked through the crowd. No George Winters. He's the main reporter for the *Ocean Alley Press*, and he likes to mention that in the six months since I moved into Aunt Madge's Bed and Breakfast I've had a role in solving two local murders.

It's not my fault. A real estate appraiser is in a lot of houses every week. I didn't put the bodies there, especially the skeleton in the Fisher's attic.

My gaze found Scoobie. He was holding the large mallet used to hit a platform to try to make a metal ball go up the pole and make a bell gong. He was imitating a body builder's stance as he showed off muscles. Ramona and Jennifer Stenner were pretending to feel his biceps.

I shook my head slightly and smiled. Scoobie is not a tough guy. Not in the physical sense, that is. In the almost eleven years since we finished high school Scoobie has fought back from alcoholism and an affinity for pot that put him in the county jail a couple times. As he once told me, he's eventually trainable and he decided to stop periodically boarding with the county.

I only went to Ocean Alley High for junior year. I stayed with Aunt Madge while my parents "worked some things out" in their marriage. I was not happy being here then, so it might seem odd that I came back after my now ex-husband Robby was arrested for supporting his gambling habit by embezzling money from the bank where he worked. I came to Aunt Madge, not the town, but the town is growing on me.

A wolf whistle caught my attention and I turned around to see if it was aimed at me. Lance Wilson is the food pantry treasurer. He's also close to ninety, so some would say he should have a bit more decorum. I would not be one of those.

He raised a small ledger into the air. "More than $400 already."

"Wow. That's really good. Who would have thought?" Certainly not me. It's the only time I've agreed with Sylvia Parrett, one of our more rigid-thinking food pantry committee members. I would never have expected so many people to sign up to be dunked. The fact that local election primaries are next month helped. Even the guy running unopposed for coroner agreed to sit above the tank.

Lance caught up to me and we stood watching the crowd for a moment. "So far you're the biggest income source, but I hear Annie Milner and Martin Small are lining up a lot of people."

Annie and I didn't really know each other in high school, but I much prefer her as the candidate to be the county's next prosecuting attorney. Small is the current one and he's a jerk and a half. "What about Jennifer?" I asked. Jennifer Stenner went to high school with us and manages to always look like she walked off a movie set. One where she has a role as a fashion goddess.

Lance smiled slightly. "She gave me a check for twenty-five dollars and said she had other responsibilities today so she couldn't get dunked."

I tried to turn my snort into a polite laugh. "Good for her."

Lance walked left, toward the dunk tank, and I continued toward the "High Striker" gong ringer game. Aunt Madge was watching Scoobie, and I considered sneaking up and goosing her, but that would be childish. And there were too many people around. She turned toward me as I walked up.

"I still have eyes in the back of my head, you know."

"No you don't." I nodded ahead of her. "You saw me in that big mirror."

"The jig is up." Aunt Madge looked toward the large mirror that distorts the images of anyone peering in it. She turned back to watch Scoobie try to get the ball up to the gong.

I stared at Aunt Madge for a second. She's actually my Grandmother Alva's sister, though she's a lot less strict than my grandmother was. At five feet six inches, Aunt Madge is about four inches taller than I am and she keeps her hair in a soft French twist. Today it's black, but not the deep black that's popular with teens and college kids. She doesn't use permanent color, so she can change it at least once a month. I don't know if it's the hair color or her continued use of her carpentry skills, but she doesn't look even close to her eighty-plus years.

The thud of the mallet hitting the bottom of the tower drew my attention back to Scoobie. "You can get higher than that!" I hollered to him.

He grinned at me and handed the carnival worker another dollar. "One for my friend with the loud mouth."

"And the wet head," Ramona added. A couple people laughed.

After another try, Scoobie announced he was just practicing and would be back in a few minutes to show off his real stuff. We hung around to watch Ramona, who diplomatically insisted she did not hit the ball higher than Scoobie.

We trailed each other to a food booth and sat at a rickety picnic table near the booth. Ramona and I split a foot-long dog while Scoobie polished off one on his own. We could see the food pantry dunk tank from where we sat, and in between bites commented on the prowess, or lack of it, of the ball throwers.

"While you were changing they tried to get Dr. Welby to take a toss at the guy who runs the eyeglass place," Scoobie said.

Ramona laughed. "Dr. Welby said he couldn't see well enough to hit him."

I nodded, still chewing. Dr. Welby (who tells you as soon as you meet him not to make fun of his name) is retired and serves on the First Prez food pantry committee. He's a take-charge kind of person, which is my favorite kind of volunteer.

Jennifer Stenner sat down next to Scoobie and jumped back up again. "It's wet." She carefully adjusting her perfectly ironed capris.

"It's just iced tea," Scoobie told her, and winked at me as he leaned over to mop up what looked to be a very small bit of tea.

"Thanks," Jennifer said as she sat down again. "I've been working at the bake sale tables and I needed a break."

"Too tempting to eat the fattening food?" I asked her.

"I have plenty of self-discipline, I'm just tired of standing."

I did an inside-the-mind eye roll. Jennifer is precise about everything. "Why don't you try the high-striker thing? Scoobie's looking for a partner."

"Am not," he said, and looked at Jennifer. "I wouldn't want to be too hard on you."

Ramona choked on her last bite and Scoobie gave her a quick pat on the back. "Come on, you guys, I'm going back to the gong for another try."

We picked up our used napkins and cups and headed over, minus Jennifer who said she'd sit a bit longer. We were almost back to the "High Striker" when Scoobie came to a sudden stop and I walked into his backside. "What are you...," I began before I caught a look at his expression.

Though Scoobie says he doesn't like being around a lot of people on a regular basis, you don't generally see him get really mad at anyone. He's more likely to leave the Java Jolt coffee shop than argue with its owner, Joe Regan, who seems to like to needle Scoobie. Right now he looked ready to hit someone and I noticed he clinched his fist for a second. I followed his gaze to the High Striker, which was now under the watchful eye of different carnival worker. A worker who was looking directly at Scoobie with a smirk on his face.

Scoobie took an abrupt left. "I'm tired of that game. Let's go bowling."

Ramona and I looked at each other and followed him to the bowling game. We've both known Scoobie long enough to expect him to work out his moods in his poetry, so we don't usually ask about what gets to him. After beating both of us hands down he seemed back to a happier self. Plus, he had won Ramona and me both medium-size stuffed animals, mine being a spotted dog that looked like a cross between a cat and a Dalmatian.

THE CARNIVAL STARTS AT NOON and ends about ten o'clock. I hadn't been to it since eleventh grade, back when it was held in the large public parking lot by the ocean. New Jersey beaches are crowded from Memorial Day until well after Labor Day, which is why it's a spring carnival. We appreciate the tourists, most of the time, but the carnival is largely a townie event. Anyone can come, of course. It's like bingo. The Catholics will take anyone's money, just like the Presbyterians will take it for a quilt raffle or bake sale.

I'd certainly never stayed all ten hours, but since the dunk tank was benefiting the food pantry I thought I should stick around and hand towels to the dunkees. If Lance could stay that long so could I. However, I insisted that he not be one of the people on the step ladder to refasten the banner reading "Harvest for All Food Pantry." The banner graced the wall behind the dunk tank. It's new. We had a contest to give the food pantry a formal name. Scoobie had several suggestions, all of them printable, none really appropriate. "Nuggets for Nourishment" was his self-proclaimed favorite. The winning entry was submitted by a fifth-grader who saw a sign about the contest at the library.

I helped Reverend Jamison steady the ladder while a church member I didn't know placed the banner's holes back over a couple hooks. I kept looking around for Scoobie and Ramona. I figured they were trying a last round at the High Striker, since Ramona still topped Scoobie's best effort by almost a foot. That's what walking two miles a day on the sand and lifting boxes in the Purple Cow will do for you.

Ramona wandered over with her sketch pad and pencil box just as I was getting ready to leave. "Where's Scoobie?" she asked.

I shrugged. "Thought you guys were back whacking the mallet."

"Nope. I finally let him win." She walked toward my car with me.

"Somehow I doubt that's how he'll portray it."

"Probably not," she agreed.

It was a clear night with little breeze and almost a full moon. We were a few blocks from the ocean so I couldn't smell it, but I figured the surf would be calm. "You want a ride?" I asked this as I avoided stepping in a blob of hotdog and mustard that looked as if it might have been in someone's stomach previously.

Ramona lives about ten blocks from the Purple Cow, the office supply store where she works. She doesn't own a car and doesn't seem to miss one. However, it was late and St. Anthony's was almost a mile from her apartment. I was glad she accepted my offer. Even in Ocean Alley it's probably not smart for a woman to walk by herself through town this late when there's hardly anyone else on the streets.

After I dropped off Ramona I headed for the Cozy Corner B&B and the room I share with my cat Jazz. When I first came to Ocean Alley from Lakewood, New Jersey my little black cat had been my biggest concern. Aunt Madge has two shelter-adopted dogs, Mr. Rogers and Miss Piggy. I was worried that Jazz would be constantly fearful of the two exuberant part-retrievers. No worries. She terrorizes Mr. Rogers by jumping on his back for a ride a couple times a day. Miss Piggy either ignores Jazz or races around Aunt Madge's great room so fast that Jazz does not enjoy her perch. Aunt Madge enjoys these antics even less, but she puts up with all of us.

Chapter Two

I WAS UP EARLY SATURDAY MORNING, since I had a couple things to do before going back to the carnival at noon and I had wanted to take a short jog on the boardwalk. When I got back, Aunt Madge had already served breakfast to her six guests, all of whom were in town for the carnival. I heard her laughing with them and remembered a couple guests were people who used to live in Ocean Alley.

It was a sunny Saturday. After my shower I gulped orange juice and inhaled one of Aunt Madge's date muffins before I thought about checking the *Ocean Alley Press*.

The paper sat on Aunt Madge's large oak kitchen table, and it had a long article about the carnival and a bunch of pictures, but none of me. George had a great one of Ramona whamming the mallet onto the platform, and the caption noted she had done better than any other woman who tried to make the ball hit the gong. I smiled. Ramona wouldn't like the photo, since her face was screwed up in concentration.

"Nuts." I was almost to the end of the article, thinking I'd made George mad enough not to mention me, when I saw the reference to "a spoiled sport" who had pulled "this reporter and his phone" into the dunk tank. Since the next sentence mentioned the food pantry as the sponsor of the dunk tank I figured anyone who knew me would guess who the spoiled sport was. "Oh well."

"Saw the article, did you?" Aunt Madge came through the swinging door that connects the kitchen with the guest breakfast room. She was carrying a tray of used coffee cups and I jumped up to take them from her.

"Yep, could be worse."

"Probably will be at some point," she said, in her usual matter-of-fact tone.

"Who were you laughing with?" I asked.

"Audrey and Jeff Inwood. Before they moved to Florida she and I played hearts with a bunch of gals every third Thursday."

"I figured it must be someone you knew pretty well." I walked to the sliding glass door to let the dogs into Aunt Madge's living area, which is a large open space, with the kitchen at one end. Her bedroom and bath are in a separate area behind the kitchen. I call the living area her great room and Aunt Madge calls it her sitting room. "I'll take them for a long walk on the beach tomorrow," I told her.

"You don't do too many appraisals on Saturdays," she commented as she rinsed the cups and placed them in the dishwasher.

"The owners told Harry they both wanted to be there, and I told Harry I didn't mind." Harry Steele owns the small appraisal company I work for. I did appraisal work when I was in college and just after that. I sold commercial real estate the last few years I lived in Lakewood, and hadn't thought about what I would do in Ocean Alley when I left the town where I had become best known as the wife of an embezzler. I consider it good karma that Aunt Madge's friend had just opened a new appraisal business, and she considers it providence. I don't think Harry has an opinion either way. He's glad to have me and I like him a lot.

I make about a tenth of what I did in real estate, but I don't have a lot of expenses and Aunt Madge refuses to let me pay rent. So I weed the small yard and shovel snow, walk the dogs, and volunteer for other odd jobs. She won't let me change the guests' sheets. Aunt Madge is easy-going in most ways, but she's very precise about caring for the B&B guests.

I grabbed an apple on the way out, told Aunt Madge I wasn't sure if I'd be back before going to the carnival, and headed out. The early morning air was crisp and a little chilly. You never know what beach weather will be like in the spring. I turned on the heater in my little Toyota and eased from the B&B's small parking lot into heavier-than-usual traffic on Seashore Street.

As I crossed Conch Street I noticed two men with a grocery store cart full of what was likely all their belongings. It reminded me of the first time I'd seen Scoobie when I came back to Ocean Alley last fall. He was on the boardwalk and had a knapsack on a bench next to him. He was putting duct tape or something like that on one of his shoes, and at first I had thought he was a homeless person, though it was kind of late in the season. Most of the people who live on Ocean Alley's streets in the summer go to a warmer climate after October.

I looked more closely for a moment and saw the grocery cart was from Mr. Markle's store. He wouldn't like that. I made a mental note to find out how the food pantry reaches out to people who have no kitchen to use to prepare any food we give them.

The house I was appraising was in the middle of Ocean Alley. The town runs along the Atlantic Ocean for close to two miles, but it's only twelve blocks deep. Still, there are a lot of homes crammed into this relatively small town, since most of the originally larger lots were subdivided long before the town had any zoning regulations.

I had driven by the large bungalow the day before yesterday, so I had a sense of what I was about to measure and come up with a value for. I had already pulled a couple of comparable recent sales to use as benchmarks. However, when I saw the interior of the house I realized I would have to look for other comps. Ben and Louise McCarthy had upgraded literally any surface that was nailed down, and they'd added a couple of skylights in the back. The house looked like a feature in a decorator magazine. *No wonder they want to be here. Probably want to make sure even the dust mites aren't disturbed. Not that I saw any dust.*

My work took about twice as long as it usually does since the McCarthys followed me from room to room explaining every aspect of the remodeling they'd done over the last eight years. When I began asking them to hold one end of the tape measure they tired of the job and left me alone for the last couple rooms. It didn't take me long to take the digital photos that are part of the appraisal package, and I was out of there by ten-thirty.

I stopped by Harry's house, a Victorian that is perpetually enduring remodeling, which also hosts his office. He was out, so it didn't take me long to enter measurements and other information into the computer and print out a floor plan. I wouldn't be able to go to the courthouse to look at recent comparable sales until Monday.

Footloose and fancy free, as Aunt Madge would say, I drove to the library to see if Scoobie was at his usual table. He has a room in a sort of permanent halfway house on F Street, but he's mostly only there to sleep. His usual haunts are the library, Newhart's Diner and, when he's not too annoyed at Joe Regan, the Java Jolt coffee shop on the boardwalk.

No Scoobie anywhere. I haven't seen as much of him since January. Scoobie's been taking a few courses at the community college to prepare for full-time enrollment in the fall. He wants to become an x-ray tech, which he believes is a job he can do without being around people every minute he's at work. He gets some kind of disability income now because of his long history of depression, and he'll likely get grants for tuition. His proclaimed goal is to "get back to the real world," which seems to mean recovering from what ails him and getting a job.

I decided to bug Ramona for a few minutes. It has to be only a few, as the Purple Cow's owner, Roland, gets mildly annoyed if too many people stop in to chat with Ramona. Half the town does. He's not rude about it, of course, as every visitor is a customer at some time or another. But he gives a pretty good evil eye.

Roland must have given himself the morning off, so I sat in one of the very expensive office chairs on display and gently twirled in circles to watch what was going on while I waited for Ramona to finish with a couple customers. The store was more crowded than on a normal Saturday. Newhart's Diner and the Purple Cow are two places Ocean Alley alums frequent when they are home for a visit. Neither is elegant, but Newhart's has great blue plate specials in the off-season and Roland has free coffee in the store.

Ramona and I had just begun to compare notes on the carnival — which for Ramona is a commentary on what people wore and for me includes a lot of questions about whether Ramona thinks I knew someone from the brief time I lived in Ocean Alley — when a black Ford sedan rolled to the curb outside the store.

"*Uh oh*." I looked at Ramona. "Do you remember me doing anything lately that would annoy Sgt. Morehouse?"

"Don't think so." We watched for a couple seconds while he slammed the car door and walked the short distance to the store.

Sgt. Morehouse and I have a sometimes uneasy relationship. If you can call me trying to get information from him when he wants me to mind my own business a relationship. He's only about ten years older than Ramona and me, which puts him in his late thirties or early forties, though he looks older. He wears more polyester than I do and he can be grouchy when he wants me to go away, but he's done me a couple big favors.

He half opened the door, and barked at us. "I need you two to come with me." As we both looked at him mutely, he added, "Now!"

Ramona gestured one arm in a circle. "I'm the only one here..."

"Roland's coming in."

The back door to the store opened and we heard Roland's voice from the storage area as he walked toward the sales floor. "I'm here. Get going."

Ramona grabbed her purse and I hitched mine on my shoulder. "What the..." I began.

Morehouse interrupted me. "It's Scoobie. He's hurt bad."

Chapter Three

MOREHOUSE SHOUTED DOWN our barrage of questions. "I just got the damn call. I told you what I know." He put the cherry light on his dashboard so we got to the hospital pretty fast. He parked the car at the curb near the emergency entrance and we ran inside.

I'm not sure why I was running. I had no idea where we were going, but wherever Scoobie was I wanted to get there fast.

"He still in there?" Morehouse nodded at the emergency room nurse standing by the "patients only" door as she opened it for us.

"They just took him to surgery."

Morehouse stopped and Ramona and I collided with each other. He pointed to a small room behind the triage desk. "In here."

I was ready to scream at him to tell us what was going on. Ramona doesn't scream, but she looked as confused and scared as I felt.

"Sit." He pointed to two of the six chairs in the small room and pulled one around to face us. "Found him about seven-thirty this morning. He was face-down in the sand under the boardwalk."

Ramona and I both shouted almost the same question. "He was out there all night?!"

Morehouse looked at the nurse, who had followed us into the small room. I realized it must be for families of people who died, since there were booklets about the stages of grief on a table. *Not a good omen.*

"I don't think we know. We can be pretty sure he was injured not too long before he was found." The woman glanced at us and back at Morehouse. "His injuries...I doubt he would have lived through the night."

"What are they operating on?" Ramona asked.

"It's okay," Morehouse said, in response to the nurse's hesitation. "These two and Madge are the same as his family. Couldn't tell you wherever the hell his lazy-assed parents are, anyway."

"There's a head injury," she said slowly. "The doctors want to reduce pressure from swelling."

"They do that here?" I asked. I'd been in this hospital briefly. Though it's been added onto through the years, it's a community hospital, not a place you'd associate with brain surgery.

"Time was of the essence." When she saw the silent tears coursing down my cheeks her tone softened. "He did make it here, that's an important first step."

Morehouse stood up. "Stay here for a second." He left and the nurse followed him.

Ramona and I stared at each other, and she dug in her purse for a handkerchief. I grabbed a tissue from the table.

"Did he stop by to see you and Madge?" she asked in between a couple good blows.

I shook my head.

"Was that a no?" Morehouse asked as he walked back in and sat down. With him was Dana Johnson, who is a more junior officer. Even Jazz would have trouble turning around in the tiny room.

"We left the carnival without him." I looked at Ramona.

"I didn't see him the last hour or so. I was back to my drawings."

"And I was over at the dunk tank," I added.

Dana pulled out a small notebook and began to read from her notes. "We got the call about seven-thirty this morning. Caller wanted paramedics to come to the boardwalk, near the steps close to Java Jolt. Dispatch said the guy who called was pretty calm, had a raspy voice. That's really all we know. Lieutenant Tortino's down there with a couple officers now."

"What did Scoobie say?" Ramona asked.

I glanced at Morehouse and he looked away. I didn't figure Scoobie did any talking if he had brain swelling.

"He wasn't conscious," Dana said, gently.

"So other than you two, who was he with yesterday?" Morehouse commanded.

We kind of played off each other, remembering the day. We both remembered that Scoobie didn't seem to want to go back to the High Striker. I said, "He looked right at the guy, and I'd swear the carnival guy was giving Scoobie a funny look."

Morehouse nodded at Dana. "Find out which one of the carnies that was and talk to him." She left.

Carnies. Why is that familiar? I racked my brain. I could almost hear Scoobie say something about carnies, or carny, or something like that.

"What?" Morehouse asked, looking at me.

"I think Scoobie said something..." I sat up straighter. "We were at Gracie's grandmother's house, on the porch. But...all he said was, like, I should remind him to tell me about his carny days, or something."

"Ocean City, I think," Ramona added, and we both looked at her.

"Ocean City, what?" Morehouse asked.

She shrugged. "He went away for a few months. After the last time he got picked up for smoking pot. Or maybe," she scrunched her face, "maybe it was after the time he got picked up for selling an ounce of pot."

I knew about the pot stuff, but not that Scoobie had left town for a while. "What about Ocean City?" I asked.

"I remember he said he wanted to be near the water but he thought he ought to get away from people here, so he worked at...I don't think a carnival, maybe an amusement park."

Morehouse wrote in his small notebook. "I'll figure it out."

A man I assumed to be a doctor opened the door. "You wanted to talk to me, sergeant?"

Morehouse waved him in. "Whaddya know?" he asked.

"It's not the worst TBI I've seen, but it's a pretty decent one... traumatic brain injury," he said, nodding to Ramona and me.

The door opened and Aunt Madge came in. She still had on the apron she wears when she's making bread for afternoon tea at the B&B. "Is it true?" she asked, almost in a whisper.

"Sit down, Madge." Morehouse gestured to the chair next to him.

We all looked at the doctor, whose name badge said he was Dr. Nobles, and he continued. "It's from a pretty severe blow to the back of the head. An injury like that causes the brain to collide with the skull, and in response the brain will swell. In some cases, the surgeon will do what's called a craniotomy, which means they will reduce the increased intracranial pressure so as to avoid brain damage."

He kind of stumbled over the last few words, which I took to mean he couldn't guarantee Scoobie's brain wasn't already messed up.

"There are choices, but whatever they choose to do, it shouldn't take long to relieve the pressure. But," he glanced at Aunt Madge, as if trying to ascertain who was a close relative. "It will be a…"

"In English, Dr. Nobles," Aunt Madge said. "What is a craniotomy?"

"Please," Ramona said, in a soft voice.

I gave her a tiny smile and we both looked again at the doctor.

"Now this sounds more dangerous than it is, plus keep in mind that there are less invasive methods." He looked at Sgt. Morehouse and then Aunt Madge. "A craniotomy entails drilling holes in the skull. Generally a piece is removed and then placed back when danger of swelling has ended."

"And the less invasive methods?" I asked.

"Another option is to insert a catheter into the brain to drain fluid. Sometimes it can be drained once, other times the doctors put in a shunt so they can use a catheter on more than one occasion."

"But you don't know which for Scoobie?" Sgt. Morehouse asked.

"That's a decision to be made in the operating room, in this case. The good news is that the surgeon who was here today has done both surgeries, many, many times. I'm actually not as concerned about the brain swelling as the back injury, which could be more problematic."

"More than drilling holes in his skull?" Aunt Madge asked.

"The brain is incredibly resilient. Crushed vertebrae in the back maybe not so much." He nodded at Sgt. Morehouse and

Aunt Madge. "We should know fairly soon if there is substantial nerve damage. I'll keep you posted."

What are we, bedpans?

As Dr. Nobles left, Sgt. Morehouse began to tell Aunt Madge what had happened. I didn't bother to wonder how she knew to come to the ER. She knows everyone. Instead, I thought about Scoobie, trying to remember if he had said anything about anybody being mad at him. All I could see was him sitting at the table in the library, head bent over a steno pad, writing his poetry.

"Hey," I said. "If they found him at seven-thirty how come we're just hearing about it?"

"He didn't have any ID on him, and he couldn't tell them who he was. When he first came in apparently they were more focused on his injuries than who he was." Morehouse looked up and then went out to talk to a uniformed officer in the hallway.

After Morehouse left the small room Ramona, Aunt Madge, and I went over yesterday again and rehashed what Morehouse had told us. Nothing made sense. We had been sitting silently for a couple minutes, waiting to know when we could see Scoobie, and I let my thoughts wander.

As far as I know, Scoobie knows half the town but he does not have close friends other than Ramona and me, and I guess Aunt Madge. I certainly never heard him talk about any enemies. A few months ago I would have said I knew a lot about Scoobie's schedule and habits, but since he started taking classes in January I've only seen him a couple times a week. I think I know most people in his life. There's an English teacher at the community college Scoobie said gets mad every time he corrects him on something, but Scoobie hasn't talked about anyone else being annoyed with him.

Who would hurt Scoobie? I remembered the man I thought smirked at Scoobie. Now, of course, it seemed important. But it could have been something simple, like earlier in the day he'd insulted Scoobie about his 1920s-era bathing suit. If Scoobie is uncomfortable with someone he usually walks away, and that's what it looked like he did yesterday with the guy at the High

Striker. All I could remember was that the carnival worker had a swarthy look and a solid build. Probably only about twenty thousand people like that in this part of Jersey.

The woman from the reception desk looked in at us. "You can go up to the third floor. When he gets out of surgery the doctor will want to talk to you." She pointed toward the elevator and added, "Walk right when you get off. You'll see a room called surgery waiting area."

Ramona and I trailed behind Aunt Madge, who knows the hospital as well as she knows every other building in town. There was no one else in the waiting room, so I helped myself to coffee and sat to one side of Ramona. Aunt Madge was on her other side and had a hand on Ramona's knee as she sobbed softly into her handkerchief. We all looked up as a tall man in scrubs and a paper hospital hat walked in.

He sat sideways on the arm of a large chair so he could face all of us. "The head injury could have been a lot worse. If I hadn't been visiting a couple old friends in the hospital ER when they brought him in we would have lost valuable time. I had the exact skills he needed."

I'm not usually keen on people who toot their own horn quite that loudly, but in this case I was thrilled.

"Exactly what is wrong with him?" Aunt Madge asked.

"He has a fractured skull..."

Ramona sobbed harder.

"...which is not as bad as it sounds," he continued, and picked up a small piece of paper and pencil from the table with the coffee and quickly sketched a skull.

I shivered, remembering a real one I'd seen last November.

"It's not a deep fracture, but it did cause swelling, and no injury to the skull can be taken lightly." He drew a tiny line from just below the crown and down an inch. "Judging from the size, I'd guess he was hit with something a couple inches wide. Not good, but it could have been much worse." He pointed to a spot on the drawing. "This is where I drilled a very tiny hole to insert the catheter..."

Aunt Madge grabbed a nearby trash can and shoved it at Ramona in time for her to throw up in it. The doctor walked out and came back a few seconds later with a wad of damp paper towels.

Aunt Madge was already patting her on the back and I was holding her hand, so he didn't say anything, just handed the towels to Aunt Madge, who gave Ramona one to wipe her mouth and placed the others on the back of her neck.

While Aunt Madge helped Ramona I looked at the doctor's name badge. Jacob Goldstein looked about my age, but lines at the corner of his eyes made me think more like mid-thirties. He gave me a small nod and glanced at his watch.

"I'm so sorry," Ramona said, sitting up.

She looked more or less done, so I moved the waste basket and its smelly contents a few feet away from us.

"He's someone you care about," the doctor said quietly. He adopted a more brisk tone as he went back to his drawing, which he had stuck in the pocket of his scrubs. "I'm really not that concerned about the head injury. Twenty-five years ago we had poorer quality imaging and couldn't be as precise when we worked on the brain or skull. They'll watch him closely, probably administer some steroids, which also reduce swelling. He should recover fine."

He leaned against a chair. "He has at least two crushed vertebrae, one cervical, one thoracic. They'll be evaluating him carefully to be sure there is no pressure on nerves along the spinal cord. Someone else will talk to you more about that."

I racked my brain. If cervical was neck area and lumbar was lower spine, thoracic must be in the middle.

"So, he fell?" Aunt Madge asked.

Dr. Goldstein shrugged. "That would be my assumption for the back injuries. If I had to guess I'd say down a flight of steps."

"But," I was groping, "you don't think that's how he hurt his head?"

"Anything is possible," he said, "but I did my neurosurgery residence in Camden and saw enough skulls hit with beer bottles to think it looked familiar." He stood. "I'm on call in Newark this afternoon. I was just down here with my kids for the carnival. If I hadn't stayed to have breakfast at Newhart's Diner I'd have been long gone."

He shook hands with me and then Aunt Madge, ignoring Ramona for probably sanitary reasons. "I expect you'll know the local doctors who will care for him," he said.

Aunt Madge gripped his hand and looked him in the eye. "I will forever regard you as a miracle."

He pulled back his hand and gave her a tap on the shoulder. "I'll tell my wife you said that."

Chapter Four

ANOTHER HOUR PASSED before anyone came to talk to us again. Once Aunt Madge made sure the right people knew where we were waiting she wouldn't let me go bug them. The cleaning person who came to deal with the trash can refused Aunt Madge's offer to buy him a cup of coffee and a roll. "Comes with the territory," was all he said.

Finally a woman in scrubs came in to say Scoobie had been moved to Intensive Care and we could go to the waiting area there. As we took the elevator to the fourth floor I wanted to scream. Didn't they know we needed to see Scoobie right now?

We sat and I scanned the room for the nearest waste basket. Just in case.

After a few moments Ramona got up and walked to the window. She stood looking out for a minute and then turned back to us. "I can't believe this is happening."

Aunt Madge looked at her and then me, and asked her question a bit differently. "You two are sure you don't know anyone mad at him, right?"

I shook my head. "Everybody, even Joe Regan, talks about how great Scoobie's doing, with school, and everything."

"And half of them say it's because of you," Ramona said, nodding at me.

"Me?" I stared at her. "What did I do?"

"Nothing annoying at the moment," Aunt Madge said, dryly.

Ramona shrugged. "You guys had a lot of fun in high school. You know Scoobie's always been..."

"A little different," Aunt Madge threw in.

Ramona nodded. "You guys hung out all the time in junior year, and you do again. You get him." She shrugged.

I knew what she meant. Scoobie and I had talked a couple of times over the winter about how unhappy we both were during eleventh grade — not that we had talked about it back then. For me only that one year was really unhappy. My life was okay once my parents got back together and I went home to Lakewood.

Scoobie won't talk to me much about his life then, but I guess his severely alcoholic mother, to use Aunt Madge's phrase, either ignored him or tried to get him to sneak booze to her when his father was not around, which was a lot of the time. I didn't know this at the time. I just figured he was allowed to be where he wanted to be when he wanted to be there. Aunt Madge, of course, kept a much tighter rein on me, but she went to bed early, so if the weather was halfway warm I'd sneak out.

Before I could say anything a nurse walked in. "Hi, Madge." She leaned against a small table and faced the three of us. "He's doing a lot better than anyone thought he would when he got to the ER, but he's got a long way to go."

"Has he been conscious at all?" Aunt Madge asked.

"Several times he responded to commands to wiggle his toes. And about the third time I asked him to squeeze my hand he scratched his index finger on the sheet, and when I looked at it he made a loose fist and then raised his middle finger at me."

I don't think I've ever cried that hard in my life, not even the night Robby told me he was going to be arrested for embezzling. It was a couple minutes before I could stop, even with Aunt Madge giving me a continual one-armed hug and Ramona pushing tissues at me.

"I'm so sorry," I hiccupped and wiped my sweaty face with a handful of the cheap hospital tissues.

"It's okay," Ramona said. She was kneeling on the floor in front of me and she grinned. "At least you didn't need the waste basket."

WE SET UP A SCHEDULE so one of us would be in the waiting area all the time. After they knew Scoobie could sort of respond to questions they had sedated him again, so we couldn't talk to him. It was supposed to help his brain heal better. The hospital would only let one of us into Scoobie's tiny room at a time, and for only a few minutes an hour. We let Aunt Madge go in first. It was her idea. She would let us know what to expect.

"He's banged up, but his face isn't bruised as badly as I expected, and only one eye is swollen." She thought for a second. "They've sedated him a lot, so he doesn't respond, but the nurse said we shouldn't worry about that." She sat down heavily on one of the stuffed, hard plastic chairs. "There's so much equipment in there a seagull wouldn't have a perch."

She stayed a bit longer, but Ramona and I sent Aunt Madge home in the middle of the afternoon so she could see to her guests. She's an early bird, so she planned to come by Sunday morning just after her guests finished breakfast.

While Aunt Madge had been in with Scoobie Ramona and I started calling a few people. We knew word would get out fast and rumors would fly, so we called Jennifer and asked her to tell some of the classmates Scoobie knows best. Ramona called Joe Regan while I called Daphne at the library, since that's where Scoobie hangs out much of the day. Neither of us called George Winters, but about four o'clock he showed up.

His demeanor was not as impassive as it usually is when he throws questions at people. George had his notebook in one hand and pencil in the other and gave us a raised-hand surrender gesture. "You know I gotta ask. Then I'll leave you alone."

If I hadn't pulled him into the dunk tank yesterday I probably would have shrieked at him. Instead I just nodded, and asked him the first question. "Did you talk to Sgt. Morehouse lately?"

"They're wrapping up at the carnival. Doesn't look like they're finding out much. Carnies are mad because they say everybody suspects them of every crime in town when they're here."

I don't give a damn about the carnies. "In other words, nothing."

"Nothing they're talking about and I can usually get something out of 'em." He flipped open his notebook and glanced at it. "Nobody saw him much after the last time he heckled people at the dunk tank about nine-thirty last night. By that time he had changed back into his jeans and a sweatshirt, and that's what he was wearing when they found him."

I nodded, thinking. I'd seen Scoobie then. He'd been trying to get Father Teehan to promise to get onto the dunk tank plank Sunday after Mass, and Father was having none of it. Reverend Jamison reminded Scoobie that Father Teehan was no spring chicken, and it had taken me a minute to figure out that there was some ecumenical hazing going on. "That was the last time I saw him, too."

Ramona described our walk to the car together and that we'd mentioned we hadn't seen him for a while.

George nodded. "It sounds as if he left shortly after 9:30, but it's kind of odd no one saw him leave. I guess someone may hear what happened and call the police later. They're putting a call out on the radio."

"Who's going to be listening to the radio today?" I asked.

"They're set up at the carnival, like always," Ramona said. "They'll mention it a lot."

"Yeah. Chamber of Commerce'll love it." George continued, "Morehouse is really irritated that they don't want to announce it on the PA at the carnival, but Father Teehan and a bunch of other people think it would "unduly upset" people."

"That's ridiculous!" I stood up and walked to the window and back. "How come it gets to be their decision?"

"It's not like they're warning about a heavy thunderstorm coming in." George glanced back at his notes. "What's done is done."

When neither of us said anything he glanced up. "Sorry," he said, taking in our stony stares. "They figure most people who were at the carnival yesterday aren't there today, except the workers, and they're talking to them. So," his tone grew cautious, "either of you seen him yet?"

Ramona looked at her watch. "I'll let you guys talk. I told Roland I'd come back to the store for a bit. He wants to take his nephew to the carnival." She looked at me. "I'll be back about six or seven and I'll bring you a pillow."

She left and George looked at me. "You're sleeping here?"

"Probably just tonight." I looked away, afraid I'd tear up.

He stared a moment, then repeated his question about whether we'd seen Scoobie yet.

"He looks, well, better than I thought he would. I thought his head would be really swollen and he'd be all black and blue or something."

"He's not so banged up?" he asked.

I thought for a second. "He is. His head is bandaged from where they put in a catheter to drain some fluid from his brain."

George winced.

"But it's not like a huge turban. He has a bruise on his face, and a puffy eye." I thought for a moment. "You can't see the back injuries."

"He awake?" George asked.

I shook my head. "They said once they knew he could hear them and follow a couple instructions they sedated him. It's supposed to help his brain heal faster."

George made a couple notes, and I looked at him more closely. "Did the police tell you what was wrong with him?" I asked.

"Yeah, sure," he said, not looking up.

"No they didn't. You're fishing, same as always." I could feel myself redden and it was an effort not to yell at him.

He stared at me very directly. "They said he was hurt in a fall and maybe somebody pushed him. You know cops keep back stuff."

"Because there's always some total ass who will print it." I regretted my word choice almost as soon as it was out of my mouth.

Since he wanted to keep talking to me George didn't show any offense taken. "I don't just work here, I live here. I'm not saying I sugar coat stuff, but if the cops have a good reason to keep something quiet I pretty much go along with it."

Too stubborn to apologize I snapped back. "You're only saying that because you want something from me."

He shut his notebook and stood. "I'll see you around, Jolie."

I SAW SCOOBIE several more times before Ramona came back with a pillow and a plastic bag of grocery store raw vegetables. While she was in with Scoobie I ate a few, wishing they were dipped and fried.

"What do you think?" I asked when she came back.

"Well, you know he's just sleeping. But I watched the numbers on the equipment he's hooked to and his blood pressure and oxygen level look good."

All I'd done was stare at him, and I felt stupid for not looking around the area by his bed.

"When my father had a stroke a couple years ago I learned what all those numbers mean." Ramona helped herself to a couple pieces of cauliflower. "I just don't get who would hurt him."

"That's the $64,000 question. It had to be a long time after the carnival shut down for the night. People would have been taking a shortcut through those trees to get to the popsicle district. If he had a fight with somebody there before he went to the boardwalk people would have heard." The popsicle district is a part of Ocean Alley with small bungalows painted in vivid colors. Thanks to Ramona's real estate agent uncle, Lester Argrow, I appraise a fair number of houses in that area.

She nodded. "I thought that, too."

"Did you hear who found him?"

She shook her head. There was a cough from the area near the entrance to the small waiting room, and we looked up to see Dana Johnson. She was out of uniform, and it took a second to recognize her in a pretty knit top and jeans.

"They're telling people at the desk downstairs that they can't come up, but I figured one of you would be here."

Ramona gestured to a chair and Dana sat. We looked at her expectantly.

"Can't tell you too much more..." she began.

"Because you don't know or you won't?" I asked.

Ramona said, "Jolie..."

Dana gave a half grimace, half smile. "Now I see what Sgt. Morehouse means about you being more than a bit pushy."

"I'm sorry," I said. "Really." And I was.

"Tough day," she said, evenly. "No one saw anything or will say so if they did. He's just really lucky someone found him and called it in."

"Who...?" Ramona began.

"Don't know," Dana said. "Just a calm male voice, nothing distinctive. Didn't sound particularly old or young." She paused. "One of the guys even thinks it might even be a woman with a raspy voice."

"As long as they didn't do it I guess it doesn't matter who they were," Ramona said.

"Sometimes people saw more than what they think they did, so we'd like to talk to him. It was an out-of -state cell number, so it could take just a bit longer to figure out who called, or at least who owns the phone."

Dana said she had mostly come to check on Scoobie and left after a couple minutes. Ramona stayed another hour and I insisted she leave. Sunday is her only guaranteed day off and I figured she should at least get a good night's sleep Saturday night if she planned to be here a lot on Sunday, which she would.

I didn't think I would sleep, but when I saw Scoobie about ten o'clock I was falling asleep on my feet. A very nice nursing assistant pulled a patient recliner into a corner in a hallway near Scoobie's small room. There were more people in the intensive care waiting area and they were acting more like it was a party room than a place to keep a vigil for their friend who was hurt in a car accident.

"Always are busy up here on a Saturday night," he said.

I thanked him, and he told me since I wasn't being "too big a pain" the staff had decided I could be closer to Scoobie during the night.

As I fell into a restless sleep I thought Sgt. Morehouse would be surprised to hear I wasn't such a big pain.

Chapter Five

I WENT HOME TO SHOWER when Aunt Madge got to the hospital about eight-thirty Sunday morning. She had explained to her B&B guests that they would be on their own for seconds on muffins and coffee so she could get to the hospital, and they were very understanding.

It felt odd to be driving through town. At first it felt as if life was real at the hospital and a mirage out here. When I pulled into the driveway I saw all the guests' cars were still there, so I stuck my tousled head into the dining area. There was one man still reading the paper, but he said he didn't need anything.

My room is in the part of the B&B that Aunt Madge rents out least, and it's usually only Jazz and me who inhabit that area. Today the room next to mine was in use and its occupants shared the jack-and-jill bathroom with me. I knocked softly, and when no one answered raised my voice to ask if it was okay if I took a shower. A woman's voice said they were done using the bathroom.

Jazz was very irritated at having been left alone so much, and I couldn't blame her. She walked along the edge of the tub when I showered and tried to get in the medicine cabinet every time I opened it, both things she knows annoy the daylights out of me. You'd think she had a degree in the psychology of irritation.

I carried my hair dryer downstairs to use in the small bathroom off the great room. This is not my usual practice, but I thought I should be where I could hear guests if they called. The dogs were glad to be let in from Aunt Madge's small yard, and Mr. Rogers barked once at Jazz when he could tell she was planning to jump on his back.

"Hey." I frowned at him, and he managed to look chagrined, for a dog. *Even the dogs know something's wrong.*

My cup of coffee cooled as I called Harry. "Thought I'd check in real fast." I hoped he'd volunteer to finish writing up the appraisal I'd done yesterday morning, but I also wanted to let him know I was okay. Harry's really good to me.

"Jolie, good," Harry said. "Madge just called to let me know Scoobie was still doing well. I'm glad to hear your voice."

Doing well? Of course, even though he's ten years younger than Aunt Madge he's still in the age group where friends kick the bucket every few weeks, so if that's your perspective I guess Scoobie was doing well.

"The nurses said he had a good night, whatever that means to them." I thought for a second. "One of them said they might reduce his sedation today or tomorrow."

"Good, good. I don't want you to think about work until Scoobie's doing a bit better."

As if. "Thanks. Listen, I have a favor to ask." The idea hadn't really formulated until I heard Harry's voice. "Are you going over to the carnival later today?"

There was a two second pause before Harry said, "Jolie..."

Harry's worse than Aunt Madge about thinking I'm a busybody. They can't seem to figure the difference between curiosity and caring. "Honest, it's an easy thing. I know you have a digital camera for the appraisals."

"And..." he said, letting the word hang there.

"There's this guy Scoobie gave the evil eye to. I want you to take his picture."

"Surely you told the police about him. You need to leave this one totally to them, Jolie."

I kept the irritation from my tone. I wanted to stay with Scoobie, not go to the carnival, and Harry was my friend, not just a boss. "I did, but I want a picture for me, and I know Morehouse won't share. I can describe the guy, and tell you maybe where he'll be working."

"No!" Harry stopped for a couple seconds, and then continued. "Do you know how distraught Madge would be if you got hurt? Hurt again," he said.

"Okay, I hear you." In the minute before we got off the phone I mentally rearranged my day. I would go back to the hospital and hope I could talk Ramona into going to the carnival to take pictures. She could use my car. I rummaged in Aunt Madge's junk drawer to see if there were any extra batteries I could use if the ones in my camera died.

AUNT MADGE WOULD WANT to go to First Prez at ten-thirty, so I didn't take more time at home than I absolutely needed to get presentable. I knew she would stay with Scoobie instead of going to church, but I figured she could use the comfort of Reverend Jamison and her friends. And maybe she could do some rumor control.

I put my camera and extra batteries at the bottom of a small canvas shoulder bag in which I also stowed a couple books and a clean pair of underwear. For good measure I threw in an apple and a couple muffins left over from breakfast, rationalizing that Aunt Madge wouldn't want them to go to waste. She makes them fresh every day.

The dogs went out again with no complaint, but Jazz was a different matter. She's really fast. After ten minutes of running up and down the back stairway and around Aunt Madge's sofa, I gave up and made sure the door to my room and its closet — where Jazz's litter box was stowed since I was sharing the bathroom for the weekend — were open.

She sat on the bottom step looking at me, poised to run again. "If Aunt Madge comes home and finds you on the sofa, you're toast." She yawned and settled herself against the step above the one she was sitting on.

Traffic around town was heavier than on a normal Sunday, likely because a lot of people were back for the carnival. I still made it back to the hospital by ten fifteen. Aunt Madge looked up, surprised. "I thought you'd take a longer break."

I shrugged. "Say hello to Lance for me." I sank into one of the uncomfortable waiting room chairs, glad that the group from last night had finally left.

She stood and picked up her purse. "I was in there for fifteen minutes last time. I think they're going to be more relaxed about us being in there today." She shook her head slightly. "I can't see any difference, but the nurse said he mostly had a good night."

I'd heard the same thing, so I merely kissed her cheek. "You're the best."

She studied me for a second. "You're up to something."

I laughed, and realized it was the first time I'd done that since we'd heard about Scoobie. "Maybe you can pray for a less suspicious attitude."

"I'll come back for a bit after church and then go to Cozy Corner." She gave me one more of her appraising looks before she left.

It wasn't a lie, really. Aunt Madge and I have very different definitions of 'up to something.'

THE NEXT TIME I SAW SCOOBIE I thought he looked calmer, somehow. Not that a sedated person looked too stressed, but something seemed different. I asked the nurse about it.

"We've changed his pain meds a couple times, trying to get the best dosage to keep him comfortable but not too doped up. I think we found the right mix." She tucked a folded towel under Scoobie's shoulder.

"What's that for?"

"We don't want to roll him around a lot, but we want to change his pressure points." She glanced at my puzzled stare. "If he lies in one spot to long he could get pressure sores, but we don't want to move his spine too much."

"Can you tell me more about his back injuries?" I asked.

"The doctor could tell you more."

"I don't know when I'll see him. Or is it a her?"

"The orthopedist is a woman, Dr. Cahill," she said.

"Are you allowed to tell me anything?" I asked.

She ignored my snippy tone. "Sure. It could be a lot worse, actually. He compressed T-3, which is about here." She pointed to a spot maybe five inches below her neck, "and C-3, which is in the neck. You know what that means, right?"

"I've heard the term, but I guess I don't know the significance of it." Plus I'd heard lots of terms the last 24 hours. I thought I remembered crushed and compressed most often.

She nodded. "A vertebra on someone Adam's size is maybe an inch tall. You want it to stay the same size, not get crunched, obviously. But," she adjusted his pillow, "If you do put enough pressure on it to compress it some, your spine can adjust. It's important to stabilize it, usually by wearing a brace for a while."

I thought about this for a moment. "And if it doesn't stabilize?"

"There are so many things that can be done now besides the major surgery, you know, the kind with pins and all that."

I must have looked relieved, because she smiled slightly. "They can even insert kind of a gel, which hardens, to keep it from compressing more."

While it didn't sound like fun, gel sounded a lot better than having pins in your spine. "Thanks for the generic explanation."

"Dr. Cahill can tell you more specifics." She hesitated. "You are family, right?"

"As far as I know he has none. I'm his best friend." Best friend. Yep, that's me.

She nodded and left the room. There was a plastic chair a few feet from the bed and I pulled it close enough that I could sit next to the bed and put a hand on Scoobie's arm. I realized his arm felt really cold and wondered if I could put it under the sheet. I studied the IV line and decided to just pull the cotton blanket higher, so it covered each arm better.

"I'm here, Scoobie," I whispered. "Nobody can hurt you here."

Was that a tiny smile? It couldn't be!

I studied him a couple seconds. "Okay, maybe they'll stick you with needles, but they won't push you down any steps."

Nothing, no tiny smile or any other sign he'd heard me. I sat looking at him until the nurse came to the doorway. "Probably time to give him a rest."

USUALLY RAMONA IS MORE REASONABLE. I had tried to get her to take the camera and look for the guy at the carnival, but she wouldn't.

"Are you insane?" She actually whispered in a hiss.

I lowered my voice even more. The parents of the kid who had been in a car accident last night were sitting on the other side of the room. "You know Morehouse. He may show us a picture but he won't give us one. I'm not going to keep the guy's face in my mind forever."

"And you want to hold that thought?"

"Well," I needed a good reason here. "What if he comes back? We need to be sure what he looks like so we can call Morehouse."

She thought about that for a moment. "That's not why you really want the picture." She gave a half sigh. "I don't want to go, but you go and I'll stay here."

THE HOSPITAL is at the far north side of Ocean Alley, less than a quarter-mile from the carnival. I tried to hold back tears, thinking about this time yesterday. *What could we have done differently? What if Ramona and I had looked for him as we were leaving?* These were the kinds of questions I'd been pushing to a dark corner of my mind since yesterday. With the initial panic subsiding they were demanding to be heard.

Logic told me that if neither of us had seen Scoobie the last hour or so of the carnival that he'd already left. Or he was someplace where he didn't want to be seen. I clenched the steering wheel so hard my fingers hurt, suddenly so angry with Scoobie I wanted to scream.

So I did.

And then I cried, and kept it up until I pulled into St. Anthony's parking lot. "This is ridiculous. You're going to walk in there with a red blotchy face and stuffed nose and Lance or Reverend Jamison will think Scoobie died." I blew my nose hard, and forced myself to think of Aunt Madge with her green hair on St. Patrick's Day. It worked, a little.

I wondered why I could park closer to the carnival entrance, then gave myself a head slap as I realized the gates wouldn't open for another fifteen minutes. "Oh well." I figured I could talk my way in by saying I was with the dunk tank. *That's not a lie, you were in it yesterday.*

I needn't have worried. There were no carnival workers ready to keep people out of the way as there had been just before the opening hour yesterday, when there were dozens of people waiting to get in.

The only two people at the dunk tank were Megan, my favorite food pantry volunteer, and her daughter Alicia. "Jolie! How is he?" Megan asked.

"They say better than he was yesterday. I guess we'll know more as time goes..." I stopped as Alicia burst into tears.

Megan pulled her daughter in for a hug, and I fought the urge to cry again. "She's been so upset," Megan said as she stroked Alicia's hair.

"I'm not upset!" Alicia wailed, burying her head into her mother's shoulder.

Teenagers. Megan and I half-smiled at each other.

"I can't stay to help, I'm sorry. We're taking turns being at the hospital, sitting with Scoobie. Ramona's there now."

Megan nodded. "This morning at church Reverend Jamison told everyone to pray for Scoobie and then asked for a couple more volunteers." She continued patting Alicia. "About a half-dozen people said they'd be over, and he told them to get together after church and come up with a way to stagger their schedules."

"Right." I had just realized that if the First Prez service was over I needed to start scouting for the man I'd seen Scoobie looking at yesterday. If Aunt Madge dropped by the hospital to find only Ramona she'd know I really was up to something. I gave Alicia a pat on the shoulder and dug out my camera.

After taking a couple photos of the empty dunk tank and the "Harvest for All Food Pantry" sign above it — which was going to be my excuse for being there, if I seemed to need one — I looked around the expansive carnival area. People had begun to arrive and I heard the Merry-Go-Round start its first cycle of the day.

"You aren't here to take photos of the dunk tank."

I jumped about three inches and turned to face an unsmiling George Winters. "And you would know that how?" I asked, and turned my back on him.

"Because, sad to say, I know you." He fell into step beside me. "Who are you looking for?"

"I don't know." I glanced up at him and could feel my eyes filling with tears and looked away.

George's tone, absent the bantering quality he often uses with me, did not change. "You'll be back at the hospital soon. If you tell me what you're looking for I can look, too."

That stopped me, and I considered his offer. When I was trying to figure out how a skeleton had gotten in the Tillotson-Fisher attic a few months ago I had considered talking to George about it. A reporter is used to ferreting out facts. I had rejected the idea then and didn't like it any better now.

I took a breath, mostly to be sure I wouldn't cry. "Okay."

"Okay, what?" he asked.

"Did you see Scoobie playing the High Striker yesterday?" I asked.

"Yeah," he grunted with a smile. "I saw Ramona hit the ball higher, too."

What had seemed funny yesterday held no appeal today. "When we were over there first a blonde guy was collecting the money. When we went back maybe forty-five minutes later, it was a different guy."

"Different how?" he asked, taking out his thin reporter's notebook and pulling the stubby pencil from its spiral binding.

"Not as tall."

George gave me a look full of sarcasm, and I flushed.

"The second guy was maybe five eight or nine, not a lot taller than Ramona. His coloring was darker, and his hair was black." I paused, remembering. "I'm not sure he was from Greece or Turkey or someplace near there, but that's what he looked like to me."

"So, Mediterranean features, then?" he asked.

I nodded and shrugged at the same time, and George looked away for a moment, and then took my elbow as if to guide me.

"Hey!"

"Enough already," he said in a low voice. "Just walk to the cotton candy lady with me. And pretend you're having a good time."

"Yeah, right." But I followed his lead.

George bought two cotton candy sticks and paid for them. "Now," he said as he handed me one, "you owe me more than a phone."

"I guess I should apologize for pulling you in," I said, grudgingly.

"Gotta love you, Jolie. You aren't sorry one bit." He nodded behind us and said, "Don't turn now, but in a minute look at the game and see if that's the guy."

I put my tongue on the candy, since you can't really bite it, and wished I'd had something other than sweet food today. Maybe I would go to the hospital cafeteria and buy something healthy.

I feigned interest in the Ferris wheel and, with George following my gaze, looked at the High Striker and then turned back toward the cotton candy stand. Same guy. "Yep, that's him."

"Okay, now walk to the dunk tank with me, and tell me what you think he did."

"It's not what he did as the way Scoobie reacted to him. He and Ramona and I were walking back to the High Striker after we had hot dogs." I thought for a moment, trying to remember Scoobie's exact expression. "Scoobie was going to try again to beat Ramona, but when we got closer he stopped, kind of without warning, and I bumped into him."

George looked up from his notebook. "Didn't shove him in a puddle or anything?"

"Don't be a jerk." I scowled at him.

"You got that cornered. Continue."

I gave him what I hoped was a look of pure dislike and continued. "Scoobie was almost rigid, and his face looked mad, but just for a second. I looked to see what he saw, and the guy was looking at Scoobie with a funny expression."

"Funny ha-ha or funny odd?" George asked.

"Odd. It was kind of a...smirk, I guess. And Scoobie turned around fast and said we were going bowling."

"That's it? You're holding back."

I tossed the cotton candy stick in the trash. "Am not. I could just tell Scoobie knew the guy and didn't like him. Didn't think about it again until yesterday morning, when Morehouse asked us about everything. Maybe Ramona would remember more."

He stuck his thin reporter's notebook in the pocket of his Hawaiian-style shirt. "Okay, I'm going to take pictures of a bunch of booths and games. You go back to the hospital."

"But, I want..."

"You want a photo. I get that. I'll email you a copy, and I'll print one off for you."

When I started to protest, he almost growled. "You were with him when Scoobie reacted to the guy. You need to get the hell out of here before he gets interested in you, too."

I left, but not because George told me to.

I BARELY BEAT AUNT MADGE back to the hospital, but she had talked to Harry at First Prez and was fit to be tied. "Can you honestly tell me you aren't going to go to that carnival to take a picture of that worker?"

"Yes."

Ramona looked away.

"I described the guy to George Winters and asked him to do it."

"After you dunked him?" Ramona and Aunt Madge asked, together.

"Yep. He likes Scoobie, and he said he would and would email me the picture." I looked steadily at Aunt Madge, grateful that she had phrased her question in a way that let me answer honestly. I was not going to the carnival, I had already been.

"How will he know what he looks like?" Ramona asked.

"I described him as well as I could. I guess if he sees more than one guy with that build and skin tone he'll have us look at more than one picture."

"That's not the point. What do you want the picture for?" Aunt Madge demanded.

I knew Aunt Madge was really mad. I figured if there were not other people in the waiting area she might even be raising her voice. I adopted an injured tone. Really, how could she doubt me?

"If Scoobie says that's the guy who hurt him, I want to be able to stay away from him."

"And not let him near Scoobie," Ramona added.

Still appearing suspicious, Aunt Madge made no comment, but took a seat and nodded at the parents of the car accident victim. Ramona glanced at me and looked away again.

There was still a frosty air to the room when Sgt. Morehouse came in a few minutes later. "Thought we might compare notes," he said, as he took a chair next to Aunt Madge.

That's a new one. He must have sensed my thought as he nodded in my direction and gave, for him, a brief smile.

"Carny guy you think Scoobie was avoiding is called Turk. You hear Scoobie mention that name at all?"

Aunt Madge said, "I never heard Adam mention that name," while Ramona and I just shook our heads.

"Figures," he said. "So, we got the name of the person who owns the cell phone that called in when Scoobie got found, but it's a dead end."

"Why..?" I asked, and stopped when he and Aunt Madge both evil-eyed me.

"The owner's a lawyer from the city who grew up here." He glanced at Aunt Madge. "You remember the Stewarts?"

She nodded. "You must mean Peter."

"Yep," he said. "Someone stole his cell phone while he was at the carnival. Had it in his back pocket, and later he remembered somebody carrying a couple helium balloons banged into him."

"And the balloons were what he noticed, not the person's face," Ramona said, shaking her head slightly. "People do stuff like that on the boardwalk all summer."

"Not bad," I said to her, as Morehouse nodded.

"Now the next part might be disappointing to you," he continued. "About one-thirty Saturday morning one of our guys was in the Sandpiper Bar and Grill. Scoobie was there."

"What was Adam doing in a bar?" Aunt Madge asked. "He gave that up years ago."

"Don't know what he was doing there, but whatever it was he wasn't happy with the guy he was sitting with. No fight or anything, but they were arguing. Not loud though, so don't know what about."

"Same guy from the High Striker, you think?" I asked.

"Can't tell. Our officer wasn't there to look at carnies, and he only saw the guy sitting down."

"Well, there was the Mediterranean guy, and there was the blonde guy there before him, but I don't think Scoobie was mad at the blonde guy," Ramona said, as I nodded.

Morehouse made a note. "I keep telling that damn bar owner to get security cameras inside, but he won't do it."

Aunt Madge almost snorted. "He won't. It's supposed to be the best place in town to buy pot."

"And you know this how?" Morehouse asked.

She shrugged and Ramona added, "Everybody knows that."

Morehouse gave a slight head shake. "Great. None of the carny workers admit talking to him other than the old guy who runs the bowling machines. And there's no way to figure why he was in the Sandpiper Bar and Grill."

"Maybe he remembers it was my favorite bar," said a woman from the doorway.

Chapter Six

IT COULD HAVE BEEN THE grey color of her eyes or the kind of oval shape of her head, but even though I'd never met her I would have picked Scoobie's mother out of a crowd. Penny "you don't need a last name I change it a lot" was polite to Aunt Madge, but did not look at all pleased to see Sgt. Morehouse as he stood to greet her.

"Penny," he said, "it's been a long time." He did not extend his hand.

"Yeah, well, I've been living in upstate New York. What happened to my son?"

The last word was slightly slurred and I glanced at Aunt Madge, who didn't notice me because she was staring mutely at Penny. So was Ramona, but her rigid posture told me she was even less happy to see Scoobie's mother.

Morehouse gestured that Penny should sit and positioned himself across from her while he gave her the sixty-second summary of finding Scoobie and the rush to provide medical assistance. "Beyond that, we know very little," he concluded.

"Seems like if you can bust people for driving with a little beer in them you could spend some time figuring out who tried to kill my son."

Morehouse reddened and was about to speak when Aunt Madge said, "I trust you don't do that anymore. Where are you staying, Penny?"

She is not going to let this witch stay with us!

Penny looked away and then back to Aunt Madge. "I'm not sure just yet."

"Why don't you join us at Cozy Corner? The last of my carnival guests will be gone by this evening." As Penny gave her a questioning look, Aunt Madge added, "As my guest of course."

With what little I knew about Scoobie's home life, including Aunt Madge's disparaging comments about his "severely alcoholic" mother, I had a hard time figuring out Aunt Madge's logic. But it is her house.

Ramona stood abruptly. "I'll catch you all later." She left.

Morehouse nodded at Aunt Madge and me, and then looked at Penny. "I'll know where to find you if we learn more." He walked out, quite fast.

"Like rats leaving a sunk ship," Penny said, misstating the analogy. She said it just loud enough for Sgt. Morehouse to hear, but he didn't look back.

She turned her attention to me. "You I don't know."

"I'm Madge's niece, Jolie Gentil. Scoobie and I were friends in high school, and again now." In eleventh grade, Scoobie never talked about his mother except to say she worked a lot. If she acted then as she did now, my guess was "working" was Scoobie's euphemism for "drinking."

"Huh." She looked around. "No ashtrays, either."

A nurse walked in and began, "He's had a good rest. One of you..." Her voice trailed off as she saw Penny.

I gave her a closer look, too. Skin-tight leotards are best left to high school students or anorexic fashion models. They do nothing for slightly overweight, almost age fifty women. Her golden blonde hair looked as if it needed a color touch-up, and her black low-heeled shoes were scuffed. Combined with the large faux-alligator handbag, Penny looked as if she could be a bag lady, minus most of the luggage.

In a brisk tone, Aunt Madge picked up where the nurse left off. "We can go in to see him about twenty minutes every hour, so we take turns. Perhaps you'd like to go now, and I'd be happy to join you."

Penny steadied herself on the arm of the chair as she stood. "Naw. I'm gonna catch a smoke." She walked toward the hallway elevators without another word.

The nurse was one who had been especially kind the day Scoobie was admitted. I recalled she also went to First Prez with Aunt Madge. She looked at us. "Is that his mother?"

"Yes," Aunt Madge's tone was grim.

"Didn't he...?" I stopped.

"Get taken away from her?" Aunt Madge said. "A couple of us talked to social services more than once, but just like that," she snapped her fingers, "his father would show up again and insist he was going to take care of Adam and get his wife into some kind of counseling."

"I didn't know that." I stared at her.

"I didn't want to bias your opinion of her that much, in case you ever met her."

"No worries there."

IT WAS ALMOST TWO-AND-A-HALF hours before Penny whatever-her-last-name-is came back upstairs. She was chewing gum and her gait was a bit more unsteady, so I figured she added a visit to the Sandpiper to her cigarette break.

I was the only one in the waiting area and she stared at me, then moved uneasily to one of the plastic armchairs and sat.

Bet she can't get out of there this time.

"I was gonna go to Madge's direct, but I forgot where it is." She wouldn't look me in the eye as she spoke.

"It's at the corner of D and Seashore."

I waited a few seconds, to see if she had a response. Aunt Madge had made it clear she wanted Penny at the B&B so we knew where she was. "Adam doesn't need her at the hospital all day," was her comment.

I figured her presence would very likely upset Scoobie, and we both thought that, as the closest relative, Penny could decide who could see Scoobie — at least until he could make his wishes clear himself. "So play nice," were Aunt Madge's parting words as she left for home.

"Would you, uh, like me to tell you how Scoobie looks, so you aren't surprised?" I asked.

She turned vicious instantly. "You think I don't know what my own son looks like?"

Play nice. "Not at all. It's just that with the bandages and IVs and stuff I think he looks worse than you might expect."

"Oh, yeah." Again, no eye contact. "But he's gonna be okay, right? Nobody thinks he's gonna die or something."

"They say the back injuries will take the longest to recover from, but yes, he should be okay."

She stood, not all too steadily. "I'm gonna go to Madge's and hit the sack."

I said nothing as she left, nothing about her not seeing Scoobie, nothing about the fact that she was about to get behind the wheel when she shouldn't. Reluctantly, because I didn't want to irritate her, I pulled out my mobile phone to call Sgt. Morehouse.

When he picked up, I began. "Penny just left. She probably shouldn't be driving..."

He cut me off. "I hear you." He hung up.

I looked at the phone for a second, wondering if Penny had done more than drive under the influence in the past.

"Is she gone or with Scoobie?" Ramona looked around the room as she walked in.

"Gone, and never saw him."

"In all this time?"

"She went out for a 'cigarette break.'" I did an air caption of the last words. "And now she's gone to the B&B to sleep."

"At four o'clock?" Ramona asked?

"Yep."

The word was barely out of my mouth when Dr. Cahill walked into the waiting area. I knew it was she because her white coat said so, and tried to hide my irritation that she had not come before, despite a couple notes I'd left with the nurses.

"You must be Jolie and Ramona," she held out her hand to shake both of ours.

We acknowledged her leap of wisdom and she continued, "The nurses and the hospital administrator have made it clear that you and Madge Richards are the three I should talk to." She sat and we sat across from her.

"His mother..." I began.

"I've heard. Sgt. Morehouse also called to be sure I knew something about her history with Adam." She ignored our raised eyebrows and continued. "The neurologist and I have agreed to reduce his sedation, starting tomorrow, so you should be able to talk to him not long after that. You will want to be encouraging, but don't encourage him to do more than what Dr. Nobles and I want him to do."

I found her tone annoying. "Can you give us some guidance there?" I asked.

"He'll wear a pretty stiff cervical collar whenever he is not in bed, and a softer one when he's in bed. Most people don't like that, but it's really important to keep his neck fully supported so the cervical vertebra can heal. He'll have a back brace to steady the thoracic vertebra, but most people don't find those nearly as annoying."

She stood and began to walk out. "You can leave another note with the nurses, with specific questions."

RAMONA AND I LET GEORGE join us for a brief dinner in the hospital cafeteria. "Let" is an exaggeration, as he was coming with us whether we liked it or not. I had to be nice, he had brought me a printed photo of the High Striker guy, and it was clear he wasn't going to show it to us unless I talked to him.

"That's him," Ramona said, holding the page of photos.

George said the High Striker guy was the only one who came close to fitting the description I gave him, though he had a couple other photos, "In case you were high or something when you described him."

"Very funny." I stared at the photo, wishing there was a way to know if Scoobie actually knew him. "Oh. Sgt. Morehouse thinks his name is Turk."

Ramona ate another bite of her salad as her eyes traveled from George to me.

"Shit. He didn't tell me that." George pushed the remains of his hamburger halfway across the table.

"That's not my fault," I snapped. I looked back at the photo, trying to think if I'd seen the man anywhere else.

"What are you thinking? Don't hold back on me, Jolie."

"I'm not." My reply was testy, but I'd had about as much sleep as I guessed Morehouse had. I looked up from the photo. "There's nothing to tell. The nurses let us see Scoobie for just a few minutes every hour and then we're back to the ICU waiting area."

"You think they'd let me in?"

"In your dreams," Ramona said, as I shook my head.

George flipped his notebook shut. "You can't think of anything else at all?"

"You mean..." Ramona threw in.

"Well..." I began.

"Cut the crap, you two."

I remembered George said he had known Scoobie a long time. "Did you know his mother?"

"Hard not to. About once a month, maybe more, Penny'd sit outside the Sandpiper and sing "Row, Row, Row Your Boat" until the cops picked her up." George looked at both of us. "Why?"

"She came by today, and..." I stopped as George got up.

"Damn. That's all Scoobie needs. I'll catch you guys later."

He was a couple feet away when I called to him. "Don't tell Morehouse I gave you the guy's name." He didn't acknowledge me, but I figured he would keep it to himself.

In cahoots with George Winters. Who knew?

AFTER RAMONA LEFT I walked over to the window and back to my chair a few times and finally decided I had to get out of the waiting room. It was at least a half-hour before they'd let me see Scoobie so I opted for ice cream from one of the machines outside the cafeteria, rationalizing that I had decided to stay until about ten PM and needed nourishment.

I found the vending area easily, but I only had a five and a ten. I had just gotten the change-making machine to accept my five dollar bill when someone tapped me on the shoulder. "Excuse me, miss."

He was a bit taller than I remembered, but I hadn't stood next to the guy at the High Striker. I was right about the Mediterranean features, and now that he was close to me they looked pretty menacing. "Can I help you?" I barely heard the clunk of quarters as they hit the change dispenser.

"I think you know my friend, I saw you with him yesterday."

He was deliberately standing closer than people usually do. "I'm not sure who you mean." I moved to go past him and he put a hand on my arm.

"At the carnival. Everybody calls him Scoobie."

My heart was pounding so hard I felt it in my temples. "I know Scoobie, yes. You must have heard he was hurt." He still didn't move.

"Yes, the police were at the carnival a lot today. I thought I would pay him a visit." He smiled, revealing a mouth that had teeth placed only sporadically.

"He's in intensive care, and they're only letting a couple of us wait up there." I pushed past him. "I'm on my way back there."

He called to my back. "Tell him Stefan was asking about him and I'm sorry I missed him. We leave tonight."

I WAS STILL SHAKING when I got back to Scoobie's floor and kept punching the wrong buttons on my cell phone when I tried to call Morehouse.

When I finally did get it right, Morehouse's reaction really ticked me off. "I got eyeballs on the guy since you think Scoobie avoided him, but I can't question him tonight just because he told you to tell Scoobie hello. And yeah," he said, in response to my sputtering, "I agree with you. He wanted you to know he knows who you are."

"If you had eyeballs on him that means you knew he was at the hospital. Why didn't you call me?"

"I said eyeballs, not a damn crystal ball. One of the guys followed him to where you were. You walked right by my guy when you left the vending machines."

I hadn't noticed anyone in particular. All I wanted to do was get away from the man Morehouse said was called Turk. "Oh, he said his name was Stefan."

"Yeah, that's what the carny manager said. He also said he's been with him for about four years and is one of his best employees."

"So now what? Where'd the guy go after he left the hospital?"

"I don't report to you, you know." Morehouse sighed. "It looks like he's going back to the sleazy motel where the carnies are staying. And Jolie."

"What?"

"You left your quarters in the change maker."

IT WAS AFTER TEN when I got back to the Cozy Corner. I'd been fighting sleep as I sat by myself or with Scoobie. I was looking forward to sleeping in my own bed again, knowing that Scoobie would be okay at the hospital. And the nurse I had nicknamed Nurse Ratched, after the mean nurse in One Flew Over the Cuckoo's Nest, had gone home.

I had just walked into the kitchen when I heard a soft growl coming from the area near the kitchen sink. Since I was pretty sure Aunt Madge and Harry had finally persuaded the two chipmunks Mr. Rogers had brought in to leave the house in March, it had to be Jazz. I stooped and opened the cabinet under the sink and she streaked out.

"How did you get in there?" I asked, turning to watch her path up the back stairway.

Aunt Madge came out of her bedroom, her now auburn hair released from its soft French twist and flowing around her shoulders. "I locked her in there."

Uh oh. "I'm sorry," I almost stammered. "I forgot to tell you I couldn't get her back in the bedroom, and I wanted to get back to the hospital."

"I guess I'll forgive you. She always wants in there, so I left it opened and she wandered in."

I stooped down again to be sure Jazz had not peed under the sink. Thank heavens for big favors.

Aunt Madge started to turn to go back into her room, but turned back and leaned on the arm of her sofa. "Penny was pretty drunk when she got here. I had to help her up the stairs, and I put her in the room next to yours. I want her as far from any potential guests as possible."

She must have read my sullen look. "And you aren't a guest." She gently tugged Mr. Rogers from his goal to smell every inch of me. "I want you to keep an eye on her. I don't want her wandering around much. She used to have a reputation for being light fingered."

I shed my jacket and sank into a kitchen chair and put my head in my hands. How could this be happening? Scoobie still hurting and his drunk-ass mother sleeping in the room next to me.

Aunt Madge put her hand on my shoulder as she sat next to me. "When I said you aren't a guest it wasn't a comment about you being here, you know."

I sat up fully and kissed her cheek. "Hadn't crossed my mind." I forced a smile. "I'm just tired and hate the thought of that awful woman bothering Scoobie."

"You better hope she doesn't vomit in the bathroom either."

Chapter Seven

AS FAR AS I KNOW Penny didn't vomit anywhere. I heard her fumbling around in the room about six-thirty Monday morning. I could tell every time she bumped into anything because she cursed a blue streak. Quietly I used the half-bath in the hall. I was not about to share a bathroom with her and was glad I had moved my toiletries into my bedroom for the weekend.

As I was coming back down the hall, the door of Penny's room opened and she literally stuck her head out. Her hair was combed, but looked as if it needed a wash.

I bet she doesn't know how she got here. "Good morning, Penny. Hungry?"

At this she stepped into the hallway. "A bit, yeah."

She was wearing the same clothes that she had on yesterday, and they were much the worse for wear. "I'll put my bathrobe on and walk downstairs with you. Aunt Madge is an early riser, so she probably already has a pot of coffee on." I opened the door to my room and Jazz ran into the hallway.

Some people are suspicious about black cats. They may tell you this or they may give a piercing scream. Penny would be in the latter category.

"It's okay!" I yelled as I heard Aunt Madge coming up the steps way too fast. I walked toward Penny who was leaning against the door jamb with her hand over her heart. "She's a sweet cat, she won't hurt you."

Aunt Madge got to the top of the steps and Penny had the good sense to look sheepish. "I'm sorry, Madge."

"Don't worry about it." Aunt Madge's tone was formal, and I saw her visibly try to look friendly, which I don't think I could have done. "Come on, Penny. Coffee's on and I was about to scramble some eggs."

They started down the steps and I looked down to see Jazz had just sat on my foot. This is her 'I'm scared' spot, so I picked her up and rubbed her head as we walked back into my room. "I don't like her either," I whispered into Jazz's ear.

I TOOK A TWO-minute shower and threw on jeans and a yellow knit shirt. No makeup. It didn't seem fair to leave Aunt Madge alone with Penny. She invited her. Yes, but she did it for Scoobie.

The dogs were sitting by the sliding glass door that leads to the small back yard. They looked as if they were on full alert for a squirrel sighting, but they were all eyes on Penny, who was holding a mug of coffee with both hands as she slowly took a sip. My eyes met Aunt Madge's for a second and I walked to the counter and pulled the toaster toward me.

"White bread or whole wheat, Penny?" I asked.

"Don't matter. What's your name again?"

"Jolie."

"Weird name," was her comment.

Aunt Madge deftly slid scrambled eggs onto each of the three plates she had placed on the counter closest to the stove. I got a sudden urge to cry, remembering how much Scoobie likes her scrambled eggs.

"Do you have a suitcase in the car?" Aunt Madge asked as she placed a plate in front of Penny.

She sat up straight. "Where is my car?"

Aunt Madge nodded in the direction of her small parking lot. "Corporal Johnson drove it home for you, and helped you in."

"Crap. Did I get a ticket?"

"I think they got to you before you started to drive," Aunt Madge said, dryly. "They're fond of Scoobie, but I don't think you'll get a second break from them."

Fond of Scoobie is a stretch. But if you were comparing it to Morehouse or Dana's view of Penny, then Morehouse might be about to propose to Scoobie.

Penny stared at Aunt Madge and downed the rest of her coffee. "I gotta check to see if my stuff is all there." She stood, a bit more steady than she was when she left the hospital yesterday.

"I can keep your eggs warm..." Aunt Madge began.

"I don't eat nuthin' in the morning." She didn't bother to look at us as she walked through the swinging door to the guest breakfast room and out the side door to her car.

It was a couple seconds before I moved to look at Aunt Madge. "Who taught Scoobie how to talk?" I asked.

She put a bit of eggs on the piece of toast I had put on her plate. "She didn't raise Scoobie. Books did."

The door to the parking lot banged and there was a plop as something hit the floor just inside the door.

"Shit," Penny said.

"Go help her," Aunt Madge said.

My bet is Penny would have gone back to bed, but Aunt Madge and I each carried a bag and walked upstairs with her, Aunt Madge letting her know that if she needed shampoo or anything she could ask.

Please let her take that hint.

The small suitcase I carried was surprisingly heavy. It was the old-fashioned, hard-sided kind I recalled my mother called a cosmetic case. I set it on the bed and, after a scowl from Aunt Madge, moved it to the small antique washstand. Aunt Madge pulled a luggage rack from the closet and hoisted the slightly larger bag onto it. Apparently not one to take a hint about what Aunt Madge wanted on the quilt, Penny sat her large purse on the bed.

"I'm going to finish getting dressed and head over to the hospital." I made for the hall.

"What are you gonna do over there?"

I glanced at Penny, who looked genuinely puzzled. "They let us into his room for a bit every hour. I like him to know someone who cares about him is there."

She bristled. "You saying I don't care?"

Before I could say anything, Aunt Madge said, "Of course not, Penny. Now why don't you get yourself together and you can go over a bit later."

WHEN I WENT BACK to the kitchen a few minutes later, makeup on and ready to leave, Aunt Madge just gave me a silent head shake. The dogs were at her feet as she rinsed the breakfast dishes. She never lets them be in the way. I wondered who was getting the most comfort from the deal.

"I forgot to tell you, Sgt. Morehouse has warned the hospital staff about Penny."

All she said was, "Good to know," so I blew her a kiss and headed out.

The air was crisp for a morning in May, and I breathed in deeply, catching the scent of the ocean for a couple of seconds. As I unlocked the car door I glanced back at the house. Penny was in an upstairs window, staring down at me.

"Creepy woman," I muttered, starting the car.

It was just a little after seven-thirty, not quite what passes for morning rush hour in Ocean Alley. As I turned onto D street to head to the hospital I saw a dark blue Ford Taurus sitting on a side street, one block down from the Cozy Corner. As I got closer, the window came down and a hand waved. Instead of continuing on down D Street I turned and pulled up next to it.

"Hey Jolie," Dana said.

I put down my window. "I heard you were a Good Samaritan yesterday."

"Hardly. Listen," she paused as if thinking, "I'm supposed to let Lt. Tortino or Sgt. Morehouse know when his mother leaves, so Morehouse can go talk to Madge."

"Can't he just call?"

"Doesn't want Penny to know he's filling you guys in. We found out what part of "upstate New York" Penny was in for the last couple years."

"Uh, okay..."

"A medium correctional facility in Bedford Hills. She was serving a five-year sentence for home burglaries, a boatload of check kiting, and other variations of identity theft. Got out early because there's so much overcrowding."

"Damn it!" I hit the steering wheel with both hands. "Scoobie doesn't need this."

"No," she said in a matter-of-fact tone, "he doesn't. If she's just here to see him and move on we'll leave her alone, as long as she behaves. Doubt she will."

My shoulders relaxed. "This might be the first time Scoobie'll be happy about police activity."

"She drinking yet today?" Dana asked.

"Not that I know of. And Aunt Madge gave her coffee."

"Great. A wide-awake drunk." Dana raised her car window.

AS I PULLED INTO the hospital parking lot I thought about how to deal with Penny if she made it to the hospital. She did come when she heard Scoobie was hurt. I decided to tell the nurses we should do only five or ten-minute visits. I was pretty sure I'd heard somewhere that people in comas later say they were aware of people talking. I didn't want Scoobie to have to listen to Penny very much.

The nursing staff sympathized, but said they couldn't treat her differently than they treated Ramona and me.

"But he hasn't seen her in years, for good reasons," I said.

Nurse Ratched was having none of it. I glanced at her name badge. I'd thought of her only as the rigid bitch. "Listen, Susan, I heard Sgt. Morehouse talked to you guys about Penny. She, uh, has a lot of problems."

We were standing at the nurses' station just outside of Scoobie's small room. She was on the opposite side of the counter and I felt like a kid looking across the teacher's desk.

"I am aware of her issues..."

There was a remarkably loud belch behind us. Nurse Ratched froze mid-sentence, staring behind me. I turned.

Today Penny had on skin-tight white pants that left no doubts about her panty lines. There's a reason people shouldn't wear white until after Memorial Day. I shouldn't have to look at this for another two weeks.

"Penny, this is Nurse Ra..Susan. She's been with Scoobie a lot."

"Hmm." Penny looked at both of us for a couple seconds. "Well, where the hell is he?"

"I've got this," I said to Susan and a couple other staff who were busily doing something and listening to every word. I said nothing as I led Penny into the room.

Scoobie actually looked a bit better. His skin tone was almost his usual, and his face was relaxed. Still it had to be hard for any mother to see her son with two IVs, a cervical collar, a bandaged head, and a deep bruise down the side of his face. Any mother except Penny, I guess. She stared at Scoobie with an impassive expression, and walked out.

Let her go, let her go.

I followed her out, barely able to keep up as she pushed through the door that led back to the waiting room. "Penny, did you..."

She turned. "I'm headin' out."

"Out?"

"Like outta town, maybe not too far. Listen," she turned to face me directly, "I don't know where I'm gonna be the next couple weeks. You think it'll be in the paper if he checks out?"

"They don't usually list when people get out of the hospital..." I began.

She gave an impatient wave, barely two inches from my nose. "Check out, like permanent."

"You mean die?" My voice was about an octave too high.

"Yeah. I'd probably come to the funer..."

"Get the hell out of here!" I yelled.

"Jeez." She hitched her ugly purse onto her shoulder. "You got a nice aunt, but you're a bitch."

Chapter Eight

I GAVE MYSELF FIVE MINUTES TO calm down and then walked toward Scoobie's room. Dr. Cahill stopped me as I walked by the nurse's station.

"For some reason, Adam's blood pressure was all over the map last night. Dr. Nobles and I think we'll wait until late this afternoon or early tomorrow to reduce the sedation. Assuming he has a good day." She saw my worried expression and smiled. "This is not uncommon. Overall he's doing very well."

I sat with Scoobie for a few minutes, and then touched his hand. "Hey, I know you're in there." No response, of course. "I'm going over to "Harvest for All" for a bit. Need to put in the order to the food bank in Lakewood. Ramona's coming over about eight-thirty. I'll be back about ten."

I looked at him, wishing there was a way to know if he heard me at all. "Scoobie, we're thinking of changing the food pantry name to Nuggets for Nourishment."

Nada.

I WAS GLAD TO GET TO the pantry before it opened. I could work on the order to the food bank without having to talk to anyone. I'd been there an hour when there was a click in the lock of the door that leads to the street in front of the storefront-style pantry. I looked up. Please don't let it be Sylvia.

Thankfully, it was Megan and her daughter Alicia. Megan stopped just inside the door. "Jolie! I'm so very glad to see you. Is Scoobie better?"

I glanced from her to her daughter as she shut the door and was surprised to see a tear working its way down Alicia's cheek. I smiled at her. The two of them had restocked the shelves together a lot in the hectic days before Christmas, with Scoobie helping and teasing. I usually saw little from Alicia other than a mildly sullen attitude. It was nice to see she cared. "The doctors say things like 'he's doing well.' And it doesn't look like he's in pain. I mean, he's not frowning or anything."

Alicia started to cry hard, and Megan drew her in for a hug. "She's still so upset." This time Alicia did not deny it as Megan stroked the back of her daughter's head. "Reverend Jamison said with so many people praying for him all over town he's sure to be okay."

Alicia pulled back abruptly. "I heard you the first time." She shrugged off her jacket, wiped her tears with the back of her hand, and stalked behind the counter to take out the jar of pencils and sign-in clipboard from where they were stored under the counter.

Megan and I shared a quick glance, hers seeming to say something like "now what?"

I turned back to the filing cabinet I had been about to open. A thought buzzed in the back of my brain, but I couldn't quite grab it. I took out a blank order form and put back the folder, and then turned back toward Megan and Alicia. "They aren't letting people up to see him except a couple of us, but everybody up there listens to Aunt Madge. If you want to peek in for a minute I bet she could arrange it."

Alicia had her back to me and turned slowly. "How does he look?" she almost whispered.

"If I didn't know how badly he was hurt I'd say he doesn't look too different."

Alicia's look of relief could only be described as enormous. "I'm, I'm so happy," she stammered.

Definitely something going on here. "Why don't you guys give my aunt a call at the B&B if you want to go visit." I remembered Megan usually took the bus to volunteer at the pantry because she didn't have a car. "I can drive you if you want."

"I may well do that," Megan said.

We left it at that, but I knew Alicia was upset about something more than a recovering Scoobie. I'd have to work out how to get her to talk about it.

I WAS GETTING USED TO THE hospital routine, enough that I was bored silly. Jennifer came by at lunch time and I was actually glad to see her.

"I've called and emailed anyone I could think of. And I said what you said, about he should get better and that people shouldn't come over here."

"That's great." I didn't know what else to say. I wasn't about to ask her how her appraisal business was going. Jennifer now runs her family's business, and they do most of the appraisals in town.

"You think he'll be all right?" she asked.

"Everybody says things about how lucky he's been. If he was going to be a mush melon they probably wouldn't say that." As soon as the words were out of my mouth I regretted them. Scoobie would laugh at that, but hardly anyone else would.

"Oh dear..." she began.

"I'm sorry, I shouldn't have put it that way."

She actually patted my knee. "You and Scoobie always have had your own...language."

Fortunately, she didn't stay long. Ramona was coming after she got off work at five o'clock, so I spent the afternoon sitting with Scoobie and calling a couple people myself. Reverend Jamison said everyone was praying for Scoobie, and Lance said he'd been by "Harvest for All" and I shouldn't worry about things there for a while.

"I'm not saying we could get along without you, but Sylvia or Dr. Welby or I could probably figure out how to do things like place orders with the Food Bank in Lakewood."

"If I need you to do that I'll let you know. Right now, it's good to have something else to think about besides Scoobie."

"Never good to dwell on the negative," he said, as he hung up.

I smiled to myself. Lance might be about ninety, but I'd already learned he knew a lot about friendship. *You could take some lessons.*

RAMONA AND I WERE sitting in the ICU lounge when Dr. Cahill stopped by at five-thirty. "We're going to wait until at least tomorrow evening to reduce the sedation." Seeing our expressions, she added, "He's continuing to do well. We just want his blood pressure to be relatively consistent for twenty-four hours straight."

Ramona and I talked again about the visit from Turk or Stefan or whatever his name is, and what to make of it. "At least they're out of town now," she said.

"Do you know where they were going?"

"There was a small article saying Scoobie's a bit better. It also said the carnival was going to Asbury Park next."

I nodded. The early home of Bruce Springsteen was only about twenty miles or so north of Ocean Alley. "I suppose kids are still in school, so they only do weekends."

"Why do you care?" she asked, clearly suspicious.

"Just glad to know they aren't here, that's all."

But it wasn't all. After she left I kept thinking about what Scoobie didn't like about Turk. It could have just been a coincidence, but I didn't think so. Maybe it wouldn't hurt to go by the carnival at its next stop. I'd need some sort of disguise...

"The hotel," I said, aloud. I had forgotten about the "sleazy hotel where the carnies stayed. Or however Morehouse had put it. It could have been one of two, either Stay at the Shore or the Ocean Alley Budget Inn. Maybe Scoobie had gone there with Turk. It wouldn't hurt to check.

"DID YOU SEE MUCH OF ADAM'S mother today?" Aunt Madge asked as I got back to the Cozy Corner about ten o'clock.

"She left the hospital almost as soon as she got there. Sounded like she was leaving town. She didn't stop by here for her stuff?"

"She went upstairs late morning and came back down fairly soon. All she said was she might stay somewhere else tonight, and asked if she could leave most of her things here." Aunt Madge was frowning now. "I always respect my guests' privacy, but in her case I made an exception."

I grinned at her. "You snooped through her stuff?"

"Some of it. Just personal items and a couple ounces of pot."

I made a mental note. How did Aunt Madge know what pot looked like?

"Since she put that smaller case on the closet shelf under the clothes she wore yesterday, I figured she wanted it out of sight. I left it alone." Aunt Madge turned off the main kitchen light.

I shrugged and started for the stairs. "She must still have friends here."

"You're kidding, right?"

"Oh. Right. It's possible that she got picked up for drunk driving."

Aunt Madge stood up. "Lucky you sleep upstairs. I'd bet a month's worth of muffins that she'll roll in here about two A.M. and pound on the door."

Chapter Nine

I GOT UP TUESDAY MORNING, glad Scoobie hadn't had to deal with Penny. Who knew where she was or why she showed up in the first place?

We were enjoying a Penny-free breakfast as we sat at Aunt Madge's oak kitchen table eating toast and eggs, since Aunt Madge didn't have to make muffins for paying guests. I had even scrambled the eggs.

Aunt Madge kept going over why Penny had bothered to come at all. "Maybe Penny saw that short piece on the early New Jersey news show on Sunday and came through town with her last vestige of maternal interest."

"And then left for a while so she didn't have to deal with Scoobie?" I asked.

"I doubt we've seen the last of her. Maybe," her face brightened, "she'll get her things and leave without spending another night."

I picked up our now-empty plates and carried them to the sink. "How come you didn't tell me you tried to get social services involved?" I asked.

"I thought Adam should be able to tell you what he wanted." She put some honey in her tea.

For about the hundredth time I wished my dear aunt did not have such scruples about privacy. Penny's luggage aside.

I DECIDED TO HEAD FOR JAVA JOLT before going to the hospital. I wanted something other than hospital coffee, and I thought if I told Joe Regan what Scoobie's status was he could pass the news to anybody who asked.

And I wanted to get on the Internet. The Cozy Corner B&B does not have cable or Internet. I suppose it's to keep costs down, though Aunt Madge says it's to give her guests a chance to fully relax. Some agree with her philosophy, some don't. She does have a good antenna on the roof, so at least there are a couple TV stations available.

I was halfway up the steps to the boardwalk when I realized these might be the very ones Scoobie fell or was tossed down. "Eeegh!" I ran up them and was a few feet from the top of the stairs before I turned around.

"Whaddya up to, Ms. Nosy Bird?"

I like Lester Argrow, really, but his choice of vocabulary is sometimes a mystery to me. I looked at him as he walked closer to me on the boardwalk. Lester is about five feet six, maybe less, and he often has a cigar in his mouth. Today was no exception. As he got closer I could see he had trimmed the hair in the mole on his cheek. Always a good thing.

"Nosy Bird?" I asked. "You think I'm going to talk to you now?"

Lester barked his usual laugh. "Ramona's been telling me what's going on with Scrubbie, Scoobie," he said. "Jeez, he almost bought it."

I nodded and fell into step with Lester and continued toward Java Jolt.

"What was you squealing about?" Lester asked.

"Umm." I hesitated.

"Come on, Jolie, you know you like me to help you when you got a case."

Lester is the only one who acts as if he thinks I think I'm some sort of detective. I've told him at least five times that I just don't like loose ends or unanswered questions, especially if they're about a friend. "Sgt. Morehouse said Scoobie fell or was pushed down some steps, and they found him kind of under the boardwalk. I thought maybe it was those steps."

"Coulda been, I guess. Why was he on the boardwalk that time of night, anyway?" He hummed tunelessly as he walked.

"Don't know, but he could have been just walking back to his rooming house."

Lester opened the door to Java Jolt, and I was almost overcome by the smell of fresh coffee and chocolate chip muffins. *I miss this place.*

"Jolie! Great to see you. How is he?" Joe displayed none of his mild heckling side, which he sometimes directs at Scoobie. Instead, his Irish features sported a furrowed brow.

"Not much change, but that's a good thing, you know?" I picked up a large disposable cup and began to fill it from the thermos on the counter. Once tourist season starts in earnest the thermoses come off the counter and everybody orders from Joe or a couple summer employees. I knew I'd miss the comfy feeling that Java Jolt has in the winter.

"Jolie's on top of everything," Lester threw in.

Joe gave me a full-out grin. "I don't know, Jolie, you don't always come out in one piece when you snoop."

"I don't *snoop*. I just...check out stuff." I don't understand why people insist on using that word.

Joe laughed and Lester snorted as he poured his coffee.

"Cut it out, you guys. We're talking about Scoobie," I said.

Joe nodded and turned back to the latte machine, which he'd been cleaning when we walked in. "Ramona's keeping me up to speed. You call anytime."

I had planned to take my carryout cup and get on the Internet and be on my way, but it would be rude to ignore Lester. He helped me out last December, after I found the skeleton in the Tillotson-Fisher attic. And Lester talks to a lot of people.

"So what's next?" Lester asked as he sat facing me, seated in one of the wooden chairs he straddled, backwards.

"There's no next, Lester," I took a sip of my hot coffee and ran my tongue over the roof of my mouth. I leaned back in the chair and consciously relaxed my back and shoulder muscles. Java Jolt, with its combined air of coffee house and beach eatery, is my hangout, and I wanted to feel normal for at least a few minutes.

"You aren't letting some assholes get away with hurtin' Scoobie, are you?"

So much for normal. "You know this is a police matter, right?" I asked.

Lester and Joe snorted in unison.

"Really. Morehouse and Tortino, they're all over this."

Lester looked disappointed. "But, you really think somebody mighta been after Scoobie, right? Ramona said something about the carnival guy who runs the gong thing."

"It's not fair to accuse anyone," I was suddenly aware that there were a few other people at a back table. I lowered my voice. "Ramona and I just thought 1aybe Scoobie saw someone he didn't like." I didn't mention that the 'someone' had been hanging around the hospital Sunday night.

"So, you got nuthin'?"

"Lester! I'm not looking to 'get' anything. Listen, I need to check my email before I go to the hospital. It's been a couple of days."

Lester stood and picked up his cup of coffee. "Ok, I hear ya. But call if you need some help. We worked good together last time." He gave me an exaggerated wink and walked out, still humming.

As I sat at one of Java Jolt's computers I realized Lester was humming "Under the Boardwalk."

SCOOBIE'S NIGHT HAD BEEN "uneventful," which in hospital code means he wasn't getting any worse and maybe was improving. Dr. Cahill had left orders to reduce Scoobie's sedation in the late afternoon. I had plans before that.

I had taken the notes I'd made at the Java Jolt computer into the hospital with me. The *Ocean Alley Press* had said that the carnival was owned by East Jersey Entertainment. It was in a story about Scoobie's "apparent mugging," and the carnival was mentioned because Scoobie was thought to be on his way home from there.

When I Googled East Jersey Entertainment I learned that it was a fairly large organization that not only had two separate "carnival teams" but also ran boardwalk games and rides in several east coast beach towns, including Ocean City and Atlantic City, New Jersey. Ramona had said Scoobie worked at an amusement park in some town, Ocean City, I thought, but I realized I didn't know if she meant New Jersey or Maryland.

A small bell dinged in my brain as I walked down the hall to see Scoobie for the first time that day. Maybe Scoobie had known Turk/Stefan at the amusement park.

THE OCEAN ALLEY BUDGET INN is worthy of its name. The so-called lobby of the two-story motel was about fifteen feet square, and in addition to the check-in desk it had a counter along the wall that had a dirty-looking coffee pot, Styrofoam cups and a toaster. Looked as if they gave their guests the least breakfast possible.

"My friends were in Ocean Alley over the weekend and one of them thinks he left his camera here."

The man at the desk looked at me through a pair of dirty glasses. "We didn't find a camera," he said. "I know the cleaning staff. If they found it, I'd have it."

"Oh. Well, maybe he was at "Stay at the Shore...""

"That dump?" the man asked. "He should stay here." He leaned across the counter and was close enough that I could smell whatever goop he had on his hair. "I hear they have bed bugs."

"Ugh. Well then, I really don't want to go over there. Can you tell me if Stefan stayed here over the weekend?"

His look, which had been conspiratorial when he talked about his competitor's bed bugs, was now one of suspicion. "Are you a cop? I told them the carnies didn't cause any trouble this time."

Bingo. "Do I look like a cop?" I gestured to my lightweight denim pants. "Stefan was going to catch up with another friend of ours, maybe you know him. Scoobie?"

He was angry now. "I don't care if you are a cop or not, I don't give out..."

There was a whoosh as the glass door to the street was pulled open very fast. I turned slightly to see the newcomer. Penny no longer had on the white pants. Instead she was dressed in a very attractive light blue pants suit and the faux-alligator purse had been replaced by an ivory-colored one that looked as if it was real leather.

"What are you doing here?" she scowled.

"Ha. Now I know you aren't a cop." The desk clerk was almost jeering. "What's up, Penny?"

I could feel myself flushing. "Hi, Penny. We missed you last night."

"Got busy with friends." She walked fully into the room. "I need another key," she said, no longer looking at me.

The manager took an actual key, not a swipe card, from a drawer and handed it to her. "Last one except the master. Make sure you leave it this time."

"Yeah, yeah." She walked toward the back of the room where a door led to a hallway, but turned before she opened it. "She's friendly with cops." She left.

"I, uh, guess I'll be going."

The desk clerk didn't acknowledge me, but pulled out a small ledger and started making a note.

I had learned only what I already thought I knew. *What a waste of time.*

MOREHOUSE CAME BY late Tuesday afternoon. "Nothing to tell," he said. "Thought I'd see how he's doin'."

"Same." I stood from the lone plastic chair by Scoobie's bed. I noticed the nurses didn't seem to apply the one-visitor rule when it was the police who wanted to come in. "They lowered his sedation, but he's not alert yet. They said that's kind of normal."

"Huh. Good he's not worse." From his pocket he pulled a dirty piece of paper that he had placed in a plastic bag. "Is this one of Scoobie's poems?"

I took it slowly. "You know, he doesn't always like people to..."

"Jolie." Morehouse paused until I looked directly at him. "This is a police investigation, not an English class."

I looked at the paper. It looked like half of a steno pad page.

As she undid the laces
Of her fragile mental health
Revealing to him places
Where she'd never been herself

Breakfast table cordial
Stage direction for the scene
Both being very careful
To not say what they mean

Struggling through the mourning
Of the night before
Juggling

I looked up, aware my face was now flushed. Scoobie had several times alluded to the fact that he thought I had 'issues' I didn't want to face. And we would eat breakfast at Aunt Madge's. *Is this about me?* I cleared my throat. *Get a grip, Jolie. Like he would write about you.*

"I haven't seen it before, but it looks like his writing. A lot." I glanced back at the page. "Not just the penmanship, but the kind of thing he'd write. Where was it?"

"Blown up against one of the posts under the boardwalk."

I looked at it again. "The way it's written, it looks as if he got interrupted."

"Yeah, even I got that."

SCOOBIE WAS MILDLY ALERT by about five-thirty, and more awake by seven. The nurses said Ramona and I could be with him together, since we were likely going to be his 'primary support team.'

His half-opened eyes rested on me first, and he said, "Yo, Jolie," in almost a whisper. He closed his eyes again.

"Hey," Ramona stood just in front of me and touched Scoobie's shoulder. "It's so good to see you back in the real world."

He looked at us both now, with his eyes fully open, and I could almost see a dozen questions forming. I went for the familiar. "Plus, you scared the daylights out of us, so you can cut that out anytime."

"I missed you, Ramona," he said slowly, but with a lopsided grin.

"Ha! See what you get, Jolie?" She was trying to heckle me, and having a hard time not crying.

We were on the same side of his bed, so he didn't have to turn his head. "You did scare us." I gave him a light touch on the knee.

He winced. "I didn't plan it."

"I think Sgt. Morehouse will have a lot of questions for you," I added.

"That windbag?" He frowned.

"He's been all over town trying to figure what happened to you."

"I'm not the one he should be worried about."

I could tell from his eyes that a lot was coming back to him at once, and he moved his legs toward the bed rail, as if he was thinking of getting up.

"Whoa," I said, while Ramona added, "No way."

Apparently he didn't need any convincing of the need to stay put, as a look of pain crossed his face. "Sheeeit."

Someone cleared a throat behind us, and Ramona and I turned to look at Sgt. Morehouse. "Good to see you awake," he said, looking at Scoobie. "Can you answer a couple questions?"

"You first. What the hell happened to me?"

Morehouse gave him the sixty-second spiel, and Scoobie said nothing as he seemed to be absorbing it all. Finally, he said, "Might go faster if I just told you a couple things. I'm going to ask them to give me some kind of a shot or something here in a minute."

"Shoot," Morehouse said, pulling a notebook from his pocket.

"I saw this guy, I knew him when I worked on the boardwalk in Ocean City." Morehouse looked up, and Scoobie added, "You heard of Ocean City, New Jersey, I bet."

Morehouse ignored Scoobie's apparent sarcasm. "Name?" Morehouse asked.

"Everyone called him Turk."

"Yeah, I heard that at the carnival." Scoobie looked puzzled, and he added, "Your buddies here said you gave him the evil eye, so I checked him out some."

"He's slick, or was. Bet you won't find a record on him." He shut his eyes for a second and then opened them. "Anyway, he saw me, too. I could tell from the way he looked at me that he was still up to his old routine."

Scoobie cleared his throat and Ramona picked up the cup of ice water with its straw and held it to his lips.

"Thanks. He sold pot, maybe other stuff. Even to kids. Ran the Ferris Wheel." Scoobie paused for several seconds. "It would look like he was helping somebody get strapped in, but they'd be passing him a ten or twenty and he'd give them a small baggie when they got off."

"Do that here?" Morehouse asked.

"Not sure. I went just inside that bunch of trees and brush and watched him for a couple hours, even after the carnival closed. Didn't see him at it. It got damn cold on that ground, and I was going to leave about eleven-thirty when I saw him and a couple guys heading for a car. I walked back into town."

"Hmm. One of my guys said he thought he saw you in the Sandpiper," Morehouse said.

"Yeah. I walked to the drive-up window at Burger King and after I got my burger I saw them leaving the Sandpiper."

Scoobie closed his eyes, and I half-glared at Morehouse. *This is too much for Scoobie.*

"Just another minute," Morehouse said, seemingly reading my thoughts.

"Turk sees me, and he starts laughing, and calls out that his old friend Scoobie should come over for a drink. The other two guys left and I went into the bar with him."

"And argued with him." Morehouse made it a statement, not a question.

"Yeah. I told him I was giving him the hairy eyeball and to stay away from the local kids. He didn't like that."

"That's enough." We all turned to look at Nurse Ratched, arms folded across her chest. "I told you two minutes, sergeant."

I've never seen anyone give Sgt. Morehouse orders. I liked it.

"Only have one more, then we can finish tomorrow," Morehouse told her. He turned back to Scoobie. "You know who did this to you?"

"Nope. We split, and I followed him over to that dive hotel on B Street."

Morehouse only nodded, and I decided not to mention my morning's foray to the Ocean Alley Budget Inn.

Scoobie had his eyes closed now. "He had an outside room, and I saw what room he went in and I was actually going to call you about him in the morning."

Morehouse smiled, "Stranger things have happened."

"Really strange," Scoobie said. "Anyway, I walked up onto the boardwalk for a kind of pleasant detour home. Hadn't gone but a few steps and somebody must have snuck up and shoved me down that flight of concrete steps, not far from Java Jolt. That's the last thing I remember, until I woke up here."

"Out!" Nurse Ratched said.

I told Scoobie I'd check in on him once more and then probably go home to sleep.

"I heard you slept here." He smiled with closed eyes. "You'd miss me."

"Nah, just your poems."

We walked down the hall with Sgt. Morehouse. A quick look in the waiting room showed it had a lively group, complete with bags of potato chips. "Come on, over here," Morehouse said, nodding toward the bank of elevators.

He leaned against the wall, and I realized he looked pretty tired. He must have been checking out a lot of people about Scoobie.

"It makes sense he don't remember much," Morehouse began.

"Why?" I asked.

"Lemme finish. Thing is, the tox screen showed quite a bit of Rohypnol…"

"He wouldn't…" Ramona said.

"What is it?" I asked.

"I said lemme finish," he scowled, including both of us in his annoyed look.

"Scoobie never did anything with needles," Morehouse said. "Plus, it was a really bad needle stick. Somebody already high as a kite might do it that bad, but Scoobie wasn't using. He didn't stick himself." He thought for a moment, seeming to choose his words carefully. "Now, don't get all hysterical on me here, but my guess is someone wanted to kill him."

"What is it?" I repeated.

Morehouse gave me a funny look. "It's a date rape drug. Usually it's not injected, but rarely people, especially stupid people, crush a pill and inject the powder. Somebody either had it with them or came back to finish off Scoobie."

"Mexican valium," Ramona said, slowly.

"How do you know that?" I asked.

She shrugged. "You work at the beach, you hear what people use." She stared directly at Morehouse, as if daring him to ask who used it.

"So, whoever hurt Scoobie is a pretty evil person all the way around…" I began.

The elevator door opened and George Winters walked out. His eyebrows went up and he grinned at Morehouse. "Been calling you."

"Yeah, I know." Morehouse gave him a fifteen second summary, leaving out the so-called needle stick, all the while walking to the elevator. "Scoobie's awake, but he don't know much about what happened. Looks as if someone snuck up on him from behind, pushed him down a flight of stairs."

As if in response to Morehouse's wishes, the elevator door opened and he stepped in, holding up a hand so George would not join him. "Get a new phone yet?" he asked, as the door closed.

Chapter Ten

SCOOBIE MOVED TO A REGULAR room on Wednesday morning, and he was allowed to sit in a chair and walk with a walker. He didn't like the walker, but Drs. Nobles and Cahill said it was for balance and to get him to do everything slowly until his vertebrae healed more. He didn't complain when the occupational therapist worked with him, showing him how to do things without straining his back or neck. That was a clue about how much pain he was in. A needed clue, since he wouldn't let on.

I went to get coffee when the occupational therapist worked with him. I know how hard "face time" with people is for Scoobie, and thought he was only being reasonably chilled about everything because Aunt Madge visits mid-morning each day. He wouldn't want her to chew him out. I know his attitudes are what work for him, but I still don't get it. Scoobie seems so at ease with Ramona and me — most of the time.

When she visited this morning, Aunt Madge had told Scoobie his mother had come and possibly gone. I waited in the hall, not sure what Scoobie would want me to hear. I wasn't eavesdropping, really, but did hear him say, "She still alive?" Then he offered Aunt Madge a piece of fruit from the basket Reverend Jamison had sent over from "your friends at First Prez." Since he never mentioned his mother, I didn't either.

Scoobie was tired after his time with the OT so I decided to go back to Cozy Corner about ten-thirty. Just before I did I remembered Alicia's reaction to Scoobie's injuries and told him about it.

"Huh. I saw her a couple times at the carnival," he said. "She helped Megan some at the dunk tank...hey, how much did we make?"

"Seven hundred and eighty-two dollars. Can you believe that?" I asked.

"Ha! Next time I have an idea don't put it down so fast."

"The most was when Martin Small was up there. He was one of the people who said he'd stay up there as long as there were people who wanted to knock him down."

"Every druggie in town?" he asked, alluding to some of the people Small prosecuted a lot.

"Nope, Lance said it was the cops. Guess they think he's a weenie."

"So, Alicia," he said, thinking. "After she helped some at the dunk tank she went off with friends. They were hanging around the Merry-go-Round a lot."

"Do you suppose..?" I began.

"Drugs? Jeez, Jolie, she seems awful young."

I gave him a look, "And you were how old when you had your first joint?"

"I guess I see your point. But why would she be so upset about me? She thinks I'm a dork."

"If you mean because you kept trying to get people to bet on how many cans of sweet potatoes would be left on the shelves after Christmas, I think she got over that."

"She's what, twelve or thirteen?" he asked.

"I guess. Did you see her talking to any carnival workers?"

He shook his head. "They were doing the usual kid stuff. Ignoring the boys, trying to guess each other's weight on that huge scale. Girl giggly stuff."

I smiled at that. "They might come visit you. Megan and Alicia."

He grimaced and then gestured at the baskets of fruit and candy. "I don't want to see anyone, but I guess they're OK. Tell Megan not to bring anything for me."

AUNT MADGE WAS really pleased that I offered to take Mr. Rogers and Miss Piggy for a long walk Wednesday afternoon.

"They're tired of the back yard." She loaded me up with plastic bags.

"And you're tired of poop patrol. Sorry I haven't been here more to do it."

"Heavens, nothing matters except Adam getting better."

The Ocean Alley Middle School is about six blocks from Aunt Madge's, so I had to hustle to get there in the neighborhood of two forty-five, which is about when I remembered being annoyed by school buses in that area. Hustling was not what Mr. Rogers and Miss Piggy had in mind, and they resented not sniffing every tree or bush.

I knew Megan and Alicia lived two blocks west of the school, as I'd dropped them off a couple evenings before Christmas when we all worked late at the food pantry. I could see the buses parked in front of the school, so I figured we were right on time. I hadn't counted on the dogs freaking out when another bus pulled up, so I was busy convincing Mr. Rogers to keep moving toward the school when the bell rang and kids started pouring out.

It suddenly occurred to me that while the dogs seemed like a good excuse to be walking by the school, I hadn't thought of how they would react to all the kids. No worries. Tails wagging and tongues out, they immediately forgot the big yellow buses and walked toward the groups of kids. I suspected there were some food smells in their knapsacks.

"Oh, they're so cute. Can I pet them?" asked a girl who looked to be about twelve.

"Sure. They love attention." *I've never seen them even nip at anyone. What if they bite?* I broke into a sweat as six or eight kids surrounded the dogs. Miss Piggy immediately plopped on the ground and put her front paws over her eyes, a trick she learned before coming to Aunt Madge and uses periodically to get attention or dog treats. She was a big hit.

Between keeping an eye on the dogs and responding to questions about how old they were and if they were siblings (*who the hell cares?)* I would have missed Alicia if she hadn't seen me and walked over.

"Jolie. You have dogs."

"Technically Aunt Madge does. I probably should have walked in the other direction this time of day." I took in her black-on-black outfit, which was nothing I'd seen her in. They didn't look like clothes Megan would buy for Alicia, but what did I know?

"Could you hold one leash, Alicia?" I asked.

She put both knapsack straps over her shoulders. "Sure." She reached for Miss Piggy's leash and urged her to stand. "You going back toward your aunt's?" she asked.

"We can go in your direction for a minute or two. I don't want to keep you from your homework."

There was general laughter at this, and the group of mostly girls said goodbye and moved in different directions.

"I hope I didn't embarrass you. That was probably a dumb thing to say."

She smiled and we stopped while Mr. Rogers smelled a bench near the school's main entrance. "It's okay. They know who you are."

That confused me for a few seconds, until I realized my picture had been in the paper a few times, and Alicia probably talked to them about helping at Harvest for All. Should I be insulted? I pushed that thought aside.

We were past the school boundaries and there weren't any more kids to talk to. Alicia seemed so relaxed I almost hated to bring up the carnival, but that was why I was here.

"Scoobie's getting a bit better every day. He was really pleased that you cared so much about him."

"Oh, uh, sure." She began to look worried, perhaps sensing this was more than a dog walk.

"The police don't really have any leads. I thought it might be this guy who seemed to know Scoobie, but I guess not."

She started to hand me back the leash. "I need to..."

I didn't take it. "Alicia, what did you see? Why were you so upset?"

Her eyes darted from side to side, avoiding my gaze. "I didn't see anything."

We were stopped now, and Miss Piggy was relieving herself on a blooming azalea bush. "Nobody'll be mad at you. I can't imagine you did anything wrong."

"I didn't." She was almost fierce, and she wiped her eyes with the back of the hand not holding a leash.

"But you saw something, something you wonder if you should talk about, but you're afraid to." When she looked away I continued. "You don't need to talk to the police. Just tell me."

She looked back at me. "You won't tell my mom either?"

That got me. "Did anybody hurt you?"

"No." She said this very quickly. "Not at all."

"Okay, I won't tell your mom." Bad thing to promise, Jolie.

She took a deep breath. "You remember when you guys were walking back to the gong thing, but then Scoobie walked away?"

That I didn't expect. "Yes."

"Well, the guy, the worker. He was looking at Scoobie, and when you guys turned away he called Scoobie an asshole, but not very loud. And then," she paused, "he sort of noticed I was looking at him, and he just gave me a funny smile, and then started talking loud again."

"Talking loud?"

"You know, all the dumb stuff they say to get you to play the games."

I smiled at that. "The guy on the loud speaker was the worst."

"Footlong dogs," she said, and we both laughed for a second. Alicia looked away.

"There's something else," I said quietly.

"And you won't tell?"

"Nope. I think I know what it is, I just want to see if I'm right."

She looked surprised, kind of as if no adult could have a clue. "Well...did you know he sells joints and stuff?"

"Scoobie said the guy used to do it years ago. It's why Scoobie didn't want to be around him."

She nodded. "I didn't buy any." She looked directly at me. "Really."

"That's good. You wouldn't believe all the crud in marijuana smoke." *To say nothing about it being illegal.*

Her eyes widened. "What kind of crud?"

Bad word choice. "Ammonia, for starters. Look on the internet." This topic was not why I was here.

Her look became resentful. "Are you going to tell me to stay away from all that stuff because of Whitney Houston?"

I sighed. "You know who Len Bias was?"

She gave me a blank stare. "The guys'll know. He was a star basketball player at the University of Maryland, supposed to be one of the best to be going to the NBA that year. He used cocaine once."

"So?" She had adopted a haughty attitude. She probably got a lot of 'advice' from her mom and teachers.

"Died." I snapped my fingers. "Just like that. So much for celebrating the basketball season."

She said nothing, and her look was almost defiant.

"Just marijuana?" I asked.

"I think maybe some pills, but I'm really not sure. I heard one of the guys say he was going to fly tonight."

"I'm not going to lecture you at all, that's not why I'm here." Though she better pay attention.

She looked back at me, probably regretting her offer to take one of the dog's leashes.

"Somebody hurt Scoobie on purpose. I just don't want it to happen again, and I definitely don't want that jerk selling drugs to kids."

"But you said you wouldn't tell!"

"I promise, I won't." I looked into her eyes, which had lost all pretense of teenage cool.

A voice came from behind us. "Jolie. Is that you?"

Megan had a grocery bag in each hand, probably walking home from Mr. Markle's store.

"I promise," I said again, quietly. "Yep. It's me. Alicia helped me organize the dogs. I didn't realize the school buses would scare them."

Megan literally beamed. "Hi sweetie."

Alicia's posture relaxed, and she handed me back Miss Piggy's leash. Miss Piggy, who had been panting on the cool brick sidewalk, stood and gave herself a good shake. I realized she and Mr. Rogers both had their eyes on Megan's bags.

I pulled their leashes closer to me. "Not for you, guys." They ignored me, still focused on Megan. She walked into the street to get around us.

"Sorry! We're just heading home. They haven't had a good walk in days."

"Of course." She frowned. "Scoobie doing okay?"

"He's getting there. It'll be a long haul, but he'll probably recover completely."

We said a couple more of the usual things, and I turned to take the dogs home. This wasn't the first time they'd helped me out, though never intentionally. "You guys get a doggie treat when we get home." They ignored me, preferring to pay attention to a nearby fire hydrant.

I VISITED SCOOBIE AGAIN LATE WEDNESDAY afternoon. Yet again he told me I shouldn't visit three times every day. "You have a life. I know it's a boring one with me in here, but jeez Jolie, if you don't have better things to do you should probably collect shells or something."

I sat my bag on his bed and plopped myself down next to it. Scoobie was in one of those hospital recliners your skin sticks to. Lester Argrow, of all people, had bought him an MP3 player, and Scoobie was trying to figure out how to adjust the sound.

"I really appreciate this, you know, but what makes him think I'd have money to buy the CDs to load onto here?" he asked.

I frowned. "I think I heard you can put audio books on it. Maybe ask Daphne."

"That would be great. Especially if I can use the library's talking books." He grinned at me. "Can't you see me taking a walk on the beach with ear buds in and getting run over by the lifeguard's cart?"

"Can you lend it to George?" I asked.

Scoobie shook his head. "I don't like what he writes sometimes, either, but you should give it a rest with him."

"Yeah, I guess." I jumped in before Scoobie could continue and told him about my conversation with Alicia. "And I meant it when I said I wouldn't tell, but I need to find a way to let Morehouse or Dana know so they can tell cops in some of the other towns."

Scoobie thought for a moment. "Just tell him, without using Alicia's name."

"And if he insists?"

"Tell him you've had a head injury and your brain is foggy."

Chapter Eleven

EXCEPT FOR THE TIME WITH ALICIA, I was either at the Cozy Corner or at the hospital. "How's the head?" I asked him on Thursday in the late afternoon.

"A lot better. I've been cutting back on the pain meds. Even Nurse Ratched says I shouldn't go so low, but I don't need narcotics in my life again."

Scoobie had adopted my reference to the nurse who was most strict, but there were times when I was pretty sure he liked her a lot. "I'm going to go over to the food pantry, probably tomorrow, and Harry says he has a couple houses for me to appraise in the popsicle district."

"I keep telling you not to be here so much." Scoobie was supervising my efforts to build a tower of cans of the meal supplements that masquerade as milkshakes. He refused to drink them, and was tired of them cluttering the table by his bed. We had opted for the window sill.

"Now that you're feeling better, I feel better." I stole a glance at him. He was rooting in a small goody bag Ramona had dropped off yesterday evening, though he had to hold it up to his face as he couldn't bend his neck to look at it. Ramona had brought him a couple candy bars, a steno pad and a few pens, along with a card from Roland that said Scoobie could have free steno pads for a year.

I was starting to feel guilty about not telling Aunt Madge or Scoobie that I'd seen Penny at the Ocean Alley Budget Inn a couple days ago. Penny had not been back to the Cozy Corner after that, so Aunt Madge had packed up her things and cleaned the room. Penny's suitcase and smaller bag were now under Aunt Madge's own bed.

It was almost four o'clock when Sgt. Morehouse came in. Scoobie had once said Morehouse was "not high on his Christmas list," and I assumed this was the result of Scoobie's marijuana arrests long ago. Now, it seemed they had established some sort of truce. When Scoobie gestured to the visitor's chair Morehouse sat down.

"Scoobie, I gotta tell you something hard to hear, and I wish I could wait a couple weeks, but I can't." Morehouse looked at his hands as Scoobie glanced at me and back to him. Then Morehouse looked directly at Scoobie. "I'm sorry to say we found your mother's body early this morning." I'm not sure yet how she..."

"You can go now," Scoobie said. His voice was stronger than it had been since before he got hurt, and pretty harsh.

Morehouse stood slowly. "I hear you." He took a card from his pocket and set it on the bedside table. "My cell and office numbers are on there. You call anytime you want to." He gave me a small nod as he left.

Scoobie looked out the window. No tears, just a stony expression.

"Would you like me to go, too?" I asked.

"I guess I need some time to myself."

"I'll come back about seven unless you call and say not to."

He glanced at me briefly and I blew him a kiss.

I STOPPED AT THE PURPLE COW, which was getting ready to close. I was pretty sure it was the first time I'd given Ramona news she hadn't heard elsewhere. Her reaction surprised me.

"That horrible woman. She screws up Scoobie's life for years, then when he's sick she ignores him, and then she gets herself killed." She slammed the cash register drawer shut and Roland looked over at us.

I left Ramona for a minute and told him what Morehouse had said. When he pestered me for details I just said Scoobie hadn't asked for any so I hadn't either. I didn't mention that Scoobie had pretty much thrown Sgt. Morehouse out of his hospital room.

"I won't stick around long," I told him.

"That's okay today. You stay out of the way when we have customers," Roland said. He glanced back at Ramona who was furiously polishing the glass top of the display case by the cash register, and shrugged.

I walked back to Ramona, and on the way noticed her white board was just inside the front door rather than on the sidewalk, and it was blank. "Where's your message?"

She stopped spraying glass cleaner and looked up. "I just can't think of anything, I'm too upset. And I'm mad at George Winters about it. He's in here every day and bugs me about it."

"I'm always mad at George." I thought this might get a smile, but it didn't. "You, uh, want me to go, too?"

"What do you mean, too?" she asked.

"I asked Scoobie if he wanted me to leave his room and he said he'd like to be alone."

"If it was two years ago I'd worry about that, but I know he can deal with it. Sort of, anyway." She stowed the cleaner in a bottom cupboard.

I walked back to my car, repeating the mental debate about whether to tell Sgt. Morehouse I'd seen Penny at the Ocean Alley Budget Inn. I knew I had to, and the longer I put it off the madder he would be. My cell phone rang and I fished it from a pocket.

"What the hell do you think you're doing?"

I recognized the bellow at Morehouse's and didn't need to ask why he was mad. "I'm on my way to the station now. Honest."

"You damn well better be." He said this at almost bellow level, so I knew he was really mad.

FOR THE FIRST TIME I didn't have to wait in the small lobby for Morehouse, he was at the counter talking to the officer on duty. "Back here," he said, and I followed him toward his tiny office. We continued past it to a conference room a couple doors down.

I knew I was in trouble when I saw Lt. Tortino. It wasn't just his higher rank. He'd hauled me to Aunt Madge when he found me smoking on the boardwalk in eleventh grade. He may not have had a "right" to do that, but I didn't know it. I felt a little like my fifteen-year old self as I sat across from him. Morehouse shut the door.

"Why were you looking for Penny on Tuesday?" Lt. Tortino asked.

"I wasn't."

"Jolie..." Morehouse began.

"I wanted to see if Turk or whatever his name is was staying there over the weekend. And maybe whether anybody saw him with Scoobie. Penny just walked in."

Neither of them said anything for a few seconds, then Morehouse did. "Let me get this straight. You called me Sunday night because you were terrified of him at the hospital, and Tuesday morning you go looking for him?"

"No. I knew he was gone." I stared directly at Lt. Tortino, who shook his head.

"See if anything she knows will help," Tortino said, standing and nodding at Morehouse.

I don't like to be talked about as if I'm not in the room, but this didn't seem the time to mention that. Morehouse sat so he was across the table from me and I thought of TV shows where the detectives question suspects.

"What did you and Penny talk about?" he asked.

"We didn't talk..."

"Desk clerk said you did," he said, evenly.

"She walked in, I told her we missed her the night before — which was a lie, of course — and she asked the guy for another room key."

"And?" Morehouse asked.

I stared at him for a second. "She told him I was friendly with cops. Which made the desk clerk guy really happy, so I left."

"And what did Penny do then?"

"Nothing. She just walked out the door into the hall. I assume she was going to her room."

"So, nothing else?"

I thought for a minute. "She was wearing a beautiful pants suit."

He looked up, probably assuming I was being facetious, and his expression changed when he could tell I wasn't. "Nice clothes? Penny?"

"Yep, a light blue outfit and an expensive purse. What was she wearing when you found her?"

It almost worked. "Her usual slovenly...I'm asking you." He paused. "Sounds like the same purse, though."

"Hmm. So she was dressed up Tuesday and back in her usual clothes by today?" I wondered what on earth she was doing that required her to dress up.

"Can you tell me anything else, Jolie?" he asked, clicking his pen.

When I said no he stood and walked out without saying anything.

I LEFT AND DEBATED calling Winters, remembering Dana Johnson said he knew how to hold his tongue. I had no idea what his phone number was, since I'd spent a lot of time avoiding him, so I had to wait until I got back to the Cozy Corner.

George was sitting on Aunt Madge's sofa, looking very out of place in his Hawaiian shirt and jeans. Aunt Madge had probably told him to wait while she served afternoon bread to her one B&B guest.

"I was going to call you just now," I sat across from him.

He gave me a "yeah, right," look.

"Honest. You know, then? About his mom?"

"Just heard. You know anything?" He flipped open his notebook.

"Scoobie didn't want to hear, so Morehouse left almost as soon as he got there. All he really said was that they didn't yet know how she died."

"Rats, that's probably true, then." My uncertainty must have showed, because he added, "That's what he told me. He wouldn't have told Scoobie that if he did know. Scoobie?" he asked.

I shrugged. "I asked if I should go and all he said was he wanted to be alone, so I left. I'm not sure if he was sad or mad or what."

He stood to go. "All I know is they found her north of town. Morehouse said her car was full of beer bottles and a bunch of other stuff and he thought she was leaving. He said something about maybe New York, but I figured it was a guess."

"I wonder why she didn't take her suitcase," I said this more to myself than him.

"What do you mean? How do you know that?" he asked.

"Because she stayed here the night she got here. Aunt Madge invited her."

"You said you'd share info," he said, his voice rising.

"Shh. The guest." I nodded my head toward the door to the breakfast room. "I honestly didn't think it was important until now. Aunt Madge wanted to keep track of her, so she invited Penny to stay here. But after she went to the hospital Monday morning Penny only came back for a few minutes. She asked if she could leave her stuff here for a few days, or something like that."

He stood and walked to the sliding door and let Miss Piggy in. "You and Madge didn't think that odd?"

"What was odd was that she was still in town. I saw her at the Budget Inn."

"What were you doing...? Oh, the carnies stay there." He thought for a few seconds. "Penny and the carnies."

"Coincidence you think?"

"Can't be," he said. "But why would she leave stuff here?"

I shrugged. "She had some other clothes. When I saw her Tuesday morning she had changed into something nicer."

"Nicer that her usual, or really nice?"

I considered this. "Really nice, blue pantsuit."

"So," he said. "Penny got some money."

"Maybe she was staying with someone who worked at the carnival."

"She could have, when they were here, anyway." Aunt Madge walked through the kitchen door.

"Why do you say that?" George asked more politely than he talked to me.

Aunt Madge put two tea mugs in the sink and walked to us. "She used to occasionally work at the carnivals when they came through the area. Sold tickets to the rides."

"You forgot to mention that earlier," I tried hard not to sound critical.

She shrugged. "Hadn't thought much about Penny in years. She was better known for being in the Sandpiper a lot."

George tucked his pencil stub back into the spiral of his notebook. "It doesn't make sense that she was in the motel but had her stuff there."

I gave him a look that I hoped said "you're kidding." Out loud, I added, "You knew her longer than I did. Did she strike you as somebody who always made sense?"

I stayed on the sofa while George let himself out through the small back yard. Mister Rogers came in as he left and trotted over to see if I was in possession of dog treats. I stroked him absently, thinking.

Where had she been since I saw her at the Budget Inn on Tuesday and today?

Aunt Madge interrupted my thoughts. "I didn't want to talk to George until I talked to you, so I gave him a cup of tea and said I'd be back." She sat next to me on the sofa. "How is Adam?"

"Could be worse."

AND IT WAS. I tried to talk to Scoobie when I went back at seven, but he answered in monosyllables and asked me to turn on the TV.

I left after about twenty minutes and said I'd be back late morning on Friday, unless he called my cell and said not to come. He just nodded.

I APPRAISED A HOUSE in the popsicle district Friday morning and when I got to the hospital just before lunch it was as if Sgt. Morehouse hadn't given Scoobie the news about his mother. He had a steno pad on the wheeled tray in front of him, though on it were mostly doodles and a few single words in a list. I carefully avoided looking at the pad.

"Would you see if the little kitchen up here has chocolate milk?" he asked, as I sat down my purse.

I came back from the patient kitchen with the milk, already opened and with a straw. "I'm not talking to you about it, but you know I'm around if you want to talk, right?"

"Yeah, I know." He held the milk even with his mouth and stuck the straw across his neck collar. "Hadn't seen her in years. I'm trying to be glad she's gone without wishing her dead. I've wished that a lot, but it's kind of pointless now."

I wasn't sure if he thought that was funny, so all I did was nod. When he didn't say more I picked up the remote and turned to a rerun of "Murder She Wrote." We'd watched MASH the afternoon before, but Scoobie said he had enough needles on his own.

We didn't talk, and my thoughts kept returning to Penny. I realized I didn't know when she actually died, only that her body was found early Thursday. I wondered if I could have been one of the last people to see her alive.

BECAUSE SCOOBIE'S MOTHER was found a couple miles north of Ocean Alley, there was just a short note about her death on the inside page of the *Ocean Alley Press*. There was no mention that she was Scoobie's mother, and I figured Scoobie had George to thank for that. I did get to learn her last name, though. It was Pittsen. I'd never heard of that name.

"Because she made it up," Morehouse said. He was at the B&B late Friday afternoon, about to go through Penny's suitcase.

"Who makes up a name?" I asked.

"Somebody who gets out of Taconic Women's Correctional Facility in upstate New York and doesn't want to use one of her prior names when she starts stealing stuff and forging checks again."

Sgt. Morehouse pulled on a pair of latex gloves.

"Why are you wearing gloves?" I asked. "You think the stuff in her suitcase has something to do with her death?"

"You saw her, would you touch her stuff without gloves?" he asked. He was carefully putting her makeup in separate plastic bags. "Might have fingerprints besides just hers," he said, in answer to my questioning look.

The suitcase was sitting on Aunt Madge's oak kitchen table and she was standing a few feet away, arms folded. She had told Sgt. Morehouse she went through the suitcase, and he was grouchy about it, so she'd gone into her bedroom for a few minutes and then come back. "Do you see much besides the pot?" she asked.

"Nope. Just trying to cover all the bases," he said, cramming Penny's clothes back into the suitcase. I was struck by the fact that she had no books. Scoobie is usually reading two or three at the same time.

"Don't forget the smaller bag that was in the closet," Aunt Madge said, as it looked as if Morehouse was readying to leave.

"Oh yeah." He reached down to the chair on which she had placed it. "Heavy sucker. What's in it?"

"Locked," Aunt Madge said.

"I thought you said you didn't look because she had clothes over it so you figured it was more private," I said.

She shrugged and we both watched as Morehouse picked the tiny lock with the small pocket knife on the end of a pair of nail clippers.

"We'll just see what was so all-fired..." he stopped.

The small bag was full of sterling silverware and money. Lots of money.

Chapter Twelve

"THAT'S WHAT THEY CALL a game changer," Morehouse said as he stared at the money and silverware.

I kept gazing at the case, unable to stop looking at the fifteen or twenty rubber-banded stacks. There was a one hundred dollar bill on top of one, fifties and twenties on others. There was no way to see if each stack was comprised of all the same denomination without looking through them. I figured Morehouse would cut off my hand and use it for fish bait if I tried.

"It's real, right?" I asked.

"Do I look like the Secret Service?" he asked.

Aunt Madge walked closer for a better look. "I can think of a lot of reasons she'd have that, and none of them are good ones."

"Ya think?" Morehouse sat on a wooden kitchen chair. "This I did not expect." He was already on his cell phone asking for another officer to help him "with the contents of Penny's luggage."

"When did she get out of prison?" I asked.

"Middle of February," he said.

"Wouldn't it be nice if all of us could accumulate cash that fast?" Aunt Madge said.

I looked at Morehouse. "Burglary and kiting checks, you said she was in for that."

"Technically receiving stolen property. I'm thinking she branched out."

"Who would trust her with this kind of money?" Aunt Madge asked.

"Nobody." They both looked at me. "She's dead, right? My guess is she wasn't supposed to have it. Or keep it, anyway."

Morehouse literally shook his finger at me. "You stay outta this."

I feigned an injured look. "You know I always do what you say."

The doorbell rang and I started for the front door, but Aunt Madge put out a hand. "I want to let the dogs out before I let anyone else in."

"I mean it, Jolie," Morehouse said.

I raised my hands in mock surrender. "She's all yours."

THEY DECIDED NOT TO UNFASTEN the packets of money in Aunt Madge's kitchen, so it didn't take long for Morehouse and Lt. Tortino to write and sign a note agreeing to the number of stacks of bills and their height, which they measured with Aunt Madge's pock-marked wooden tape measure. Each stack was about a half-inch tall.

"You want me to donate money for you to get a new measuring tape?" Tortino asked her, with a humorous smirk.

"It was Gordon's." Her expression did not change.

That shut them up. Uncle Gordon's been dead more than twenty years.

I walked them to the front door. When I got back to the kitchen Aunt Madge was sitting at her oak table, hands in her lap, doing nothing. She had not even turned up the lever on the electric tea kettle, so I did, and sat in a chair at the head of the table so I could face her.

"You okay?"

She shook her head. "Someone killed her, probably looking for that money. They could have come here looking for it."

I nodded. "Guess they didn't know she stayed here that night. Cozy Corner is a little beyond her usual price range." I was trying to get Aunt Madge to look less worried, but it didn't help.

Both dogs barked and I looked toward the sliding glass door. Jazz was strutting back and forth in front of it, as if to emphasize she was in and they were out. I let them in. Aunt Madge's phone rang and she answered, saying only "hello" and "I'll tell her."

She looked at me. "Sgt. Morehouse says he assumes we know not to talk about the money."

As if.

NOW THAT WE KNEW Penny had all that money there was no pretending, as I had tried to do, that her death was random. I didn't give a damn about Penny, but I was nervous about what finding this out would mean for Scoobie.

I put it out of my mind as I pulled in front of Harry Steele's Victorian home early Friday evening. I hadn't been there but once since last Saturday, and was stopping by on my way back to the hospital. Last fall Harry had replaced some boards on the front porch and he had been trying to get the paint he put on them to turn out the same color as the paint he put on older boards. This spring he apparently had gotten over that desire, as the porch and first story were all freshly painted a dark green, with slight color variations in a few places. It looked as if the paint stopped at the point Harry could reach standing on a ladder.

Harry's house had not been as well cared for through the years as Aunt Madge's. She repaints hers every three years, white with blue trim and shutters. Harry's grandparents had owned his place, but it had had other owners for more than twenty years when he bought it. They had divided it into three apartments and the last owner had taken as much care of it as slum landlords take care of inner-city duplexes. Harry says, quite proudly, that he bought it "just in time to save it." I'd have razed it, but he has put on a new roof and hung drywall throughout. Only the first floor looks really good, but he says he's in no hurry.

I let myself in the side door nearest to the large first-floor office he and I share and hollered as I walked in. I heard him yell that he'd be down in a minute, so I walked to the pile of files that represented appraisals yet to be done. It's usually only one or two deep, as I grab them pretty fast. Harry pays me half of what he gets as the appraisal fee, and he doesn't mind if I do most of them. Since I hadn't done but one for a week there were four files.

Two were from the popsicle district, courtesy of Lester; one was a multi-unit rental on C Street, and the other a larger single family home about 20 minutes north of town. A note on the folder said it was the home of the son of one of Harry's college buddies. I studied that one first. Manasquan was on the way to Asbury Park, almost at the halfway point between Ocean Alley and Asbury Park. I wouldn't have to explain why I was heading out of town. As a matter of basic courtesy I usually tell Aunt Madge my plans for a day. I'm not saying I'm always one-hundred percent truthful, but I do live under her roof. For free.

"Hey, Jolie." Harry looked as if he'd been painting. He had a large butcher-type apron, which had several colors of paint on it, over a pair of cotton pants and a long-sleeve tee-shirt. "I'm really glad to hear Scoobie is doing better."

"He got your card. That was nice of you." Harry had stuck two tens in the card with a note that said "in case hospital food gets to you." I could tell Scoobie was mildly offended at first, but then he had grinned and said if I took money from Harry he could, too, and he stuck the bills in a book.

"You sure you can do this?" he asked as he finished wiping his hands on a paper towel and threw it in a waste basket. "I was about to do a couple of those, but I'd rather keep painting."

"Yep. I think I'll do a couple of the in-town ones next week and maybe do the one in Manasquan tomorrow, if that's okay." Because the carnival will be open on Saturday.

"Sure, as long as that's okay with the clients. None of the settlements are for at least a month."

We talked for a couple minutes more about the houses and Scoobie, and then I left. As I drove I realized I'd have to look in the Monmouth County courthouse for the house in Manasquan. Usually I'd do it the same day I did the house, but the courthouse would be closed on Saturday. I wouldn't mind going to Manasquan twice, and piously assured myself I would not charge Harry mileage for the second trip.

I WAS DRIVING to the hospital Saturday morning when it hit me. If someone killed Penny for that money they'd still be looking for it, and they might know she'd been to the hospital to visit Scoobie. They wouldn't know the stupid woman never talked to her son or left him as much as a get well card.

A plan began forming in my head. I know enough about myself to know that's not always a good thing. But still...

Scoobie was walking in the hallway with a physical therapy staff member when I got there, so I helped myself to a page from his steno pad and one of the pens on the table by his bed.

What I know
- Scoobie is getting better
- The carny guy was Turk/Stefan
- Penny's been in prison
- Penny likely knows some carny people
- Penny was up to something
- The carnival is in Asbury Park
- Morehouse and Aunt Madge would be ticked at me if they saw this list.

What I need to know
- Who hurt Scoobie?
- Why did they hurt him?
- Why did Penny come to the hospital?
- Where did Penny get all her stuff?
- Who killed Penny?
- Why was Alicia upset about Scoobie?
- Did whoever killed Penny know Scoobie was her son?

I studied the list. Someone else might say Penny came to the hospital because her son was hurt, but I thought she was a narcissistic woman who would only come if she saw something to gain. I left this off the "what I know" list because there was no way to know. I figured Scoobie would agree with me. Not that I planned on showing him the list.

"Yo, Jolie," Scoobie and his walker came slowly into the room. I watched the therapist help him into bed and replace the large, stiff collar with a softer one.

"Thanks," I told him as he placed Scoobie's walker near the bed.

Scoobie had his eyes closed for a half-minute, then looked at me. "I saw you slip that paper into your pocket. What are you doing?"

"It's my grocery list."

"Bull." He stared at me for several seconds. "You better leave this one alone. I won't be available for ass-saving for probably a few weeks."

Scoobie has every right to take some credit for my well being, but that doesn't mean he's my boss. "I'm not going to do anything dumb."

"Yeah, right." George Winters came in and walked toward the bed. "Had a brain transplant, Jolie?"

I was about to suggest he leave when I noticed Scoobie seemed really pleased to see him. What is that about?

"Thought I wouldn't come by too often 'til you got your sea legs again," George said, looking directly at Scoobie. "Morehouse was actually sharing some info, so that helped me out."

"Yeah, he's been by a couple of times. I keep telling him I don't remember anything after I got hit or pushed or whatever it was."

Since I wasn't needed, I said I was going to get a cup of coffee and, to be polite, asked if Scoobie or George wanted one. George did.

"And I won't offer to pay, since my new phone costs about $120. *Gulp.* "Uh, why so expensive?"

"Cause I'd only had it a few months and didn't buy insurance."

"That might be a good thing to buy in your business," I said.

At this he turned toward the chair I was in, just across from the foot of the bed. "I've been a reporter for more than ten years. Guess how many phones I broke?"

I was about to give a smart-ass answer when I noticed Scoobie looked pained by the conversation. "Tell you what George, I'll buy you coffee every time you come by." And then I'll leave.

He just grunted.

I sat in the cafeteria nursing my coffee for about ten minutes, and then headed back to Scoobie's room. The door was open, per usual, so I walked in. George and Scoobie were sitting with their heads close together talking quietly. Unsure if I should barge in, I backed out.

After a few second, Scoobie called, "Come on in, Jolie."

George was standing and he pushed shut the top drawer of Scoobie's bedside table as I walked in. I handed him the coffee.

"One down, 119 to go," he said.

"Don't push it." I said.

"Catch you later, Scoob," he said, and left.

"Scoob?" I asked.

"Don't push it," Scoobie said.

Chapter Thirteen

THE GORGEOUS MAY seemed to say summer would bring a lot of tourists to Ocean Alley very soon. A gentle breeze came from the ocean so that when I walked to Java Jolt to get coffee for my drive to Asbury Park, the air smelled marvelously clean. I felt a little guilty for being glad I wouldn't be at the hospital as much, and told myself I only thought that because it was Saturday.

I walked back to Cozy Corner and was on the road by eleven-thirty. The house in Manasquan was a large cape cod, but the site visit was quick, even though the owners were there. They were mildly annoyed that I had asked to come on a Saturday and I hoped they wouldn't mention this to Harry. Ordinarily if someone implied they wanted a different time I would accommodate them. Harry would expect me to put the customer first. *I put Scoobie first.*

I was en route to Asbury Park and its carnival by two o'clock. On the seat beside me were a New Jersey Knicks hat, large sunglasses, and my trusty digital camera. I decided I wouldn't tell Morehouse what Alicia said, I'd get proof myself. What other teenager am I around besides Alicia? He'd figure it out and talk to her. Half of me wanted to keep my promise to Alicia and the other half wanted to dodge Megan's wrath if she learned I had talked to Alicia about something so important behind Megan's back.

I thought the carnival should be crowded enough that no one would pay attention to me. The town of Asbury Park had made it easy to find the carnival; there were signs at every possible corner telling me which way to turn. I pulled into the large parking lot that abutted the carnival, then pulled back out and parked on a side street about three blocks away. I had my sleuth thinking cap on. If a carnival worker followed me to check out my license plate, I wanted to make it hard to do that. A worker probably would not walk a few blocks away from his post.

Asbury Park is a good bit larger than Ocean Alley and the beach area is twice the size of ours. The businesses close to the municipal lot, which housed the carnival, were the same as Ocean Alley's. Beach apparel, small food vendors, tarot card readers, and saltwater taffy outlets. And of course, the casino, which I'm pleased Ocean Alley does not have. *Like I need any reminders.*

There was also a fairly large storefront church, which I didn't recall seeing on previous visits. A large sign in the window read, "God is everywhere, keep your pants up." They were apparently going for the teenage and young adult crowd.

I sat on a bench a couple hundred yards from the carnival entrance. It looked as if there was a roped area around the entire carnival, except for that one spot. I couldn't see the back, of course, but since the Ferris Wheel was there I couldn't imagine an entrance just next to it. If kids today were anything like I was, there would be an occasional peanut drop from the top of the wheel, so it's not a good place for people to congregate.

The size of the carnival was larger, and I saw a kiddie roller coaster that had not been in Ocean Alley. I supposed it made sense to put up fewer rides in smaller venues. A city bus pulled up on the street nearest me and disgorged about ten kids, ranging in age from about eight to fifteen. I followed the kids and caught up with them as they walked in.

"Get your footlong dogs," boomed the overhead speaker. *I should have brought a BB gun.*

I took out my camera so it wouldn't look like the only photos I was taking were of Turk or whatever his name was. Two younger teenage boys immediately asked me to take theirs in front of the pop-a-balloon-with-a-dart game. They wanted me to email them copies of them with the stuffed animals they had won. For a few seconds I was irritated, then it occurred to me it would be good to look as if I was with some of the kids.

"Why don't you put the tiger between you?" I said, getting into the spirit of things.

"Because it's a cocker spaniel," said one of the boys.

"Really?" I looked more closely. As with the stuffed animals Scoobie had won for Ramona and me, it was oddly shaped. I took a couple photos and stopped when they started sticking their tongues out.

One of the boys wrote his email address on an envelope I pulled from my purse. *Damn, I meant to mail that.* Oh well, the student loan people were going to get paid a couple days late.

A cursory look around did not show Turk at any of the rides. Maybe I wasted the better part of an afternoon. I was sitting on a bench to drink an iced tea when I spotted him leaning against the rail that surrounded a ride across from the Ferris Wheel.

It didn't take long to figure out his routine. He called out to clusters of kids, seemingly daring them to go on a ride called the Inverter, which turned them upside down. When my two stuffed animal buddies got close he did his spiel, and then added something. They stopped to talk to him, then shrugged and moved on. He did the same thing to a couple of tall girls, then again to a group of three kids who might be termed misfits.

I chided myself for the term, especially since I was one in high school in Ocean Alley and had been really unhappy about it. But, I was seeing a pattern. He zeroed in on young people who, on the surface, were not part of the 'cool crowd.' Kids who might think his attention was special.

About ten minutes and another iced tea later, Turk took over operation of the Ferris Wheel. I couldn't see where he would keep a supply of anything to sell. Then I noted he often wiped the steel bar that went across riders' laps. Every now and then he set the cloth on a tiny table, then picked it up again.

I was roasting. I never wear hats, certainly not with my hair folded into one. Aunt Madge's face drifted into my mind, with her telling me to wear a hat in winter because twenty percent of a person's body heat goes out through their head. Mine was stuck there. And now I had to go potty. My two iced teas, bought to help me stay cool, were having an unintended consequence.

One last look before I went in search of a restroom told me what he was doing. He slid the bar over the two tall girls' laps and one of them passed him what looked like a piece of green paper. OK, he has the money, now what? The wipe rag was still in his hand and he fooled with it for a couple seconds as he watched the riders. He walked over to the lever that would slow or stop the ride, and reached behind it. When he stood up, Turk was holding the rag differently.

That's all? Something that simple? I wasn't sure what I had expected, but could not imagine that he could keep a small stash of anything right at his work space. As the next couple chairs of riders got off he shook their hands, pointed back to the chairs as if urging them to ride again. When it was the two girls he shook one of their hands with both of his. As they walked away, the girl kept her hand at her side and they went toward the haunted house. *They'll be in the dark. No one will see if they look at it or take a pill.*

I just made it to the port-a-potty before I peed my pants. At St. Anthony's the bathrooms near the church community room are easily accessible, much to my distinct pleasure after I pulled George into the tank. Here they didn't even have wipe-and-dry disposables. Yuck. I bought a bottle of water and washed my hands. *Don't touch anything.*

I took my small camera from the pocket of my capris and took a couple pictures of kids on the Merry-go-Round, waving at them as if I was with them. I ambled toward the Ferris Wheel. I wouldn't get a photo of any money or products, but I thought I could show Morehouse how Turk's system worked, and he could share photos with his police pals in Asbury Park.

It was annoying to take pictures with my big sunglasses on, but no way would I take them off. I got one of Turk reaching behind the lever and another of him shaking hands with my two stuffed animal buddies as they got off the chair. *Is it that easy to sell this crap?*

Satisfied with my feat, I bought a candy apple to eat as I walked back to the car. I was taking a bite when a tall man carrying a bunch of helium balloons bumped into me.

"I'm so sorry," he said, and kept walking without a backward glance.

I'd gone about ten steps when I remembered the guy's stolen cell phone in Ocean Alley, and reached into my pocket. No camera.

Chapter Fourteen

IT WAS AN EXPENSIVE way to learn I might be on to something. It could also be a coincidence. I had used the camera and made no effort to conceal where I stowed it. The man was out of sight when I turned around. There were plenty of places he could duck into and I didn't want to call attention to myself. Because it confirmed what I thought I knew, I chose to believe the camera was more than the target of a casual pickpocket.

I sat on a bench on the boardwalk and thought about it. If I complained, there would be interviews and my name would be associated with the complaint. "Drats!" I went into a dollar store and bought a disposable digital camera. I hoped the owners of the house I'd just appraised would be willing to let me back in.

I wasn't sure whether to tell the homeowners the camera had been stolen and decided to say it was stolen at the farmer's market just south of Asbury Park. I had an uneasy thought about pictures of their home now being in someone else's hands. The carved wooden sign on their front lawn would likely be visible in at least one of the photos. "Parker House, Manasquan, New Jersey."

TO SAY HARRY WAS SUSPICIOUS of my story would be an understatement. I stuck to it. I told him I'd stopped at a farmer's market on the way home and somebody lifted the camera. For good measure I brought him back some strawberries, and took Aunt Madge strawberries and rhubarb. I remembered to take off the grocery store price stickers.

What to tell Morehouse was harder, but I had to let him know that Turk was selling something to those kids. I settled on telling him that I'd gone to Asbury Park to take a picture of Turk so I could remember what he looked like. Morehouse didn't know George Winters had given me photos. *Lying is much more complicated than telling the truth.* The bottom line was that he'd be ticked no matter what I told him. And if he told Aunt Madge I'd be in deep kimchee.

"You got a death wish, or what?" he asked.

"I doubt a carny would kill me."

"That's just because they don't know you too well."

How rude.

He pulled a piece of paper from a drawer and had me tell him exactly what I'd done when I was at the carnival. I was in the middle of telling when I suddenly stopped. "I guess it's not just the pictures of the Manasquan house, those two boys were on that camera card, too."

Morehouse jabbed his pen in the air in my direction. "This is why you have no business, no business at all, pulling the shit you do."

I looked in my purse. The student loan payment envelope was still there. "At least the thief didn't get their email address."

"Did you hear what I just said?" he asked.

"Yes."

"Will you butt out?"

"Probably."

He would have thrown me out, but he wanted to hear the rest of what I had to tell him. At this point I didn't care what he did with the information. I knew Turk would have a reason to want Scoobie to keep his mouth shut. *But why try to kill Scoobie so he could sell a few joints?*

ON SUNDAY I FOUND OUT THAT Morehouse had "accidentally" ratted me out to Ramona, which was like telling the entire town why I'd gone to Asbury Park. Harry said I had "abused his trust" and Aunt Madge said she "needed some peace and quiet" when I tried to tell her why the carnival visit had been a good idea.

"Maybe it's more than joints," George said. We were in the hospital cafeteria by ourselves for a few minutes Sunday evening, ostensibly in search of some healthy food for Scoobie, who maintained that the hospital wouldn't serve anything green that wasn't canned.

I shrugged. "We'll never know. It makes me worry about Scoobie being by himself every night."

"It wouldn't be smart to come back down here. Besides," he pointed to the corner of the room, "the hospital has cameras everywhere."

I felt a bit better. At the moment George was the only person not mad at me, and that was probably just because he wanted to keep learning what I found out. And the promise of free coffee.

"These small-time sales could be part of something bigger," George said. "They get the kids interested and maybe they find a few customers who want something more expensive. Wouldn't take too many of those to make a lot more money than you make running carnival rides."

His words reminded me of Penny's stacks of bills. I hadn't told George about this. Keeping my word to Morehouse seemed less important after my most recent visit with him, but I thought whatever Penny had been dealing in was way above my pay grade. And I did promise, sort of. *He talked to Aunt Madge on the phone, not me.*

"What?" George asked, suspicion clear.

"I was thinking about Penny." I was. "I can't believe her murder and the attack on Scoobie are unrelated."

"Puns aside," George said, and I made a face at him.

We were in the elevator now. He carried a huge bowl of salad and I had a plastic baggie of vegetables that cost more than two candy bars. "Who in the world," I stopped, I had been about to ask who would trust her with all that money. "Would even know they were related at this point? Scoobie said he hadn't seen her in years, their names are different."

"I've been trying to find where Penny was in the couple months after she got out of the prison in New York," he said. "Since she didn't check in with her parole officer but one time, that's kind of tough."

"Jeez. Wouldn't that mean there'd be a warrant out for her?" I asked.

"Eventually, but it's not like she's a violent criminal. Damage to Scoobie aside," he said as we walked off the elevator. I started to ask what he meant, but he continued. "She was paroled in New York. I don't know anyone there. In fact," he grinned at me, "I took a page from your book and made up a name. Told her PO I was a friend of Scoobie's, and he was very upset about his mother's death, and I was helping him reconstruct his mom's last few days."

I ignored the barbed reference to my one-time impersonation of a reporter. "So did the parole officer talk to you?"

We were getting close to Scoobie's room now. George lowered his voice when he said, "He said the one time she came in she said she was about to come into some family money, so Scoobie might want to check into that."

Uh oh. She got money, all right.

I STAYED AWAY FROM Ramona for a couple of days. I was mad at her for repeating what Morehouse told her. She probably knew I was mad, because she sent me an email and told me he didn't tell her not to tell. There was no point staying angry with her, she's the closest thing I have to a friend in Ocean Alley besides Scoobie. She's also my best source of local news.

I thought Roland might be able to get me a deal on a camera, since the Purple Cow carries a few. Plus, it would give me something to talk to Ramona about besides her tattling on me.

On Tuesday the white board was back in its place on the sidewalk in front of the Purple Cow. Today it said, "Failure is simply the opportunity to begin again more intelligently." Henry Ford.

Ramona saw me coming and stopped straightening the sale table. "Are you still mad?" she asked.

"Nope. If he didn't tell you not to tell, how would you know?"

"I think he did it on purpose," Ramona said.

"You bet he did. He's lucky I haven't stopped by the station with a grenade." I caught Roland's eye. "Or a water balloon." I smile sweetly and he shook a finger at me before he walked over to unjam the copy machine for a frustrated customer.

I told Ramona I needed to replace my digital camera and we walked over to the glass sales case that houses stuff Roland has deemed popular to lift, like cell phone batteries, cameras, and fifty dollar fountain pens. Some people have way too much money.

"What about this really thin one?" Ramona asked.

I took it from her. "Lightweight, too." While she took a couple batteries from the bottom shelf I shifted the camera's weight from one hand to the other and put it in my purse to see how much heavier it would make the purse feel. I barely noticed the difference.

Ramona put the batteries in the camera and I took a few pictures in the back of the store and near the front, since I need to take photos in all kinds of light. They were all good shots. I thought I heard someone bump into Ramona's white board, but when I looked out the window I saw only the back of someone hurrying away.

"Sold," I said to Ramona and we went to the cash register together.

As I walked out I glanced at the white board and laughed. It now read, "Failure is simply the opportunity to try, try again."

Ramona looked out the window, scowled, and came out with her small foam sponge and the erasable marker. "I was beginning to think it was Scoobie, but that's the second time this week that someone has changed it."

That stopped me. I knew it was Scoobie. So who was doing it now? "At least Scoobie's off the hook."

I HEADED TO FIRST Prez for a meeting of the Harvest for All committee, the first one since the carnival. Though not an official member, because he won't agree to be, Scoobie is usually there. Reverend Jamison invited him to help me get the perspective of someone who sometimes uses the food pantry.

Although his intentional hazing of some of the stuffier members can get the meeting off track, I knew I'd miss his presence.

Dr. Welby and the mild-mannered Monica were already in the church's small meeting room. Despite the pleasant seventy degree temperature, Monica had on her usual cardigan and carefully ironed blouse. She gave me a small smile.

"Good morning, Jolie." George Welby often speaks at boom level, though he tones it down once a meeting starts.

"Thanks a lot for coming," I said, still wishing I didn't have to.

Sylvia Parrett walked in with Lance Wilson, my only tenth-decade friend. Sylvia is another matter. She was dressed as severely as usual, though she did have on a decorative pin, which is a major fashion statement for her.

"I'll give Aretha another minute to get here." She's tied with Lance for my favorite committee member. Reverend Jamison roped her in when she asked for signs to hang at laundromats, a place she believed would have a lot of people who would use the food pantry's services. As we sat chatting an accapella rendition of "Amazing Grace" floated down the hallway and as she walked in Lance waved a finger as if conducting.

"Lance you are one talented man," Aretha said as she sat next to me.

I took a breath and got started. "Okay everybody. First, congratulations. We made more money at the dunk tank than..."

"First?" Lance said.

"How is Scoobie?" asked Aretha.

I'm not sure I've ever turned a brighter red. "Well..." I began.

"I stopped by yesterday," interrupted Dr. Welby.

Uh oh.

"Didn't stay long. But I am pleased to report that Scoobie is recovering well. It'll be awhile before he's one-hundred percent, but he'll get there.

I let out a breath. It didn't sound as if Scoobie had asked him to leave. There's a no visitors order for him, his choice, but as a physician, albeit retired, Dr. Welby wouldn't ask about that and no nurse would volunteer the information.

"Thanks, Dr. Welby." I cleared my throat and blinked back a couple tears I thought were trying to leak out. *You're done crying about this!* "I did let Scoobie know we made almost $750, and he has already said 'I told you so' a couple of times."

Aretha let out a laugh and Monica almost cracked a smile. Sylvia said nothing. I've learned she mostly participates when she has a specific idea, and she had the idea of creating a name that would define our role but not look as if we were a charity. Which we are, but some people are not comfortable coming to the food pantry, and there's no point emphasizing that they can't buy food. It was a good idea.

I had a simple agenda for the meeting. We would discuss the positive reaction to our new name and whether the ten-year old who submitted it should get a plaque or something. Then I planned to ask Lance to give a treasurer's report, which would lead into ideas for another fundraiser. As I walked into the meeting I had remembered I wanted to ask if we did anything special for homeless people, and I jotted a note in the margin of my small notebook.

That was my plan until I heard the door to the street open, followed by a familiar 'plop, shuffle, plop shuffle' sound in the hallway. "Go slow, man," George Winters' voice drifted down the hall.

"Bite me," came the familiar voice.

We were all on our feet in less than a second and Sylvia, of all people, led the way into the hallway.

"Hold your applause, hold your applause," said Scoobie. He grinned but he looked beat.

Thank goodness it's a short hallway. I was trying to hold back tears. *This is ridiculous. You aren't a crier.*

"Listen guys, I need to get off my feet or I'll be on my ass."

I held the door, but Scoobie didn't look at me as he walked in. All his attention was on getting to the chair the Dr. Welby was holding. From the look of self-satisfaction on Dr. Welby's face, I figured his hospital visit had to do with seeing if Scoobie could come to the meeting.

George caught my eye. "You can drive him back, right?" When he saw my hesitation, he added, "You don't have to really help, just provide the transportation."

"Yeah," Scoobie said. "Because she's a great helper. Never any problems in her life."

Now he was looking at me, a big grin on his face. I nodded to George and just gave Scoobie a raised eyebrow. I still wasn't too sure about tears.

There were murmurs of "you look good," and "so glad to see you."

"Ahem." They quieted as I spoke. "Now that Scoobie has finished disrupting a meeting once again, we can get back to business." They knew I was kidding. Not about the disruptions, but about being irritated about them.

"Lance, you want to tell us where we stand with money?" He explained that we had almost $3,000 in the checking account and he was looking at commercial refrigerators, which we would be able to buy because of a separate generous bequest that can only be used to upgrade our facility. If you can call a large room with shelves a facility.

"So we can have eggnog next Christmas?" Scoobie asked.

"Zip it," I said, and he grinned again. This was my Scoobie. He also looked one-hundred percent comfortable with all of us.

"You're buying," Lance said. "Since most of the food we get from the food bank in Lakewood is without charge, we have enough cash to buy apples and carrots almost every week, probably as long as we need to, since we are bringing in money more steadily."

I nodded. Until we got a refrigerator we could only get fresh food that could be stored in cool temperatures rather than cold. "OK, thanks. I want to spend most of our time on other fundraising or food donation ideas."

Scoobie gave me a huge grin. "I'm going to be quiet until everybody else says their ideas."

"That's a first," I said, and he pretended to be offended.

Dr. Welby spoke first, as is the tradition. "I've talked to Mr. Markle at the market, and he is willing to let us place a couple of pickup trucks with "Harvest for All" signs in the grocery store lot, and he'll give people ten percent off on items shoppers say they are going to donate. We would stand outside with the truck."

"We'd need a lot of volunteers," Sylvia said. "We could ask at the other churches in town."

"Or at the high school," Aretha said. "Get them used to helping us."

Monica favored a bake sale and Dr. Welby gently suggested combining it with the 'truck day' at the market. I was glad of that. People would donate items, but bake sales always seems like a lot of work for not so much money.

After a couple more ideas and a brief lull in the conversation, Lance said, "You're up, Scoobie."

Scoobie had begun to look increasingly tired, but he perked back up. "I'll bet none of you know that September 19th is 'Talk like a Pirate' day,' Scoobie began.

Sylvia sat up straighter and pursed her lips, something you read about in books but very rarely see someone do.

"What kind of a pirate?" Monica asked.

"Well...I guess any kind. Did you have something in mind?" Scoobie asked.

"Oh my. Well, I don't think there were any lady pirates anyway."

"You need to get out more, Monica," Scoobie said, but he winked at her and she gave him a small smile.

"What exactly do you do on 'Talk like a Pirate' Day," asked Dr. Welby.

"I can only imagine," Lance said, dryly.

"There is water involved in this, too, but you don't actually have to get in it."

We didn't exactly go downhill from there, but to say our concentration was broken would be an understatement.

SCOOBIE KEPT HIS EYES shut for most of the drive back to the hospital. "I can't believe you came to this. Thanks."

"Sure. I needed to get out of there for a while anyway." He grinned, but still didn't open his eyes. "Plus, I knew you'd like the pirate day idea."

Scoobie had a list of ideas for the day, all of which would cost small amounts of money for participation. The final item on his list was to pay to be allowed to not talk like a pirate. "Do they give you a pass or something?" I asked.

"Heck no. They said George could wheel me to the cafeteria. I have to get back before supper or they'll come looking for me."

No head slaps when you're driving. "You really are nuts."

"I gotta admit, I'm way more tired than I thought I'd be. And my back's killing me."

"How's your head?"

"It mostly only hurts when I'm up for a while."

"Kind of like now?" I asked.

"You don't miss a trick, kiddo."

We drove the last few blocks in silence. I hadn't told Scoobie about the money his mother had, and I gathered Morehouse had not either. While I knew Morehouse didn't want me to talk about it, it felt like there was an elephant in the back seat, and I didn't like it. I figured Scoobie would be really angry that I hadn't told him, and I was getting closer to confiding in him. But not now. He looked exhausted.

I snagged a wheelchair from the lobby and stood next to it as Scoobie got in it, then parked the car and carried in his walker, which I placed across his lap. He insisted he didn't need it and only used because one of the therapists threatened to beat him with it if he tried to walk without it.

We were just getting off the elevator on his floor when Nurse Ratched came walking down the hall really fast. She stopped when she saw us. "Adam, we've been looking all over for you."

"George and I traded him," I said. "I thought he might like some fresh air."

"Hmm." The nurse stared at me for a second or two.

I sensed she didn't believe me. I suppose Scoobie had been gone well over an hour.

"Dr. Cahill has come and gone for today. Now that your head is healing well, she and Dr. Nobles are going to release you for rehabilitative care, and..."

"I'm not going to a nursing home," Scoobie said.

"You don't have to," she said, in what for her was probably a gentle tone. "We have a rehab unit on the second floor, near where you already go for physical therapy."

"Good," he said. The three of us were walking down the hall toward his room. "I like old people, I just don't want to be with them all day."

"You'll prefer it to alternatives when you get up there yourself," she said.

IT WAS ALMOST five-thirty when I got back to the Cozy Corner. In the parking lot was a rental car with New York plates, so it looked as if the tourist season was picking up. Aunt Madge was in the kitchen making dough for the next morning's muffins and her greeting was slightly less chilly than it had been for a couple of days.

"New guests?" I asked.

"Guest. He's a writer who said he wanted a few days of peace and quiet while he finishes a book."

"What kind of book?" I asked, wanting to have something to talk about with her besides my trip to Asbury Park.

"Murder mystery, he said. He can't tell the title, something about being under contract."

"Does he know you don't have Internet?"

"He does now. He almost went to one of the newer hotels, but I told him about Java Jolt and he has Internet on his phone."

Since Aunt Madge didn't seem inclined to talk more I went upstairs and jumped out of the way as Jazz ran out of the room. She used to be content to have our bedroom and bath as her space and just go downstairs when I did. No more. "Nuts." Apparently her psychology of irritation is branching out.

I walked halfway down the back stairs and called down to Aunt Madge. "The door to the breakfast room is closed, right? I don't know if your guest will want to see a cat."

"No problem at all."

I jumped and turned to see the smiling face of a man with snow white hair but a face that looked more like someone in his late thirties or early forties. His close-cropped hair made me think of the military, but his wire rimmed glasses said scholar. "Oh. When Aunt Madge said you were a writer I expected someone with a pony tail."

"I've heard there are no molds for writers." He smiled. "I'm just on my way out. Your aunt has recommended Newhart's Diner."

He turned to walk down the hall to the main stairs and I called after him. "Try the crab cakes."

MOREHOUSE WAS SO IRRITATED with me that I was no longer privy to his thinking about Penny and her murder. It was annoying, but was more like how he usually treats me.

I was in the courthouse Wednesday morning looking up recent sales to use as comparables for the multi-family house I had just visited when I spotted Morehouse coming in the door of the courthouse. I couldn't leave the material I was using on the table to chase after him so I finished quickly and sat on a bench in the main foyer to waylay him when he came back down.

After about twenty minutes I figured he must be there to testify in one of his cases, so I stood to go. I was about to push the glass exit door when he came down the steps from the second floor.

"Hello, sergeant." I used my best formal voice.

"Cut the crap," he said. "You been doing anything you shouldn't the last couple days?"

"Just working, visiting Scoobie, and figuring out how to run the food pantry." When he didn't say anything, I asked, "Anything new on Penny's murder?"

I could almost hear his brain working for a few seconds and he finally said, "Not really. Has Scoobie talked about it?"

"Nope. All he said is he's trying to process it without...without thinking ugly thoughts about her." I wasn't about to say Scoobie had said he wished her dead many times. When Morehouse didn't say anything else I asked if he knew more about the money and silverware Penny had placed in the closet.

"Not a damn thing. I was hoping someone would at least report the silver missing. If Penny had it she was doing something hinky."

I suddenly remembered George Winters said her parole officer mentioned Penny said she was about to come into family money.

What she told him was surely a lie, but it meant she knew she was going to do something that would get her some money, whether she was supposed to keep it or not. But, that was George's business, not mine.

"Drugs, you think?" I asked.

He shrugged. "Or maybe somebody's poker winnings. Who knows? Bills aren't sequential, so they likely didn't come straight from a bank."

WHEN I GOT BACK TO the Cozy Corner there were two more cars in the small parking lot and I could hear Aunt Madge laughing with them on the second floor. She came down as I was pouring myself some milk.

"Sounds like you like your guests."

"Mark and Nancy Sapperstein. They live in Pennsylvania now and their daughter's getting married this weekend. They thought they'd stay here so they didn't put a damper on their daughter and her friends at the hotel."

"A damper?"

She shrugged. "Usually the bride's parents live in the town, so they aren't at the hotel."

"So are the groom's parents a couple of swingers who get to stay at the hotel?"

"Don't think so. They're checking in later." She turned off her tea kettle. "We're all going out to supper."

"Sounds like fun." I started up the back stairs to my room. *My aunt has more friends than I do.*

I COULDN'T SLEEP, so at midnight I still had my small bedside lamp on and was trying to read the newest Sue Grafton book. Daphne knows I like the books, so she had put my name on the waiting list and called to say it was in. Leave it to a librarian.

My eyes were finally getting heavy and I was about to turn off the lamp when I thought I heard a noise in the hall. It wasn't my imagination; Jazz had lifted her head and looked toward the door. It wouldn't be Aunt Madge, and I couldn't imagine it was the guests. Their rooms weren't near mine. Why don't you lock your door?

I gave myself a mental scolding. A noise didn't mean something bad. "Maybe it's a mouse," I said aloud to Jazz. "You want to look?" She curled herself back into her usual ball at the foot of the bed.

I walked to the door and put my hand on the knob, and then thought better of waltzing into the hall in the middle of the night. I locked my door and for good measure locked the one that led into the bathroom I share with the now-vacant room that adjoins mine. *Get a grip Jolie.*

I DIDN'T WAKE UP THINKING about the noise, but by the time I went downstairs on Thursday I had remembered it and told Aunt Madge about it. "You haven't let a ghost move in, have you?"

"Not knowingly. I have been thinking of getting the plumber to look at one of the third-floor bathrooms. The pipes have started to creak. I don't want water cascading down the walls."

Pipes. Of course.

Chapter Fifteen

I CUT BACK MY VISITS to Scoobie to once a day. Rehab meant physical therapy would be morning and afternoon for at least a couple of hours. Though they still thought the vertebrae would heal without surgery, he had a lot of other sore back muscles. He said the therapists were doing some great massage and teaching him ways to sit, stand, and lift without putting too much stress on his back or neck. They would get to "the really hard stuff" in about a week, according to Scoobie.

"I mean, I think if I were going to be a veg that would already have happened, but why take any chances?" He was cutting up an orange I brought him, and the steno pad was open on his wheeled table. Since he had to hold the orange almost level with his face, it appeared to be a challenge not to drip on the paper. Of course, he would accept no help.

"Looks like you're writing again," I said.

"Yeah, I had a poem in my pocket. I was working on it when I sat in the bushes watching for Turk. Don't know what happened to it."

Uh oh.

"You might want to talk to Sgt. Morehouse about that."

He stopped cutting. "What do you mean?"

"He showed me part of a poem that had blown against a piling under the boardwalk. I told him it looked like..."

"And Morehouse still has it?"

I shrugged. "I assume so. Why don't you call..."

"Could you please leave?" he asked.

No doubt the shock showed in my face as I picked up my purse.

"I'm not mad at you, or even him, Jolie. I just," he paused, "well you know I don't let just anyone read my stuff."

"Right. Call him." Seeing his still stony expression I blew him a kiss as I left.

I debated calling Morehouse. Scoobie is a full-fledged grown-up, he can handle himself. And I sometimes have trouble leaving things alone.

I was glad I called. "I can't give it to him, Jolie, it's evidence and has to stay with us."

"You mean it's, like, in an evidence room?"

"That is where we tend to put stuff," he said, and I detected amusement in his voice.

"That might not be something you want to say to Scoobie. He'd have a hard time with the idea that a lot of people could see his poem." *Hard time? Could set him back a lot.*

Morehouse sighed. "Thanks for the warning." He hung up.

I STOPPED AT THE *Ocean Alley Press* on my way home from the hospital. I had never been in the two-story building and thought it looked very much as it might have in the 1950s. There was a long wooden counter just inside the door and behind it was a row of metal desks, maybe six or eight. There was a partition that stood about two feet tall on the top of each desk, but the concept of privacy clearly did not extend to this news room. And I hated the smell. Ink, I supposed.

I could swear the woman at the desk smirked at me when she heard my name, but maybe I was imagining things.

George came out, looking harried. "I'm on deadline whaddya need, Jolie?"

"I don't need anything. Just wanted to talk to you about Scoobie and stuff. Call me." As I turned to go I caught the receptionist's eye. Definitely smirking. And I could swear I heard George chuckling to himself as he walked back to his desk.

GEORGE CALLED ABOUT SIX-THIRTY. "I'm frustrated as all get out," I told him. "The state police aren't going to keep after Penny's murder. They have nothing. And what if someone thinks Scoobie has the money and goes after him?"

"What money?"

Crud, crud, crud, crud.

"Uh, Morehouse didn't tell you?"

"Jolie. We were going to help each other, remember?"

I sighed. I honestly had not meant to tell him about Penny's mountain of money. I just plain forgot. "I wasn't supposed to tell anyone. Morehouse made Aunt Madge and me swear."

"What money?" George's voice had gone up a few decibels.

"She had a small bag in the closet, and Morehouse came and got it after they found her. He opened it and it was packed with cash and silverware." There was perhaps ten seconds of silence. I wasn't sure if George was counting to one-hundred or about to explode.

"That kind of puts her murder in a different light," he said, sarcasm almost dripping through the phone.

"I'm sorry, George. Morehouse was pretty firm about not talking about it."

"Yes, he was," said Aunt Madge, from behind me.

Uh oh. I dropped the phone and bent over to pick it up.

"What the hell are you doing, playing pick-up sticks with the phone?" George asked when I put the receiver back to my ear.

"I was talking to Aunt Madge." I looked at her, stony expression and hands on her hips, something she rarely does.

"Oh boy," George said.

"I gotta go." I hung up.

There are times when I assert myself as an almost-thirty year old woman with a responsible job, and there are times when I feel about twelve. This was one of the twelve-year-old times.

"Think of all the times you were furious with George Winters for printing things you would rather not have had half the town read." Her voice was quiet, but that was almost worse. "And here you are, babbling to him about something you have no business telling him."

She turned and walked back toward her bedroom.

I ALMOST SLUNK OUT OF THE HOUSE Friday morning. Certainly I left a lot earlier than I normally would. Aunt Madge was sitting in the breakfast room with her old friends, and the mystery writer guest was telling them about the time his computer crashed, and he lost a nearly complete manuscript. He retyped it from a printed copy and then learned that there was a way to recover it from his lifeless machine. I know this because I listened at the door. Reaction to his riveting story sounded more like polite acknowledgement than interest.

I left Aunt Madge a scribbled note that said I'd be back in the late afternoon. It was only eight o'clock, but I thought Joe Regan would be open so I drove down to Java Jolt. I normally walk, but it seemed better not to stroll back to the Cozy Corner to get my car until Aunt Madge had a lot of time to cool off. I figured I'd find things to do around town all day.

As I walked down the boardwalk I saw the two homeless men I'd seen last week. Today they were sitting on a bench a couple doors down from Java Jolt. They didn't have the grocery cart now, so I hoped that meant they had a place to stay. On impulse I stopped in front of them. "Hi, I'm Jolie. Can I talk to you for a second?"

The younger of the two said, "I guess," but the older man, whom I judged to be about thirty-five, just stared at me mutely.

"I hope I don't offend you, but I work with the "Harvest for All" Food Pantry. I wanted to be sure you know where it is."

Nada.

"Okay. If you do want to stop by, it's at First Prez, First Presbyterian Church."

"We know," said the younger man, who appeared short for a guy. "We've been there already." He spoke very fast, and then seemed to be self-conscious and shut his mouth very deliberately.

After a few seconds I turned to continue toward Java Jolt.

"Thanks," said the older man.

I was doing an internal cringe as I walked into Java Jolt. Did I offend them? Would it look like the "rich" lady was being condescending? I decided I couldn't worry about that. At the food pantry meeting last week I'd learned we didn't have any outreach to the homeless, and I had planned to think more about that. You have other things on your mind.

I paid for my coffee and a chocolate muffin, my favorite and a treat to myself, and sat in front of one of the two computers. I didn't know what I was looking for, but I had to be able to find out something about Penny or Turk or somebody. I wasn't sure why I thought I'd be able to find something the police couldn't, but I told myself my mind probably worked differently than the state police or Morehouse's. I almost giggled. He'd certainly think so.

First I searched for the name of the prison Penny had been in, Taconic Women's Correctional Facility. *Correctional facility. Who are they kidding? You couldn't correct her in twenty years.* The facility web site was little help. There were descriptions of how the women were housed, what kind of work they did while incarcerated, and how much time they could spend "recreating" each day.

There was a link to inmates, which showed their prisoner number and some info about their sentence. I keyed in "Penny Pittsen" before I remembered Morehouse implied she made up the name after she got out of the facility. I wasn't sure if the information would help even if I knew her name.

"What are you doing, Jolie?" Joe asked. "You've been scowling at that screen for twenty minutes."

"Trying to figure out more about Scoobie's mom."

"Why?"

"How many people do you know who get murdered soon after visiting their son in a hospital?"

"The key word there is murdered," Joe said. "I'd stay the hell out of this one."

"Nice to know what you would do, Joe."

He went back to making some fresh coffee.

I decided to try a different tack. I googled various combinations of Penny, check kiting, New York, Taconic Women's Correctional Facility, forgery and sentenced. Plus a few other terms as I thought of them. If I could just get her name I could look her up in the "courts on line" database. I was about to give up when I substituted Ocean Alley for New York.

Bingo. One article had a photo of Penny Marks, formerly of Ocean Alley, who had been arrested for forging a total of eighteen checks that she had stolen from a woman's purse. The woman had foolishly left her open purse in the top of a grocery store cart and Penny helped herself. She had bought a lot of stuff with the checks and then tried to sell it. "Wow."

"Find something?" Joe asked.

"I'm not sure," I lied. "I was just looking at some of these identity theft articles. Makes you want to bury your money in your backyard."

"Unless you live near the ocean," Joe said.

I found a couple more articles, including one from the Binghamton paper that had mug shots of Penny and two others who were arrested with her after they tried to sell, on eBay and to pawn shops, some of the items they bought with the forged checks. Who knew Penny could use a computer? The other woman's hair was even more unkempt than Penny's, though Penny had a better smirk for the camera. The man looked a lot younger than the two women, but it was harder to gauge his age because he had brown hair longer than mine and facial hair that could have been a true beard or just a week's stubble. He squinted as he looked at the camera.

I entered Penny's name in the "courts on line" database and was rewarded with a list of court cases for everything from public drunkenness in Brooklyn to forgery in Manhattan to possession of stolen property in Binghamton. She certainly got around. There was not a statement of resolution for every case, and I could tell she had pleaded guilty to lesser charges in several cases. The Binghamton article noted she was considered a habitual offender and probation was no longer an option. I remembered Dana thought Penny would likely still be in the women's prison if it weren't for overcrowding. *Too bad for her, she might still be alive.*

So, I knew what she had been arrested for — though probably not everything — and had no idea what to do with it. If I had to guess, I'd say she was funding a drug habit, but I supposed it could have been just plain old unwillingness to work. Despite the joints in her luggage, there weren't any drug arrests.

I jotted down the web addresses of a couple articles and was irritated that I didn't have a printer. That meant the library.

DAPHNE TOOK MY MONEY for the article copies I printed and didn't even ask what I was doing. Since we would generally chat about such things, I had been prepared to tell her I was looking up articles on Ocean Alley's growth. After all, a real estate appraiser should know something about a town's economic history.

I had the articles on Ocean Alley on top of my small pile and stood to one side of the front desk as Daphne checked out books for a mother and two young sons. After they left, Daphne began to tell me about the many comments about Scoobie's attack. "Sign the card, Jolie. Everyone except Elmira signed it."

Elmira Washington is a first-class busybody who made sure everyone knew that I moved to Ocean Alley because my ex-husband embezzled money from the bank where he worked. In Newhart's one evening I let her know I knew this, and she didn't like that. She probably wouldn't sign Scoobie's card because she considered him guilty by association. Of what I don't know. The card was one of those foot-tall ones, so there was a lot of room left. I signed it, "Yo, Jolie," and drew a smiley face.

I was about to leave when Aunt Madge's writer-guest came in. He saw me and his face lit up. "Jolie, I hope you can vouch for me."

I might if I knew your name.

"I went to the coffee shop to use the computer and it's packed and noisy. Joe, I think that was his name, didn't think I could use these because I'm not a card holder."

I turned to Daphne. "You know Aunt Madge has the B&B, right?"

"Of course. And still no Internet I take it?" She looked from me to writer man.

Daphne's smile is always dazzling, in part because her perfect white teeth are offset by her coffee skin tone. The guest responded with an equally large smile and I felt as if I was in a toothpaste commercial.

"No Internet. She says it's to give guests time to relax, but this gentleman is here to work. Finishing a book, aren't you?"

"Yes." He reached across the desk and Daphne took his hand for a firm shake. "Marcus Hardy, mystery writer."

"We have that cardholders-only policy so we don't have every wet bathing suit in town coming here to check their email." She came from behind the counter and walked toward a computer, with Marcus-the-mystery-writer following her. "Now, if it was next week, I'd probably have to enforce the policy or people would accuse me of favoritism."

I realized this weekend would be Memorial Day. I was about to be reminded of the element of Ocean Alley I least like — tourists. I said a quick good-bye as Daphne was asking Marcus-the-Mystery-Writer if he had a web site so she could read about his books.

I HAD THOUGHT HARRY would have gotten over his snit about me taking pictures in Asbury Park, but I was wrong.

He was literally pacing around his large office as he talked. "The house in Manasquan? Burglars hit it last night. You think that's a coincidence?"

I looked him in the eyes. "Probably not. I'm really sorry, Harry. What can I do?"

That took some of the wind out of his sails. "I already told them I'd pay the deductible on their homeowners insurance. Your half would be $250."

"I'll pay all of it," I said, with as much meekness as I could muster. "I agree it's because of the photos on the camera card. What, uh, makes them so sure?"

"Because everything taken was visible in the rooms where you took photographs, and that's all that was taken. Mostly electronics. They didn't look in closets or even take her purse, which was on the dining room table." He ran his hands through his salt-and-pepper hair. "The police think they planned based on the photos and were in and out in less than ten minutes, while the Parkers were walking on the beach."

"I'm really..." I began again, and he interrupted.

"You know what makes it worse? You lied to me, Jolie. I thought we were friends."

I haven't felt so thoroughly miserable about my own behavior since I "borrowed" my sister Renée's high school class ring. I was twelve and tired of hearing about proms and graduation parties. I gave it back, of course, but not for about a week. After my mother found it in my sock drawer.

"We are friends. I didn't want to worry you. I shouldn't have..."

"You're damn right you shouldn't have. As of right now I'm not worrying about you one bit. You don't come back from an appraisal on time it won't be me looking for you." He stopped, having noticed my wide-eyed expression. "I might look after a couple of hours." He walked to his desk and pushed the button to turn on his computer's monitor.

I swallowed hard. I didn't want to tear up. "I promise I won't lie again." I paused. "I can't promise that I will always tell you what you want to hear."

He gave me a shrewd look. "Fair enough."

Chapter Sixteen

I SAT IN NEWHART'S to read the articles again. It was the middle of Friday afternoon and it was crowded with "first day of summer" beach-goers. Even so, I figured I wouldn't see as many people I knew as I would in Java Jolt. In case someone did join me, I kept the Ocean Alley articles on top of my small pile.

I pulled out the most recent article about Penny, assuming it could be most relevant to what happened to her. *You know what it means to assume. Makes an ass out of you and me.* It was one of the few things I could remember Uncle Gordon saying, probably because it was the first time I, at age five, heard an adult say 'ass.'

The article in the Binghamton paper was from slightly more than three years ago.

Local Woman Sentenced to Five Years

Penny Marks of Binghamton was sentenced to five years for forgery and possession of stolen property, third offense. In her two years in Binghamton, Marks has become a fixture on the police blotter, with regular arrests for public drunkenness.

Though never charged with a violent crime, Judge Patterson warned her in June, when she was arrested on a prior charge of receiving stolen property, that he was giving her only one more chance and would then order her incarcerated. In announcing the sentence, he said he was "outraged by the sheer volume of your thefts in the last three months."

Marks would place an ad for work as a cleaning lady, work long enough to know a family's schedule, and then return at a time they were out and steal laptops, jewelry, cash, silver, and any collectible items, such as baseball cards or glassware. Because she worked in different parts of the city it took police almost two months to associate the thefts with her work in the homes. Marks is originally from Ocean Alley, New Jersey and has also lived in New York City and Albany.

Arrested with Marks in August were Alex "Fun boy" Masterson and Gina Rathway. Masterson was given thirty days in the county jail for his second offence, and Rathway, with no previous record, was placed on probation.

I reread the article. I would never have guessed Penny was smart enough to orchestrate a series of burglaries. On the other hand, Scoobie had to get his brain from somewhere. Hers probably worked better before she pickled it.

George Winters had agreed to meet me at Newhart's, but he was almost a half-hour overdue. I ordered another glass of iced tea and looked at the desserts. If he didn't come soon I would be forced to order the warm brownie with vanilla ice cream.

The door banged open and George scanned the room for me. "Sorry. Got a couple calls."

"That's okay. Look at these." I shoved the articles across the table.

"Before you buy me coffee?" he grinned. Spring had officially morphed into summer temperatures, and George was wearing his usual Hawaiian style shirt, but with what I think of as long shorts for men, rather than jeans.

I signaled to the waitress and mouthed "coffee" and pointed to George as he started to look at the articles.

"Jolie, I wrote the one on the change in the local business climate."

"Not the top ones. Underneath."

He flipped through them and looked at me wide-eyed. "I was searching under Pittsen," he said. "I never found these."

I repeated Morehouse's explanation about her changing her name to make it easier to start forging checks again. "I just googled combinations of words until I found this. I thought you might be able to get someone to look up the other two people she was arrested with. See if any of them are around here."

"Morehouse must have done this." He said this almost to himself.

"You'd think. But she wasn't murdered in Ocean Alley, so how hard would he look? Even if the state police shared stuff, they might be focused on crime scene stuff for the murder rather than her history in another state."

"Did you show these to Scoobie?" he asked.

"Nope. He doesn't want to talk about her at all."

"Can't blame him."

I remembered something he said earlier. "What did you mean about Penny not being a violent criminal, damage to Scoobie aside, or something like that?"

He drummed his fingers on the table for a moment. "It's his business," he said slowly, "let's just say she is supposed to have neglected him a lot when he was too young to take care of himself, and one of his arms got broken twice. That much is in the public record."

I sat back on the booth bench. "He only told me she drank a lot. Aunt Madge said a couple people tried to get the state to take custody and his dad would show up and make a lot of promises."

George nodded. "You'd need to talk to Scoobie about anything else."

I wondered how George knew about anything that wasn't "in the public record," but figured that a lot of gossip, true or not, made its way around the newsroom. After an awkward few seconds I asked, "Now what?"

"You're the snoop," he said. "I usually just follow you around."

"Very funny." I picked up one of the articles and pointed it at him. "There's a lot more to this than some of the other stuff I've..."

"...butted into?" George added.

"I'm serious. I can't think of anything to do with this except give it to Morehouse."

"The only article with any real substance is the one about her sentence three years ago. The others somebody picked up from a police blotter." He paused. "There could be a good reason not to look into this more, for you, I mean. Scoobie *really* doesn't want to talk about this. He probably doesn't even know the names she's used the last few years."

"I hear you."

George added about four teaspoons of sugar to his coffee. "No you don't. You think you're doing something that needs to be done. You think it may help Scoobie in some way. All I'm saying is he may really disagree with that."

I bristled. "I don't want those guys coming after him again. They don't know he doesn't know..."

"They may not even know there is a Scoobie." He leaned across the table and lowered his voice. "You could be putting him in danger, not keeping it from him."

George had a funny look on his face, as if he was trying to decide whether to say something or not. *You don't know him. Maybe he's just trying to pass gas quietly.*

"The thing is, Scoobie has helped you out a few times. But it's also true that he never had his life in danger until you came back here. There was that stuff at Christmas, then..."

"That's ridiculous." I tried to keep my tone neutral, but I could hear it sounded pretty argumentative.

He leaned across the table and spoke more quietly. "This is a different kind of crime. It's not a couple people who know each other taking pot shots or something. Penny wasn't killed in a hit-and-run, she was killed by somebody probably a lot meaner than she was. You gotta think about Scoobie, not just what you want to do."

I'd heard enough. I was half way to the door before he could finish his sentence.

I GUESS WHAT UPSET me the most was that George had a couple of good points. I wouldn't go so far as to say he was right. People might tell me I'm "good for Scoobie," but I have gotten him involved in some dangerous stuff. I pulled into the hospital parking lot and turned off my car and let my seat go back so I was looking at the car's dome light. On the other hand, he's gone back to school, and I think I helped him get the courage to do that. Or know he could, anyway.

What difference did it make who hurt him or killed Penny, as long as they wouldn't be back? And you would know that how? Since I had no answer to that question I sat up and pulled the car seat into a sitting position and sat staring at the hospital entrance. George was probably right. Scoobie was relatively safe when he was in the hospital. It was only in the movies that bad guys snuck into hospitals to finish off somebody.

But he wouldn't be there too much longer, and when he got out he would eventually walk along the boardwalk, sit in the library, and take classes. I knew the end of May was a break in classes, but I didn't know when they started up again. That would give me a neutral topic to talk to Scoobie about.

I knew Scoobie was in his room because the walker was at the bottom of his bed. I leaned my arm in, waving a tissue.

"And people think I'm the strange one," he said. "Come on in, Jolie."

"Thanks." I tossed another orange onto the bed near him and sat in the guest chair. "You look beat."

"I'm doing a lot better. Rehab is a lot of work though. They have stuff for me to do but I have to do it in exactly the right way so I don't hurt myself more, especially the one in the neck."

I nodded. "Do they think you'll be able to go back to school in early June?"

"Maybe, if I only take one class, and if I make it a one-day-a-week class. All I'm doing now is taking electives so I can concentrate on the x-ray stuff when I start that program in the fall."

"So, what'll you take?"

He grinned. "How are you at college math? I haven't had any since high school, and I wasn't so great then."

I shrugged. "I didn't take a lot in college, but I did okay. I can try to help if you need it."

"I probably will. It's the only math class required for my associate's degree, and I need to get it out of the way." He looked at me more closely. "You look funny."

I looked down at my tan capris and dark green top and back at him.

"I don't mean your clothes. I mean your expression."

"Aunt Madge is mad at me about something. I hate that."

He gave me a questioning look and I realized I didn't have a follow-up for that bit of information, and I didn't want to tell him the truth. Or not the whole truth.

"What did you do now?" Scoobie asked.

"Why do people assume I did something?"

"Because they know you," he said, with a brief smile.

"She heard me on the phone. I asked Morehouse if he had any news on what happened to you." *It's half true, I used Morehouse's name. Well, maybe less than half true.*

He frowned, and I continued. "It makes me nervous that you're in here, where anyone could walk into your room. I want them to catch whoever did it."

"That'd be okay with me, but there's nothing you can do about it. Or me either. Remember what I told you about the Serenity Prayer?" He looked at me with suspicion. "You aren't doing anything to look for bad guys, are you?"

"All I did was walk around the carnival when it went to Asbury Park."

"Jeez, Jolie, what for?" He looked as if he would like to shake me. Not that he ever has.

"I wanted to see if that Turk guy tried to sell drugs to kids."

"And..."

"Looks like it. I told Morehouse so he has a reason to tell his police buddies to keep an eye on him."

"And that's all?" he asked.

"I never want to see that guy again." I wasn't saying that's all I had done, and I definitely did not want to see Turk again. Though I wouldn't mind having my camera back.

He didn't say anything for a moment. "I guess it let you talk to Morehouse without ratting out Alicia, but you really, really need to stay away from those carny guys."

That reminded me of what I wanted to ask Scoobie. "You said, when we were on the steps at Gracie's grandmother's house, that I should ask you about your carny days sometime." I studied his face as he took this in.

"Yeah, well, I planned to tell you the funny stuff, not the bad stuff."

"So, tell me a funny thing."

He started to say something, probably to tell me to quit bugging him, but seemed to change his mind. "There were some nice people. Couple families that had worked at the Ocean City Amusement Park for years, and their parents did, too." He paused. "I didn't actually work too much at a carnival..."

"Yeah, Ramona said she thought it was the rides in Ocean City." He scowled and I continued. "When you get your head bashed in people talk about you." I smiled at him. "If you don't want to, Morehouse makes you."

"I suppose." He stuck his finger under the soft collar he was wearing. "I hate this thing."

I said nothing, just met his eyes and raised an eyebrow.

"So I worked on the carnival for a few days when it left St. Anthony's a bunch of years ago, but then I got on with them at the amusement park. I told you that."

I nodded.

"So, there were some nice people, and some of them were really good with kids." He smiled to himself. "You know that game, where the kids pick up a plastic duck that's in water, and the writing on the bottom says what prize to give them?"

"Yep. I loved that."

"Me, too. Anyway, this old guy ran it. He thought the prizes were pretty cheesy, but he didn't pick 'em. Skinflint owner did." Scoobie frowned. "Anyway, this old guy, Sam I think, he wrote over a bunch of the writing on the bottom of the ducks so there were more ducks that let the kids have better prizes. Then he had this box under the counter, and when the owner groused about spending too much money on the prizes he'd stick a bunch of the better ducks — that's what he called them — in the box for a couple days and get them out again later."

"What if the owner found them in the box?"

Scoobie shrugged, and then winced. "Sam put a bunch of the prizes on top of them."

"But not everybody was a Sam," I said, softly.

"There were jerks," he said, "but most of the people at the amusement park were long-time employees. Carnivals have a lot more temporary workers."

A thought occurred to me. "Who owned that amusement park?"

"What do you care?" His look oozed suspicion.

"Just wondering if it was the same people who ran the carnival that was here when you got hurt." I tried to look innocent.

"There weren't signs about who owns it. How do you know who ran the carnival?" Scoobie asked.

"Think George."

"Oh, right. I think they were called East Jersey Entertainment."

AUNT MADGE HAD TWO more guests by Friday evening and her calendar for the next few weeks was pretty full. That boded well for me, less time for her to focus on being mad at me. Mister mystery-writer-Marcus seemed to see himself as an unofficial tour guide. I heard him offer to walk the parents of the groom, who had never been in Ocean Alley, over to Java Jolt on Saturday morning.

I sat in the rocking chair in my bedroom and reread the articles about Penny, and then went over my list again. The only question I'd answered on my "need to know" list was why Alicia was upset about Scoobie.

"You need two lists," I said aloud.

Need to know about Scoobie
- Who hurt him?
- Why would anyone hurt him?
- Who found Scoobie?
- Why didn't they wait for police?

Need to know about Penny
  • Why did she go to Budget Inn?
  • Did she know Carny people there?
  • How was Penny killed?
  • Where did she get the silverware?
  • Why leave her luggage here?

In some ways it was easier to make guesses about Penny. She probably stole the silverware herself. It might be hard to resell it as tableware, but there was probably a market for it simply as silver. I recalled silver sold for a great deal per ounce and people melted it down or something.

It made sense that Penny left her luggage at the Cozy Corner. If she didn't have the money and silver with her no one could steal it from her. There didn't seem to be anything in her larger suitcase that she could not easily replace, especially if she had a good bit of money in her ugly purse. *What happened to that purse?*

Penny and the carnival. Penny and the carnival. I'd never seen her with anyone from the carnival. If only I'd been a fly on a booth at the carnival. George's pictures. He had taken a lot of them. Suppose Penny was in some of them?

"Damn, Jolie. You took pictures." I didn't take many on Sunday, but I took a bunch on Saturday. Probably not too useful, as they were generally of people sitting above the dunk tank. With a sinking feeling I realized they were on the card in my stolen camera.

A lot of people took pictures. I called Ramona and Jennifer. I was mad at George and wasn't going to call him, but since he likely took the most pictures I called him, too.

Chapter Seventeen

WE CERTAINLY COULDN'T meet at the Cozy Corner with our smart phones or cameras, so Jennifer, George, and I met at the paper at noon on Saturday. Ramona was working, and said the only picture she took was of me on the dunk tank plank, but it was a "really good one," just as I was falling in. I didn't want George Winters near that one.

I'd forgotten that traffic quadrupled overnight between Friday and Saturday of Memorial Day weekend, so I got to the newspaper office about five minutes after the other two.

"You really should be on time for appointments you set," Jennifer said, as she smoothed the hem on her expensive-looking skirt.

George grinned widely, and stopped when he saw my face.

"Sorry, I had an appraisal appointment and it went longer than I thought." This was not true, of course, but, I figured this would keep her from giving me any more advice.

George turned on a computer that had a large monitor so we could see the pictures better. He had taken more than one-hundred. Some we could rule out quickly. Even if Penny was on the top chair on the Ferris Wheel we wouldn't be able to tell who she was. Turk's back was to the camera for the only one he seemed to be in besides the ones George deliberately took of him on Sunday.

"Why didn't you take any of the ticket booths?" I asked. I was tired of sitting on a hard stool as George inspected every picture for what seemed like forever.

"Oh yeah, that would be a fascinating picture for the front page of the paper," he said.

I leaned forward to pay better attention. "Hey, go back one."

In the center of photo forty-four was someone holding several helium balloons. The person's face was in profile. "There was someone with helium balloons who stole at least one cell phone." I put my nose close to the screen.

"We have this amazing technology, it's called zoom," George said, as he put the back of his hand on the front of my shoulder and pushed me away from the screen.

Jennifer giggled.

"Do you think it looks like someone we know?" I asked, looking at the now slightly blurry photo, in which the helium-balloon holder's head was almost an inch round.

The three of us looked at the person intently. I was pretty sure it was a white woman who had her hair pulled back from her face, but I could tell nothing more.

George clicked the mouse and the next photo had the same person, this time looking straight ahead. As George and I said, "Penny," Jennifer asked, "Is that Scoobie's mother?"

I sat back and stared at George. "She was actually at the carnival."

"Why does it matter if she was there?" Jennifer asked. "The police don't think she was killed there, do they?"

"Nope," George said. He looked at the date on the bottom of the picture. "I took that Friday afternoon at four-thirty."

"It means she likely knew the carnival people pretty well." I stared at the photo. I didn't know Penny from a hole in the wall at that point, but even if I had I might have walked right by her. She had on a jumper, as a clown might wear, but it was unadorned. Because of the balloons a carnival goer might think she was part of the show, but I thought it more likely she was dressed to simply give that impression, likely so she could walk around and pilfer.

"She wanted to be there to steal stuff," George said, quietly.

"Go through more," Jennifer said, and we sat quietly as George moved quickly through the rest of his photos. When there were no more Penny sitings. Jennifer held out her camera's card and he took it and popped it into a slot on the computer.

"Mine are all from Friday night," Jennifer said. "My batteries were dead when I turned it on Saturday."

The lighting wasn't quite as good in her photos. The camera was not a professional one like George's, and it looked to be about six o'clock or thereabouts. There was no time stamp on her pictures.

"Oh my God," I said quietly. Penny was leaning against the railing that surrounded the Ferris Wheel. She wasn't talking to Turk, but he was maybe five or ten feet from her, carefully helping an older woman out of the Ferris wheel chair.

AFTER GEORGE PRINTED COPIES of the photos for each of us and uploaded Jennifer's to his computer, she said she had an appointment to get her nails done and left.

"So," George said. "Penny seems to know Turk. She might have carried those balloons so she could distract people and steal stuff."

"And she might have stolen the cell phone used to make the 9-1-1 call for Scoobie. You think she…?" I couldn't say it out loud.

"Tried to kill Scoobie?" he asked, and thought about his own question for a few seconds. "I doubt it. For one thing, he said he didn't hear someone come up behind him, and she's as graceful as penguin on ice skates."

"But maybe she knows who did," I said.

"Knew, the key point is she can't tell us," George said.

"I can't believe she just 'found' Scoobie. It's too big a coincidence."

George nodded. "I wonder what else she took?" He printed a couple more copies of the photo Jennifer took. "Ocean Alley has three pawn shops. I'll see if she got rid of anything."

"I can…" I began.

"No you can't," George said as he turned off the computer.

"You can't be in three places at once."

"The shop owners all know me." He looked at me. "They mighta heard of you, but they wouldn't talk to you."

I supposed he was right, much as I hated to admit it.

SO I MADE OTHER PLANS. I took a detour to go by the police station. I doubted Morehouse would be there, since it was a Saturday. On the other hand, it was the first big summer weekend, so that might bring him in.

"And you think I would let you listen to that tape why?" he asked.

"Because I think you said the voice of the person who called 9-1-1 was raspy, or somebody said that. Maybe I'll know the voice."

"No."

"Come on, sergeant. I talk to a lot of people. Maybe I'll know the voice."

"Something made you think of this. Tell me what and I might play it for you," he said.

I wasn't about to tell Morehouse that George and I had Penny's picture at the carnival. It wasn't just that I might spoil George's story if Morehouse deemed it evidence that couldn't be in the newspaper. I might even like that. It was more that George had connections I didn't, and I wanted to keep hearing about them.

"Penny smoked. Her voice was kind of raspy," I said.

"It was a man, in case you forgot." Morehouse tapped his pen on his desk.

"How can you be sure?"

He stared at me, impassive.

"It could be her," I insisted.

He sighed and turned to his computer screen. "I'll play it once."

"From your computer?"

He gave me a withering look. "It's all digital."

The voice was slow and sounded fairly calm. "You need to come to the boardwalk. Near the steps by Conch Street. A man is hurt. Come now."

"You ever hear Penny sound like that?" he asked.

"What if she wanted to disguise her voice? She lowers it. Calm would be a disguise for her, too. So would good grammar."

He grunted and played it again, concentrating more than he appeared to the first time he played it. Then he played it again.

"What do you think?" I asked.

"Maybe, but a really big maybe." He sighed. "I don't have anything to compare it to."

"I think it's her." I stared at him directly.

He stood up. "Tortino arrested her a lot, for drunk and disorderly. I'll get him to listen again, but I don't know what it gets us."

"It might mean she knew to look for him."

His look was skeptical. "As in she knew someone hurt him? That's a stretch, even for your imagination."

"Maybe the person who hurt him didn't like that she got him help. Somebody didn't want her around anymore."

"A lot of people probably didn't," Morehouse said.

I DON'T THINK SHE meant to cause trouble, but Jennifer nearly ended my friendship with Scoobie. If I had just gone there before I went to see Sgt. Morehouse I might have stopped Jennifer from talking to Scoobie about the photos. How could she have even thought of telling Scoobie?

I walked into Scoobie's room ready to toss him an orange and stopped in the doorway. His face showed a combination of rage and hurt that I'd never seen before.

"So you and George want to know if my mother knew Turk," he said.

"I, we thought…" I began.

"No, you didn't think. You didn't think about whether I would want you to dig into her life. Or I guess I should say her death. That's your thing, isn't it, Jolie?"

I swallowed, but no amount of swallowing would moisten my throat. "It's possible she was traveling with the carnival."

"And what, she decided to sneak up behind me on the boardwalk and erase the mistake she thinks she made by having me in the first place?"

"No, not that. Not that at all."

"And you know this because you were such pals with my mother? You never met her until she came to the hospital."

"She may have saved you, Scoobie."

He stared at me for a couple seconds. "What do you mean?"

I started to sit in the chair by his bed.

"You don't need to sit."

Scoobie isn't usually petty. If he hadn't picked that time to be, I might have continued to stumble through the conversation, making excuses as I went. But he ticked me off, so I found my voice.

"You want to know, I'll tell you. I don't need your snotty attitude." I glared at him. My guess was his face mirrored mine. If he had been able he would have stormed out of the room.

"You know what? I don't want to know. I didn't ask you to dig around in my life. Or hers. You can tell George that, too."

"Tell him yourself." I walked out.

THE WORST THING WAS, I couldn't even walk on the beach or take a run on the boardwalk. Every inch of beach was covered by well-oiled bodies sporting bikinis or Speedos. And half of them shouldn't have come within five yards of a swimsuit without losing forty pounds. I sucked in my tummy and wiped tears of fury from my eyes.

Ramona was working, and she'd just say she told me to back off. Jazz. She was never mad at me. I pulled into the Cozy Corner B&B and got the last parking spot in Aunt Madge's small parking area. I rationalized that any guest who wasn't in the B&B would be at the beach for many more hours.

"Rats." The side entrance was locked. Aunt Madge is fastidious about locking it once the beach season is in full swing. I hadn't carried a key all winter, since she only locked the door at night in the off-season, and I didn't want to knock. However, since it was now summer rental season, the front door would probably be open.

I walked around the side of the house and onto the front porch. Since I was in that part of the house I went up the main staircase and walked toward my room, which is closer to the back stairs.

As I walked from the staircase landing onto the second floor, I saw Marcus Hardy in the hallway just outside the room I still thought of as Penny's room. *Why is he here? His room is on the third floor.*

He looked startled for a second and then gave me his wide grin. "I should never drink in the middle of the day. I'm on the wrong floor." He steadied himself on the door jamb.

He didn't look really drunk, but then again I didn't know how drunk differed from sober for him. "I can relate to that," I said. "You, uh, need directions?"

"Nope. Ta taa." He gave me a four-fingered wave and walked past me and climbed the stairs toward the third floor.

"Ta taa?" I repeated, softly.

When I opened the door to my room Jazz darted from under the bed and tried to charge out, but I scooped her up and shut the door behind me. While she would usually swat at me for impeding her exit, this time she put her front paws around my neck and snuggled in.

"What's with you?" I sat in my rocking chair stroking her, still thinking about Mr. Mystery Writer Marcus. As an occasional sneak myself, I recognized the guilty look. *What did he want in another guest's room?*

Chapter Eighteen

I CARRIED JAZZ DOWN THE back staircase and walked into Aunt Madge's living area. She was at her oak table with a cup of hot tea and a recipe book.

"Going to try something new?" I hoped she wasn't still too mad.

She didn't look up. "One of the guests gave me some special flour for his muffins for tomorrow. He's allergic to gluten." Her tone was cool, but not totally unfriendly.

"How long is Mr. Hardy staying?"

"Marcus is going back on Tuesday or Wednesday."

Marcus. She never calls her guests by their first names.

"How's his book coming?"

At this she did look up. "I don't know. The way he chit chats and goes to Java Jolt I can't imagine he has a lot of time to write."

"Does he strike you as a bit…odd?"

"Odd, how?" she frowned.

"I don't know. I just found him on my floor wandering around. He was by Penny's room."

"I'm not sure I like your nomenclature," she said, dryly.

Nomenclature? Sometimes I forget Aunt Madge was an art history major with an English minor. "Yeah, me either." I sat next to her. "He said he guessed he was on the wrong floor."

She thought for a moment. "That is about where his room is on the third floor. And he does seem kind of fickle sometimes." She shrugged. "Aren't all writers a bid odd?"

"I guess. Makes me want to lock my door."

"You should in the summer." She went back to her recipe book.

I stood. "I'm going to the library. You have anything that needs to go back?"

She looked up for a second. "I don't think so."

"I'm getting some books for Scoobie."

At that her fact brightened. "I'm so glad. He said just yesterday he wasn't reading much because the pain medicines make it hard to concentrate."

Nuts. Caught in a lie I didn't even have to tell.

DAPHNE SAID SCOOBIE had been reading a lot of Agatha Christie novels just before he was hurt. "Agatha Christie? That doesn't sound like Scoobie," I said.

"He reads anything, but, personally, I think he's trying to figure out what makes you tick." She shrugged at me.

"I can't even do that." I started toward the mystery section. "Can you tell me what he's read?"

"Only if he says I can."

I looked back toward her. "Privacy." She turned toward a child who wanted to check out a book.

"Rats," I mumbled. I'd just have to guess. I picked out two that were near the end of a listing of her books, rationalizing that he would have started with her early ones and worked forward. Then I went to the racks that had the last month's newspapers. It made sense to me that Penny had been pilfering while she was in Ocean Alley. I hoped I would see a crime with her initials on it.

The crime report is usually on the second page of each day's *Ocean Alley Press*. There's no Sunday paper, so Monday's is a long list, especially in the summer. I went to the Saturday of the carnival weekend. There were several DUIs, one public indecency arrest, and two car break-ins. Not too bad for a weekend. I looked at the break-in locations, noting they were nowhere near the carnival.

Monday was a different story. In addition to the usual post-weekend number of DUIs, three people had reported "items stolen from person," which I figured meant pick pocketing. Two were "location unknown" and one said only "church parking lot." I thought for a moment. The unknown locations likely meant someone noticed the theft but didn't know when it occurred. There were no names with the listings.

"That's no help," I muttered to myself. There were two more indecency arrests (you can always tell when the weather's warm) and there had been a fistfight outside the Sandpiper on Sunday. That wouldn't be Penny, she was passed out at the Cozy Corner.

Since I didn't know much about where Penny was after her last appearance at the hospital, I checked Tuesday through Thursday. Nothing looked relevant.

I looked at Friday, which had the very short note about Penny's death. At the top of that page was a two-paragraph article about the Landon family arriving home after several days' absence to find "a number of items missing from their home. "Among them were a set of all of the state quarters, an "unknown amount of cash," and the "family silver service." Someone had gained entry by making a slit in the screened porch and then going in the unlocked door that led from the screened porch into the house.

Why didn't Morehouse say anything about that after he saw the silverware in Penny's bag? Because he would consider it none of your business.

I usually thought of "silver service" to be a tea service, but I'm hardly an Emily Post kind of gal. It could be silverware. My instinct said "an unknown amount of cash" didn't necessarily mean the amount Penny appeared to have in her small suitcase, though I didn't know exactly how much she had.

My mind wandered. On Friday, Scoobie saw Turk and told him to stay away from local kids. Turk was mad and maybe beat up Scoobie, and maybe Penny found her son. Penny left her stash at Aunt Madge's, surely planning to return. Then someone killed her. Was it someone who knew she had called an ambulance for Scoobie? Someone who wanted her stash? Then I remembered the nurse said that Scoobie's head injury probably was inflicted not long before he was found. How did that fit in?

My cell phone chirped and I jumped. "Hello?"

"Why are you whispering?" George asked.

"I'm in the library."

"Meet me at Newhart's." He hung up.

I fumed as I gathered my books. Who does he think he is, ordering me to meet him at Newhart's?

GEORGE HAD TWO MILKSHAKES sitting in front of him and was almost bouncing in his chair. "Bow to the master," he said, as I sat.

"In your dreams. What? What did you find out?"

He pushed the chocolate shake toward me and opened his thin notebook. There was a list of items. "The Friday of the carnival weekend Penny pawned a laptop, two solid silver picture frames, a very old men's pocket watch, a bunch of Hank Aaron baseball cards, and two smaller flat-screen TVs."

"Didn't the pawnshop owner wonder where she got all that?" I asked.

"If she had taken it to one place, maybe, but she went to all three shops."

"So…she came into town with all that?"

"My guess would be that she steals stuff one place and pawns it in another."

I nodded. "Makes sense." I paused. "She might have stolen some silverware while she was here."

"Why do you say that?" George asked.

"Short article in the paper the Friday after the carnival. Family had been away and found some things taken when they returned."

"That's right, the Landons. I saw that."

"I figured you wrote it," I said.

"Nope. Newbies do the police blotter and stuff like that."

"So, she steals stuff and pawns it. Wait! Maybe that's why she was wearing better clothes the day I saw her at the Budget Inn."

"Yeah, makes sense," George said, slowly. "I don't know what we gain by knowing that."

"Doesn't matter. It gives me a reason why she might have had money for better clothes."

"Oh yeah, 'cause if you have a reason everything's okay." He said this with a sarcastic look.

"Cut it out." I drank more of my milkshake. "So, we don't know if she still sells on line." I paused. "Nuts, even if she pawned stuff and sold it other ways, it doesn't sound like a lot of money, nothing like how much was in her little suitcase."

"I thought you didn't know the amount," he said, suspicious.

I shrugged. "I don't. Just looked like a lot." I shrugged. "Maybe some was from selling stuff she stole and some was in one of the houses she broke into."

He slurped his milkshake and then sat back in his chair. "Maybe she was working with someone."

"And they were dumb enough to let her hold the money?" I asked.

"Yeah, they'd have to be pretty dumb," he agreed.

"Did you ever find out what happened to the two people she was arrested with in New York?"

"They haven't been arrested again, that I could find out, anyway." He flipped back a few pages in his notebook. "Guy got out of the county jail after his thirty days and wasn't on any kind of parole. Girl was on probation, but her time was up more than a couple years ago."

We stared at our respective milkshakes. "I made Morehouse play the 9-1-1 call about Scoobie. I think it could have been Penny."

"You're kidding. He would never do that for me."

I shrugged. "Maybe he has different rules for reporters."

"And…?" he said.

"I thought it sounded like it could be her, making her voice really low."

"What would make her even look for him?" George asked.

I shrugged. "Maybe she followed Turk?"

"Followed from where?" George said.

"The Sandpiper," we said, together.

"My favorite joint," said Lester Argrow.

I looked up at him. "I thought you liked Burger King."

Lester motioned that I should move over and he slid into the booth next to me. "I knew you was gonna do some detecting about Scoobie. You shoulda called me."

From the look on his face, George was about to lose his milkshake.

"We're just talking," I said. "Kind of odd that Scoobie gets hurt and then his mother gets killed."

"Scoobie getting' hurt, yeah, but I woulda off'd that broad if I coulda gotten away with it. I had to watch out for her every time I went to Burger King to meet clients."

George grinned. "I forgot you use Burger King for your office."

"Saves me makin' coffee in the office. Course I gotta buy them theirs." He frowned. "I was goin' to Java Jolt for a while, but the coffee's a lot higher."

"What do you mean watch out?" I asked.

"If it was the end of the month she always wanted to 'borrow' a couple bucks," he said. He got a food server's eye and mimed drinking coffee.

I remembered George saying Penny used to sit on the curb outside the Sandpiper. "Hey, Lester." I pushed my milkshake away and turned to face him. "Your building is kind of catty-corner to the Sandpiper, right?"

"Yeah, which is why I gotta walk by it to get to Burger King, brainchild."

George's eyes lit up. "Brainchild?"

"Do you have cameras? Security cameras, I mean?" I asked.

"Couple, yeah. Mostly just to scare people off…"

"Do they show the Sandpiper entrance?" George asked, catching on.

"Sure, somebody gonna piss on the sidewalk near the steps up to my office or throw up in the planter on the ground floor they're probably coming from Sandpiper," Lester said.

I almost asked why he was concerned about that, but I didn't really care. "How long do you keep your tapes?"

"I don't keep any," Lester said.

My heart sank.

"But the company monitors them keeps them for a few weeks, then reuses them. Why?"

LESTER ARGUED WITH THE security firm for ten minutes. They were not going to go through the tapes to find the ones from two weekends ago, not on the Saturday of Memorial Day Weekend.

"How about for a hundred bucks?" he finally said.

When whoever he was talking to didn't seem to respond immediately I knew we were going to get to see those tapes.

WE COULD SEE THEM, BUT ONLY IF WE WENT through them ourselves. Sitting between Lester and George was kind of like being squashed on the New York subway on a hot day. Plus, they were crabby, each wanting to be the alpha male of security tape screening.

George had expected an organized box of videotapes so we could watch in some order, but the security firm box said only "Argrow, May" on the side. "I can't believe they don't put dates on these," George fumed.

I couldn't either, but I kept my mouth shut and put another VHS tape into the player. After the fourth tape, I said, "You know, Lester, if you get a security firm that uses digital recordings they could label the files more easily and keep them on a computer indefinitely."

"So I could watch people barf on the curb over and over?" he asked.

Charming. "Good point."

Penny was on the seventh tape we fast forwarded through. Thankfully she had on the same leotards she'd worn to the hospital that first Sunday Scoobie was in there, so she wasn't hard to spot.

"Okay," George said. "She's in, now we have to see when she goes out."

"You learn that kind of thinkin' in college?" Lester asked.

"And we need to see who walks out before her," I said, before George could respond.

We were still fast-forwarding, but more slowly. After about ten minutes I'd guess maybe an hour of time had passed on the tape. Turk and two other men walked out of the Sandpiper, and Turk pointed in the direction of Burger King. For Lester's benefit, I said, "Scoobie said that Turk saw him and called that Scoobie should join him for a drink."

"Scoobie don't drink no more," Lester said.

"No kidding," George said, looking at the screen.

Scoobie entered the frame and he and Turk walked into the Sandpiper. "He knew that guy before," I said.

Though the tapes weren't timed in any way, my guess was less than ten minutes went by before Scoobie came out, walking fast and looking angry. "From what he said, I think that's about one or one-thirty," George said.

I nodded. Turk came out less than a minute later and followed Scoobie, and soon after that came Penny. She looked up and down the street and then walked in the direction Turk had gone. She looked steadier on her feet than she did when I met her on Sunday, but she was not a fast walker.

George ejected the tape. He nodded at Lester. "I'd like to keep this, if it's okay."

"For the hundred bucks I paid you can have five of them," Lester said.

I'd had enough of Lester and George to last me for a month. It took awhile to ditch Lester, but George I needed to talk to. I finally said I had Scoobie's library books in my car and George said he had to finish a story on Memorial Day traffic headaches.

Without agreeing in advance, George and I drove to the hospital. He walked over to my car as I was getting out.

"I need to tell you about Scoobie," I said.

"You mean like he's in the hospital after someone tried to kill him?" George asked.

"No, I mean after Jennifer was at the paper with us she told him we were looking at pictures of Penny and Turk. He's really, really angry with us."

George stopped walking and faced me. "She did what?"

I just nodded. "Really mad."

He leaned against a car. "Damn. I never trust a woman who gets her nails done."

Doesn't sound as if George dates too many women. "He already basically threw me out. Why don't you try talking to him?"

GEORGE WAS BACK in the lobby in less than ten minutes. "Ramona's with him. They ganged up on me."

"Yeah, she thought I should leave it all alone, too."

"He'll get over it," George said, seemingly more to convince himself than me.

It was well into Saturday evening, and the drive to the hospital had been slow because Ocean Alley's streets were teeming with beach-happy visitors. I wanted to go home.

"I'm ready to call it a day," I said. "I don't know where to go with any of this except the police."

"Uh, uh," George said. "I've got a story here."

"I thought you were worried about bad guys learning more about Scoobie."

George gave me a look that seemed to imply I could drop dead anytime. "I'm holding it until I can say who they are and maybe help get them arrested."

I HAD FORGOTTEN ABOUT Mystery-Writer-Marcus, but when I got back to the Cozy Corner Saturday evening he was playing Scrabble in the kitchen with Aunt Madge.

"There she is," he called, giving me his toothpaste-commercial smile. "I heard you tattled on me."

I tried not to look as surprised as I felt. *A guest in the enclave?* "You did surprise me, that's for sure."

"I have promised Madge I will learn to count better."

He missed Aunt Madge's eye roll in my direction. But when he turned back to her she smiled.

She's having fun.

"Are your friends at the wedding?" I asked.

"Yes, the reception should be more than half over by now," she said.

Marcus grinned at me. "I tried to talk Madge into crashing the reception with me, but she didn't seem to think that was very proper."

"I'm not too interested in going where I'm not...expected." She gave me a meaningful look.

I ignored her barb and nodded at the board. "She usually wins."

I begged off their request to join them in a new game and was brushing my teeth, with Jazz keeping me company on the edge of the sink, when I heard Marcus climbing the back stairs to his room. I didn't especially like him using "my" stairs, but if Aunt Madge was willing to play Scrabble with him that was good enough for me.

Chapter Nineteen

THE BEST THING ABOUT the Internet is you can find information almost instantly. A not so good thing is that sometimes I need more time to think before I act, and instant information kind of hinders that.

I walked over to Java Jolt Sunday morning to use the Internet. East Jersey Entertainment's web site said its two "carnival teams" would be in Point Pleasant Beach and Atlantic City for Memorial Day weekend. Atlantic City was not practical for a quick visit. It is a long way south of Ocean Alley. More important, I had no intention of setting foot in the town where my ex-husband said he "lost big at the tables." Point Pleasant was even closer than Asbury Park, so I hoped Turk was at that carnival.

I know George goes to Saint Anthony's on Sunday morning, so I had no one to talk to about my idea. *No one to talk you out of it.* Besides, he might want to do something his way, and I generally preferred mine.

It was ten-thirty. Aunt Madge wouldn't be home from First Prez until at least noon, later if she stayed for coffee. I would leave her a note saying I was visiting Scoobie and it would be awhile before she wondered where I was. I would have time to go to the carnival in Point Pleasant and get back to Ocean Alley before she thought about me. Much.

I figured Scoobie was still mad at me, but I did have the Agatha Christie books for him, and if I stopped by the hospital I would not be totally lying to Aunt Madge.

It was almost eleven when I got to the hospital. Scoobie's room was empty, so I looked down the hall. He was dressed in sweatpants and a tee shirt and was walking along the hall holding onto the handrail. A nursing assistant was trailing him with Scoobie's walker. When they turned to walk back toward his room, Scoobie took the walker from the nursing assistant.

He concentrated on his walking and I noticed Scoobie's gait was more natural now. Apparently he was in less pain. He saw me from about fifty feet away and just shook his head at me. He said nothing to me as the nursing assistant walked him back in the room and helped him settle in a chair.

"You don't have to talk to me," I said, when I was sure the man was out of hearing distance.

"Thank you for reminding me I have freedom of speech, and it includes not speaking to anyone," he said.

I put the two books on the bed. "Daphne said you like Agatha Christie."

"I'm tired of her," he said.

I felt my mouth twitch and tried to look serious again.

"I'm seriously mad at you, Jolie," Scoobie said.

"I know. I'm just here for a minute and I'll leave you alone."

"That would be good."

I left.

I HAD ONE STOP TO MAKE en route to the carnival. Two really. I bought flowers from the small refrigerator of flowers in Mr. Markle's store and plopped them in a vase that was in my trunk. I had taken it from Scoobie's hospital room a couple days ago. After his flowers had died, of course.

It looked as if Manasquan was as crowded as Ocean Alley for the holiday weekend. The Parkers were on the deck at the back of their house, which faced the street, when I pulled into their driveway. Bob Parker was on a chaise lounge and had a laptop in front of him. With guilt I figured it was probably a replacement for one stolen when their house was burglarized.

"Jolie, is that you?" asked Mrs. Parker, as I got out of the car.

I had meant to look up their first names. My brain seems to be foggy about half of everything since Scoobie was hurt. "Yes, Carol, it's me."

"Caroline," she said, still smiling.

Mr. Parker, whom I thought was named Ralph, stood and placed the laptop on his lounger. "What brings you back again?"

He didn't look especially happy to see me, and I didn't blame him. What appraiser loses her camera and comes back with a throwaway camera to redo the pictures? And then has her stolen camera become the apparent basis for a home burglary.

I reached into the floor of my car's back seat and pulled out the vase of flowers. "I thought I'd bring a peace offering."

"Goodness, it wasn't your fault someone stole your camera," Caroline said. She was walking the few steps down from the deck and held her hand out for the small vase. "They smell wonderful." Caroline Parker was petite and lithe at the same time and her light brown hair practically shone in the sunshine. I sucked in my tummy a bit.

"Come on up and have some iced tea," Ralph said, gesturing to one of several chairs on the deck.

My flowers seemed to have wilted his reserve, so I sat and Caroline placed the vase of flowers on their expensive-looking picnic table on the deck. "I appreciate your attitude, but I still feel very badly about the burglary. You had so much taken."

Ralph waved his hand. "Nothing that couldn't be replaced."

"They even left my purse," Caroline said.

"I heard that." I took the tea she poured for me. "Harry said that's one reason the police thought they studied the photos and planned from there."

Ralph nodded. "We've decided that our next house will not have our name on a sign out front. Though I suppose they could have found us anyway. I'm sure Harry told you we declined his company's offer to pay our five-hundred dollar deductible."

Funny he didn't mention that. All I said was, "That's generous of you." *I wonder if Harry cashed my check?* "I know money can't fully replace what you had."

Caroline's face lit up. "Oh, we're getting a lot of it back. They found it in a pawn shop in Newark. It will be awhile, though. The police said they want to see if it's tied to any other thefts."

"They seem to think there could be a few thieves working together, stealing things and pawning them in different towns," Ralph said. "In fact, they borrowed our security tapes to see if they can identify anyone." He shrugged. "I doubt they will. I looked at them. The people had on hooded sweatshirts and huge sunglasses. You can't even tell if they're men or women."

TWO DAYS AGO I'D never thought of looking at anyone's security tapes, and now I was interested in two sets of tapes. Not that I'd be able to see the ones from the Parker's house. I was still thinking about who I could convince to let me see their tapes when I pulled into Point Pleasant. My plan was to let Turk see me and hope he wouldn't ignore me. I'd find a way to tell him Scoobie was doing much better but couldn't remember what had happened after he left the Sandpiper the night he got hurt. For effect, I'd say he couldn't even remember much of that entire day. That would let Turk know he didn't need to worry about Scoobie saying anything that would implicate Turk — whether about selling joints or pushing people down stairs. Scoobie would be safe.

In the meantime, George's story aside, I needed to find a way to tell Sgt. Morehouse about Turk seeming to follow Scoobie out of the Sandpiper and Penny definitely following Turk. I hadn't worked out how to let Morehouse know I knew this. If Lester told Ramona about the tapes, then Morehouse or Tortino would know the same day, and I could honestly tell George I didn't mention the security tapes to the police. I hoped Lester would tell her.

One month ago I'd have ratted out George on anything that would get him in hot water. Now that he might find out something I wanted to know, I'd have to keep my more petty inclinations to myself. And Scoobie did seem to like him a lot.

My cell phone chirped as I got out of my car at the Point Pleasant carnival site, which was on a large lot at the edge of town.

"Where are you?" George asked.

"I'll be back in town in a bit." I turned off the car.

"You're up to something," he said.

I didn't bother to ask why everyone said the same thing to me. "I thought of a way to keep Turk away from Scoobie."

"So where are you?" he asked.

"Not too far out of town."

"Damn it, Jolie. I don't know whether to be madder because you're being shady or because you might get to part of the story before I do."

"It's not a story to me." I slammed my car door. I could feel my face redden with every step I took toward the carnival entrance. "It's not a game, George. It's about…"

"Keeping Scoobie, all of us, safe. I get that. Did you stop to think what you're doing could work against that?"

"I'll see you later, George." I hung up the phone and did not answer when he called three more times.

THIS CARNIVAL SITE WAS more similar to the set-up in Ocean Alley than the one in Asbury Park. It was smaller, without the kiddie roller coaster. The booths were more crammed together, so that I sometimes had to step sideways to pass a cluster of people buying tickets for the rides or waiting in line for food.

I hadn't bothered with my baseball cap or large sunglasses. I wanted to be seen. After a quick walk-through I spotted Turk at the Ferris Wheel. Idly I wondered why he'd been at the High Striker in Ocean Alley, if only briefly, and decided carnival workers need potty breaks, too. *If only he hadn't been there, if only Scoobie hadn't seen him.*

There were no obvious indications that he was selling anything, but I didn't really care about that. Alicia's face floated into my brain and I decided I did care about kids having easy access to drugs, but I cared more about getting this guy to forget about Scoobie.

Unlike amusement areas that sit on or near the boardwalk, there were few children in wet bathing suits or parents running after them with sun screen. There were more groups of families, some of whom looked as if they might have come from church. I sat on a bench across from the Ferris Wheel and chatted for a few minutes with a young mother who had a two-year old on her lap and looked ready to deliver another kidlet any day.

After about fifteen minutes Turk finally saw me. I smiled and gave him the kind of four-finger wave Marcus had bestowed on me. He stared for at least five seconds and then turned to slow down the Ferris Wheel so riders could get off and on. I hoped I made him nervous.

After a few minutes I bought lemonade from a nearby food vendor and took my seat again, this time next to a couple of teenagers who couldn't keep their hands off each other. A couple of times Turk glanced at me, careful to pretend he was looking at something else.

After another half-hour went by, the blonde carnival worker who had also overseen the High Striker walked over, seemingly to give Turk a break. I stood as Turk walked out the small gated area that surrounded the Ferris Wheel. He ambled toward me, hands in the pockets of a pair of faded blue jeans that had a streak of grease across one knee. His expression was a combination of cocky and cautious.

"Hello, Stefan." I used the name he had introduced himself with when he came to the hospital. "I thought you'd like to know how Scoobie is."

His expression grew less wary, but he still looked uneasy. "Yeah, I've been thinking a lot about Scoobie."

I bet you have. "He's walking, doing a lot of physical therapy, and he'll likely be able to go back to college for the summer term." I gave him what I hoped was a sweet smile.

"College? Scoobie? You're kidding."

"Of course not. He's very smart. Surely you remember that from when you worked together before."

The wary expression returned. He seemed to realize that I had talked to Scoobie about how they knew each other. "Yes, very smart," he said.

Maybe I shouldn't have said that. "It's too bad his memory isn't as good as usual. He has no idea how he hurt himself a couple of weeks ago. Can't even remember most of that day."

"That's, uh, too bad," Turk said. I thought he looked relieved.

"I'll let you get back to work." I started to turn, but he reached out and gripped my right hand with both of his.

"Tell him I think of him often," he emphasized the last word, then let go of my hand and quickly walked away.

Though I was a bit flustered by the handshake, I gave myself a mental pat on the back and walked toward the exit. This had gone even better than I had hoped, and I'd be home by the middle of the afternoon.

As I unlocked my car a man's voice said, "Please turn around slowly."

For some reason I wasn't scared. It was daylight and I was in a carnival parking lot, not a dark alley. I turned to look at a man in his mid-forties who was in shorts and a knit cotton top. "Ok, who are you?"

"I'm with the Point Pleasant Police, and we'd like to ask you a few questions."

I SAT IN THE SMALL POLICE STATION, and cursed inwardly. I was pleased that local police were keeping an eye on Turk, but collaring me was not what I had in mind when I told Morehouse I thought Turk was selling drugs to kids.

Officer McMichaels listened to me when I said why I was there, but he still drove me to the station in his unmarked car. He didn't make me sit in the back seat, but he did make me show him the contents of my purse before we got in his car. McMichaels said he would call the Ocean Alley Police to verify that they knew me and I was not likely to have talked to Turk about buying drugs. I hoped that was what he was doing. I wanted to get home. I heard him laugh as he came back down the small hallway.

He looked at me and grinned. "Sergeant Morehouse says I'm supposed to ask you how it feels to be hoisted on your own petard."

The exact meaning of the expression eluded me, though I thought it meant to mess up big time. "I take it he vouched for me?" I stood.

"I wouldn't go that far, but he did say you wouldn't be buying anything illicit." He grew more serious. "He also said to please call him when you get back to Ocean Alley."

"He said please?" I asked.

"Actually, no. He said to get your ass in gear and call him when you get back to town."

I WAS NEVER GOING TO hear the end of it. Morehouse was furious with me for "yet again butting in," and he apparently thought that the best way to get me to at least consider minding my own business was to tell Aunt Madge where I had gone. He must have called her as soon as I left the station.

"When you were young your mother and I would just say you were hard-headed. Your father actually thought you were adorable when you insisted on wearing what you wanted when your mother wanted you to wear a dress." She was mixing the dough for the next morning's muffins, and it looked as if she would stir so hard the wooden spoon would soon poke out of the bottom of the bowl.

"But…" I began.

"There are no buts!" She waved the spoon at me and a splatter of dough fell to the floor. Mr. Rogers beat Miss Piggy to it.

"It's just…"

"I can't even imagine how your mind works. Do you know how dangerous it could be to talk to a man like that? And on your own, no less?"

"I was making it less dangerous for Scoobie." I stared at her, determined not to be made to feel like an errant child any longer.

"You don't know that. You might just as easily…"

There was a knock on the door that led from the kitchen to the breakfast room and we both turned toward it. Mr. Mystery-Writer-Marcus stuck his head in. "It doesn't usually sound like a war zone around here."

Aunt Madge looked aghast. She had probably thought all of her guests were at the beach. "I'm so sorry, Marcus."

I didn't mind seeing him. "Come on in."

He nodded at me, but his attention was for Aunt Madge. "Are you okay?"

"Yes, of course," she replied. "I'm just mad at Jolie about something. Families get that way sometimes. I'm sorry if we alarmed you."

We? I wasn't yelling.

"I can occasionally be annoying," I said.

"Occasionally?" Aunt Madge said, under her breath, as she returned to stirring her muffin mix.

I looked at Marcus. "I was doing something on behalf of my friend who's in the hospital. Aunt Madge thinks," she shot me a glance, "that I should perhaps leave well enough alone."

Mystery-Writer-Marcus's expression was sympathetic. "I know you've both been very concerned about your friend."

"In fact, I'm on my way to see him now." Pleased with the opportunity to escape Aunt Madge's ire I picked up my purse and walked through the guest dining room to the side door and out to my car.

I should have hidden in my room.

George Winters was about to knock on the Cozy Corner front door, and he looked like the cat who swallowed a canary. "I can't believe you pissed off Sgt. Morehouse again."

"How do you hear this stuff so fast?"

"You know how I make my living, right?" When I just looked at him, he added, "I'm friends with a couple of the younger cops."

Once he'd heard about the conversation with Turk it was fairly easy to ditch George. I went to the hospital and told Scoobie what I had done.

He wasn't angry with me, "Since it wouldn't matter to you anyway," as he put it. Scoobie accepted that I had been "acting in good faith. But you might want to try a different religion or something."

I was sitting in his guest chair with my feet on his bed. He was in the patient recliner eating supper, carefully raising his fork so he could extend the bites of food across his cervical collar. "Personally, I think it was pretty smart to go see him in broad daylight, in front of God and everybody," I said. "He can't come looking for me now, everyone would know I maybe made him mad."

"Maybe?" He dropped mashed potatoes on his tray and tried another scoop.

"I don't care if he's mad at me or anybody else. He's the one who pushed you Scoobie. And the nurse said your head injury was probably long after you fell down the steps, so he must have gone back in the morning."

He regarded me stonily. "You don't know that." He considered his words. "Not that I'm sticking up for the son-of-a-bitch." He laughed, wryly. "Wait, that's me!"

"You really are sick," I said.

"And you think I'm in the hospital for the food?" he asked.

I knew I had to tread carefully. "I listened to the 9-1-1 tape. I think it was Penny who called it in."

That stopped him. He sat down his fork. "And you know her so well you recognized her voice? Hey, Morehouse told me a couple days ago that it was a guy."

"Sounded like her, disguising her voice. Morehouse was going to have Lt. Tortino listen. I guess he knows her better."

"If she was so hell-bent on saving me, why didn't she even stick around to see me?" He considered this. "Not that I wanted to see her."

I didn't know what he knew of his mother during the past few years, and I certainly hadn't told him anything about where his mother lived until earlier in the year and what she'd done to land herself in prison. And I wasn't about to. "I'm not saying she was a good person or anything."

"How do you make the leap to even think it was her on the phone?"

"For one thing, it was a stolen cell phone…"

"That sounds like my mother."

"Belonged to a guy who had it stolen at the carnival. And the pictures George and Jennifer took of her at the Ocean Alley carnival make it look as if she wanted people to think she worked there, but she really didn't." I told him about the unadorned clown jumper and helium balloons, and that the phone's owner said someone carrying balloons had bumped into him and likely taken the phone at that time.

"Humph. That was one of her tricks of the trade." His voice grew bitter. "She thought she made everything all right by bringing me a balloon."

"I'm sorry, Scoobie," I said, quietly.

"It's not an 'I'm sorry' deal. She was a lousy mother, a lousy person. I don't wish anybody dead. Well, maybe Hitler." He paused. "But I'm really glad I never have to see her again."

I decided to skip telling him about the security camera tapes. Lester surely would. I felt guilty for avoiding the topic, but I didn't need to be thrown out of Scoobie's room again.

Ramona came in and stood looking at me. "Tell me you didn't."

"OK," I said. "I didn't."

She looked at Scoobie. "I can't really nod," he said, "but she did." He looked at me. "Don't lie to Ramona."

I'd had enough of being told off. I sat up in the chair and turned to look directly at Ramona. "He won't bother Scoobie now. He wouldn't dare."

She just stared at me.

"How did you know, anyway?" I asked her.

"George. I think he's working on a story."

Chapter Twenty

I KNEW IT WAS TOO GOOD to be true. George Winters was going to be sure I was in a story and I wouldn't come out of it in a good light. He asked me to meet him in Java Jolt and said he wanted me to read something.

Though it was Monday of Memorial Day weekend, Java Jolt was not as crowded as I'd expected. There had been a large concert in the municipal parking lot the night before and a number of visitors were apparently sleeping in. As I'd walked along the boardwalk it looked as if some of the sun worshippers were actually sleeping it off on the beach.

I ordered an iced coffee and selected a table that was not close to others. George banged the door as he came in and plopped a page of text in front of me. He stared at me until I started to read.

Acting on her belief that a carnival worker was responsible for serious injuries an Ocean Alley resident sustained two weeks ago, local real estate appraiser Jolie Gentil went to Point Pleasant on Sunday to confront the man she believes shoved the resident down a flight of concrete steps. (The *Ocean Alley Press* does not identify crime victims if doing so could endanger them.)

Though the carnival worker's behavior has not been determined, Gentil made a point of visiting him to let him know the local resident was recovring. She believed this would annoy the crap out of the man and he would stay the hell out of town.

"I've been thinking about what you did. This," George said when he saw I had finished reading, "is what I'll write if you do anything that stupid again."

"You aren't my mother. And you misspelled 'recovering,'" I said, smiling with what I hoped was an innocent expression. We were talking in hushed tones, since Joe Regan seemed very interested in our conversation.

"Look, you can get yourself killed whenever you want, but for Pete's sake, go out doing something exciting, or noble, or at least interesting. Then I'd have a story." He got up to order from the counter.

As Joe passed George his coffee he winked at me. "Lester was looking for you, Jolie."

"Great." I needed Lester like a barefoot beachcomber needs sharp shells on the beach. On the other hand, I did appreciate his insistence that his security firm let us see the security tapes.

George sat back down. "Listen," he began.

"Are you going to show Sgt. Morehouse those tapes?" I asked.

"When I finally write a story he'll hit the ceiling and my editor will turn them over."

"I'm surprised he hasn't made you already. It shows Turk following Scoobie and Penny following him. You guys aren't in the business of covering up crimes."

"I'm not dumb enough to show them to my editor yet. Besides, the tapes might qualify as a lead, but they don't show a crime." He added more sugar to his coffee. "And I checked businesses near those steps Scoobie got pushed down. None of them point cameras there. And back when it happened, for two days running I talked to people who have businesses there. No one saw anything. It was too early in the morning."

"Except maybe Penny," I said.

"And she's not talking," George said.

"You do your thing George, I'm done."

"Whaddya mean you're done?" His voice rose. "We don't know who did anything!"

"All right, George," Joe Regan said.

George scowled at him.

"I know what I think I need to know," I lowered my voice even more, "to keep Scoobie safe. Everything about how Turk acted at the hospital that night and at the carnival in Pleasant

Point yesterday tells me he went after Scoobie. And now he thinks Scoobie won't tell anybody about that."

"But you don't know why," George said.

"I don't need to know why, that's your department. Besides, I have a lot of fences to mend, starting with Harry." *And I want to know if he'll tell me the Parkers won't take my money for their deductible.*

"Damn, Jolie. Just when I get used to you, you turn everything upside down. You're being a spoilsport."

"Nope. I'm just willing to read all about it in your paper."

"See, you are still interested." George's expression reminded me of a kid asking for just one more piece of candy. "Come on, Jolie, you like working with me," he said.

I considered that as I stood to leave. "I don't know if I'd go that far, but I like it when you're focused on somebody other than me." I gave him my four-fingered wave. I'd have to thank Marcus-Hardy-mystery-writer for giving me that little gem.

MOST OF MONDAY I did homebody things like laundry, walking the dogs, and beating Aunt Madge to the sink to do the dishes from the afternoon tea she served her guests. She could tell I was sucking up to her, and a couple times I could swear I saw something like a smirk on her face.

I decided I wouldn't go to the hospital until early evening. Better Scoobie should have a chance to miss me. When I got there Ramona was sitting across from Scoobie in a patient lounge area. They were playing chess and I could tell Scoobie was beating her. I wouldn't bother to play with him. He'd beat me in six moves.

"Hey guys," I plopped into a chair.

"How's the mayhem maker?" Scoobie asked, without looking up.

I took his tone to mean things between us were back to normal. It felt good.

The chess game was over in short order. We spent more than an hour playing a game of Trivial Pursuit that was in a bookcase in the lounge, which has a more homey environment than the rest of the hospital because the rehab patients can be there for weeks rather than days. We finally realized that it was the original version of the game and a lot of the answers had been superseded by time. Pluto is no longer the smallest planet and most of the sports records had been overtaken in the last couple decades.

I HAD STAYED LATER than I'd planned at the hospital and it was nine-thirty when Ramona and I walked to my car. I popped the locks and was pulling open my driver's side door when Ramona shrieked and tumbled out of sight. I ran around the car and saw Ramona sitting on the ground with her ankle in the grip of a gloved hand.

I kicked at the hand and missed and got Ramona in the thigh. "Ow!" she shrieked.

I reached for the hand and it disappeared under the car. I looked toward Ramona and got half a face full of pepper spray.

"My eyes!" I stood up fully and jumped in place. One eye was almost completely shut and the other streaming with tears.

I could hear Ramona getting to her feet. Someone grabbed my shoulder and I wrenched myself away, not sure if it was Ramona or whoever belonged to the hand. The hand felt much bigger than Ramona's. It seemed to run halfway down my back.

"Hey, are you okay?" It was a man's voice and I could hear feet running toward us, but all I could think about was my burning eyes.

"Jolie, I'm so sorry. I have some water in my bag."

I could hear Ramona fumbling in her shoulder bag and I groped in my pocket for a tissue. The only thing streaming down my face more than tears was mucus. What little I could see told me an orange man was running toward us. All orange. I shrieked.

A man's voice said, "We need the police in the visitor parking lot at the hospital."

LUCKILY I DIDN'T have access to a mirror. I could only imagine what I looked like. At least my eyes burned less. I didn't get to the ER for a few minutes. Whoever the orange man was he led me to the ladies room just inside the hospital front door and told Ramona to keep my head under the water running in the sink. Ramona told me later he stood outside the door until the police came.

"Oh my God," Ramona said for the fifth, or twenty-fifth time. "I'm so sorry."

"Was that guy really orange?" I asked.

"Orange?" she asked.

"It can be a side effect of pepper spray," Sgt. Morehouse said as he walked into the ER cubicle. "Makes you confused and afraid for a few minutes." He nodded at Ramona. "Better make sure you don't let Winters near her with a camera. Even I wouldn't wish that on her."

"That's not funny." I could hear how stuffed up my nose was.

"You're right. I'm sorry."

From what I could see of Morehouse's face through my puffy eyes, he was trying to hide a smile as he pulled out a notebook. "How come you're wearing shorts?" I asked.

"Barbeque," he said. "Called me at home. Big fight outside the Sandpiper so all the guys are down there."

"It's my fault," Ramona said, blowing her nose.

"It's the hand's fault," I said. "The hand under the car."

"Was it attached to a person," Morehouse said, patiently.

"Yes," Ramona said. "It was wearing a glove. A black glove."

"Okay…What else?" Morehouse asked.

"We got to the car, and I popped the locks on both sides. I guess…Ramona did you open your door first?"

"I'm not sure, but when I started to pull it open, somebody grabbed me from underneath."

"I thought she fell," I said, "so I ran around the car, the front of the car. And I tried to kick the hand…"

"But you got me," Ramona said. "In the thigh." She raised the hem of her skirt and I could see a bruise had formed on the side of her thigh.

"Yuck. Now I'm sorry. And then, then what? Oh, I reached down, I was going to grab the hand."

"But I'd gotten my pepper spray," Ramona said. "I was trying to spray under the car, but Jolie bent down just then and I guess I got her."

"I think so," Morehouse said, dryly. "You always carry pepper spray, or somebody been bothering you?"

"Nobody. I just, you know, I walk everywhere, even at night." Her voice trailed off and she looked at me. "I'm so sorry."

"If you say that again, I'm going to get my own pepper spray."

"Damn, I should think so." George Winters was in the doorway.

"No camera," Morehouse said. "And you gotta wait in the lobby."

George walked over and pulled me into a hug. "Damn, Jolie." He held on for several seconds and then pulled back. "Will you talk to me after?" he asked Morehouse.

"Yep," was all Morehouse said.

I think I was more in shock from the hug than the pepper spray for the next couple of minutes. Sgt. Morehouse found it hard to believe we hadn't seen anything of the attacker. Well, almost nothing. We saw the hand, and Ramona had a glimpse of his back, but all she knew was he was tall and seemed to have short hair.

"He had on a knit cap," Morehouse said. "The guy who brought you back inside saw that much, but not much more."

"Who brought us in?" I asked.

"Larry Budd," Aunt Madge said, from the doorway.

Morehouse gestured her into the room. "I'd say we gotta stop meeting like this, Madge, but she'll probably do it again."

"I didn't DO anything." I blew my nose hard.

"Who's Larry Budd?" Ramona asked.

"He works maintenance at the high school," Morehouse said.

"His wife just had twins," Aunt Madge said.

We talked for another twenty minutes, with Morehouse making Ramona and me go over the last few hours of our day. He wanted to know if we had seen anyone 'hanging around,' as he put it, or noticed anyone paying attention to us when we were visiting Scoobie. Ramona and I were clueless.

"Whose hand was on my back?" I finally remembered to ask.

"Mine," Ramona said. "I guess you didn't know it was me."

"It felt huge." I looked at her hands.

"Side effect of pepper spray. Like I said, you feel confused." Morehouse closed his notebook.

"You think it could have been the guy from the carnival?" Morehouse asked.

"Turk?" I said. "I kind of don't think so."

"Because you made sure he didn't have any suspicions about Scoobie?" Aunt Madge asked, irritated.

"Because it looked like a bigger hand." I tried not to sound annoyed with her.

"I think that, too," Ramona said.

"You two an expert on hands?" Morehouse asked.

"I draw them, you know," Ramona said. "It looked like the hand of someone larger. The Turk guy wasn't much taller than I am."

Morehouse stood. "I asked hospital security to check around. Not likely they'll find anything." He yawned. "I'm gonna talk to Winters. If you're gonna get cut loose soon, I'll follow you home." He walked out.

"Thanks," I called after him. I looked at Aunt Madge. "I was not 'up to something.'" *Not all day.*

Chapter Twenty-One

THE GOOD THING about "the hand attack," as Scoobie christened it, is that no one thought I had done anything to bring it about so no one was mad at me. Because it was Memorial Day weekend, Sgt. Morehouse thought it might have been a drunk or drug-addled vacationer. I might have agreed with him if it hadn't been for the glove. What drug-addled robber hides under a car with gloved hands? In the summer?

The best thing was that Harry Steele was talking to me without apparent reserve. I always know Aunt Madge will forgive my transgressions eventually, but I knew I'd wounded Harry by lying to him and I hadn't figured out how to get beyond that.

"So, anyway," I said to Harry, "the Parkers said some of their stuff turned up in pawn shops and they may eventually get it back." It was Tuesday morning and I was sitting in Harry's office at the small table I use to work with the computer-aided appraisal software.

He opened his bottom desk drawer and reached for something. "They also said they wouldn't accept our offer to pay their deductible." He slid my $500 check across his desk and I took it.

I looked at it for a few seconds, then slid it back. "Why don't you use at least some of it to make a donation to Harvest for All?" He looked at me. Usually you can tell which direction a person's train of thought is headed if you know them well and look at them closely, but I couldn't guess his thoughts.

He slid the check back. "I'll pay you one hundred instead of $200 for your next two appraisals, and then I'll donate $400 from the company to the food pantry — half from me, half from you."

I grinned at him as I felt my stress melt away. *Harry isn't mad at me anymore!*

THAT SAME TUESDAY Marcus announced that he had finished a first draft of his book and would be leaving on Wednesday. Aunt Madge seemed almost relieved. Even though she seemed to like his company, guests generally don't hang out with her. She's friendly, but she likes her privacy.

"So, when can I read your book?" I asked him. Since he was leaving soon I decided to be friendlier and was sitting with him in the breakfast room Wednesday morning.

"It takes longer than you'd think," he said. "My publisher will edit it, work with people to design a marketing plan, lots of other steps."

I held out my hand as I stood. "Please let Aunt Madge know when it comes out. She'll tell me."

When I walked back into the kitchen Aunt Madge made a zipping gesture across her lips. Maybe she wasn't interested in hearing a lot more from Marcus-the mystery-writer.

ON MY WAY TO HARRY'S after breakfast on Wednesday I stopped by the police station to see what Sgt. Morehouse would tell me. It was the last thing I planned to do in connection with Penny's murder or Scoobie's attack. Other than helping Scoobie recover I had decided to put everything that had happened out of my mind. I was working on believing the hand under the car was a random attempt at a carjacking or robbery. That was harder, but I wanted life back to my version of normal.

As a professional courtesy, which was Sgt. Morehouse's term, the state police were keeping him up to date on Penny's death investigation. There wasn't much to tell. For a reason she couldn't tell us, Penny had stopped at a small roadside picnic area just north of town. The general police assumption was that she planned to meet someone there. "She obviously did meet someone, right?" I asked. "I mean, somebody killed her."

Morehouse gave me a withering look. "Good one, Sherlock. It almost had to be someone stronger than she is. Penny was no pixie, and it takes a lot of strength to strangle someone."

"Ugh."

"You asked," he said. "There were two recent sets of fingerprints in her car, Penny's and the man she was arrested with in Binghamton, Alex "Fun Boy" Masterson."

George had said he couldn't find anything recent on Masterson. Sounded as if there was something going on, he just hadn't been caught yet. "Just two?" I asked.

"I thought you just told me you were going to butt out." I said nothing, so he continued. "There were a number of latent prints, but I gotta agree with state police theory, which was that they belonged to prior owners. There were no matches to the fingerprints in any databases. And because someone scratched off the Vehicle Identification Number there's no easy way to find a prior owner to provide prints we can match or rule out."

Sgt. Morehouse opened a file on his desk. "They did give me a more recent photo of Masterson than when he and Penny were arrested. You see this guy around?" he asked.

I shook my head. The stringy brown hair was shorter and he had a mustache instead of a beard. The seemingly perpetual smirk was the same. "Half the guys who hang out on the boardwalk have hair like that." I started. In a way the photo looked like the shorter of the two homeless guys I'd talked to.

"Yeah," he agreed. "I asked the state cops why they don't look harder for him, but they seem to think if they put out a BOLO for him he'll leave the area, even if he had nothing to do with Penny's murder. They've passed this photo to all the local departments."

"BOLO?" I asked.

"You don't watch much TV," he said. "It stands for 'be on the lookout for.' It's a cop term, which you don't need to know because you aren't in law enforcement."

I took that as my cue to leave and headed for the hospital. I was familiar enough with Scoobie's therapy schedule to know he'd be done soon, for the morning anyway.

I kept going back to the conversation with Morehouse and the newer photo of "Fun Boy" Masterson. I would have to be really certain about that before I mentioned the homeless guy. The police would certainly haul him in for questioning, and if he wasn't Masterson it would probably be hard on the guy. *What if he is Masterson?*

I shook my head to clear it. I wasn't going to deal with anything except Scoobie. The police had photos of Masterson. If it was the homeless guy they'd figure it out. *Maybe I'd plant the idea with George.*

SCOOBIE WAS IN THE hallway and his walker had been discarded in favor of a cane. "Arrgh!" He pointed it at me and made a gesture like a sword fighter. I did note that he kept his other hand on the hallway hand railing.

"What are you, a three Musketeer?" I asked, as we walked into his room.

"Have you forgotten about 'Talk Like a Pirate' Day?" he asked.

"I did, but I doubt Monica and Sylvia have."

He grinned. "They'll come around. Anyway, we have time to plan, it's not until September." His face lit up. "You think your aunt will make me a costume?"

"Probably." I plopped in his chair as he sat on the edge of his bed and then swung his legs up so he could lean back against the raised head of the bed. "How long do you have to use the cane?" I asked.

He winced as he bent his knees. "Not too long. I favor my right side a lot because the pain from the lumbar vertebrae runs down there. They want me to use the cane so I walk sort of normal."

"Can they fix it?"

He gestured at himself. "Don't I look fixed?"

"You look terrific." And he did. After more than two weeks his face was no longer bruised. His hair was shorter than usual, his concession to "even things up" because the doctors had shaved his head in a couple places where they'd gone in to place the catheter to release the pressure on his brain.

"I might get out at the end of the week," he said, and looked out the window.

I noticed he had ignored my question about whether they could fix his pain. I remembered a nurse saying something about putting gel in a crushed vertebra, or something like that. "I know Aunt Madge'll say come to the B&B."

"It's summer," he said simply. "She needs to rent all her rooms."

I thought about this for a moment. "You can sleep in my room and I'll sleep on the couch downstairs. She won't care."

"I can't make you move out of your room."

"My clothes and stuff will still be there. You might get Jazz, too. She's pretty used to the other pillow on my bed."

He nodded slowly. "I'll talk to Madge."

"About what?" She walked into the room.

Aunt Madge has an uncanny ability to walk into a room just when you're talking about her. My sister Renée and I have talked about that since we were little kids.

I let Scoobie go over our idea, but he only got it halfway out when she said, "Why Adam, I just assumed you'd stay at Cozy Corner for a while." She placed a foil-wrapped muffin on his bedside table. "Then Jolie can drive you to therapy or the library when you need to go. It will keep her out of trouble."

Chapter Twenty-Two

THE FRIDAY OF FOURTH OF JULY weekend Scoobie, Ramona and I walked along the boardwalk admiring the easels that had local artists' work. It's a Fourth of July tradition in Ocean Alley, and gives locals a chance to sell their work to the tourists. Ramona had six black and white, pencil drawings on display. They ran the gamut from seagulls on the beach to a single, gloved hand reaching up from the bottom of the frame. I knew where that idea came from.

We were also celebrating Scoobie's return to the real world, as he called it. He moved back to his room in the F Street boarding house the day before. He had wanted to return since the middle of June, but Aunt Madge kept encouraging him to stay "just a bit" longer. They finally agreed that when he stopped using the cane he would leave the Cozy Corner. I knew for a fact that he used it some, but not where Aunt Madge could see him.

"Hey," Scoobie said. "Let's go over here. Every time I see a bench my ass faints."

"I wonder how you'd capture that in a drawing?" I asked Ramona.

"I wouldn't be willing to try."

We sat on the bench, with the ocean to our backs. It was a balmy eighty degrees, a real pleasure in July, when New Jersey temperatures can easily rise to the mid-nineties. The boardwalk was packed with the usual eclectic bunch of middle-aged lovers, young teenage girls pretending to ignore the boys, or vice-versa, and kids of all ages waiting in line for boardwalk fries and talking about the evening's upcoming fireworks.

I had on shorts and a loose tee shirt and Ramona had on a paisley sundress, a real change for her. I noted half the men on the boardwalk gave her a second look, but she appeared oblivious.

Scoobie laughed and I stared in the direction he was looking. Lance Wilson was walking out of one of the knick knack shops wearing a child's pirate hat on his head. He ambled over and Ramona stood to give him her spot on the bench, which he refused.

"Glad to see you getting in the spirit," I said.

"Can't let Scoobie have all the fun." He adjusted his hat. "I actually got this for Sylvia."

"Madge is already working on my costume," Scoobie said. Lance gave us a salute and headed for Java Jolt. I've seen him there several times this summer. He's not big on coffee, but he likes Joe's raspberry tea.

"Hey Scoobie." I followed the direction of the voice and saw two men walking toward us. It took a couple seconds to realize they were the two homeless men I'd seen around town. After a summer spent largely outdoors they were tanned and had shorter hair. I felt a sense of unease. I hadn't talked to anyone about my thoughts about whether the shorter guy could be Masterson. *You're not a detective*. I studied the shorter man. The more I looked at him the less he looked like "Fun Boy."

"Hey, guys," Scoobie said. "Long time no see."

"Saw you a couple weeks ago," the taller of the two said, "but you were busy writing poetry outside of Java Jolt."

"And you had your cane," the shorter one said. "Your cane."

"Yeah, it's good to get back to my usual routine, such as it… Hey, do you know Jolie and Ramona?" When we shook our heads Scoobie continued. "Ramona works at the Purple Cow, and Jolie does real estate appraisals." Scoobie looked at me. "Josh plays bongo drums down at Ferry Street, and Max helps oversee the operation."

I knew this meant that Josh played on the boardwalk in the hope that someone would put money in a jar or hat, and now that I took a good look at them in summer clothes I thought I'd seen them there when I did my fast-walk one evening. Why do we make the homeless invisible to our senses?

The two men had looked uncomfortable as they walked up and when Scoobie started to introduce them, but Josh, the taller of the two, relaxed as Scoobie finished.

Max stared at me. "You're the lady with the food people," he said.

"I am," I nodded. "Scoobie helps."

Max kept staring. Scoobie's tone changed slightly, and he said, "Max and Josh are helping me spread the word that it's okay for people who sleep on the beach to go to Harvest for All."

I held out my hand to Max. "Thanks. To both of you."

At that he seemed to let down his guard a bit. "Yeah, well, okay." They both told Scoobie he looked pretty good, and then walked toward the small carnival that sets up near the boardwalk every 4th of July. Josh had his bongo drums in a large knapsack. I figured they would play there, at least until the police made them move, which they would if the guys were playing on a really crowded part of the boardwalk.

"Thanks for telling them," I said to Scoobie.

"There but for the Grace of God," Scoobie said, quietly.

Ramona leaned over to pat him on the knee. "You did a lot of your own work to get sober, you know."

"I think Josh liked your dress, Ramona," Scoobie said. "He was looking pretty closely at the front, anyway."

"Shut-up," we both said.

I STILL SERVED AS Scoobie's chauffer a lot, so I took him back to F Street to rest for a couple hours before firework watching on the beach. When I got back to the Cozy Corner to change into something a bit warmer for evening beach time I was surprised to see Marcus-the-mystery-writer in the kitchen with Aunt Madge. She was just putting three loaves of bread in the oven.

"I didn't realize you were going to be here this weekend." I'd have remembered that. He's the only person who's ever mixed up the floors.

"Alas, the inn was full." He grinned. "I brought a mock-up of the book's cover to show to my two favorite Ocean Alley women."

Mental eye roll.

I sat next to Marcus at the oak table and looked at the eight by ten photo paper he pushed toward me. The cover of *Cash Out for Murder* was a lurid green with an antique-looking silver cash register in the middle. "That's, uh, great." I hoped the interior was better than the cover. "When do we get to read the real thing?"

"November," he said. "In time for Christmas sales."

I stayed for a couple minutes and made for the back stairs just as Marcus suggested a game of Scrabble.

AUNT MADGE TOLD Marcus he really couldn't stay for afternoon tea, as it was for paying guests only. Much as she seemed to like him, I thought Aunt Madge might want a Marcus avoidance plan, so I told her she could go to the fireworks with Scoobie and Ramona and me.

She had other plans. "Harry's son from Maryland is here. I'm going to sit with them."

"Ooh la la."

"Don't be a twit. I would appreciate a ride to the beach, but no chaperone needed after that," Aunt Madge said.

The fireworks are at the far northern end of the boardwalk and most people sit on the beach to watch them. They're lit in a large municipal lot. There's lots of space so they can cordon off a fireworks-only area, but it doesn't leave much room for parking. Normally I'd walk the twenty blocks but, despite his assertions otherwise, that would be too long a walk for Scoobie.

"So, I told him you didn't want to walk it. Back me up," I said to Aunt Madge as we left the Cozy Corner's small parking lot.

"He knows I can out walk you," she said.

I shrugged. "I suppose, but his manhood will be intact."

Aunt Madge almost snorted.

Very unladylike for someone over eighty.

I dropped Scoobie and Aunt Madge near the boardwalk and parked about five blocks away. Ramona met Scoobie and me on the beach and we traipsed over to where Aunt Madge was sitting with Harry, son Ken, and Ken's two sons, who were named James and Avery.

"So, which one of you two guys looks like Harry did when he was a kid?" Scoobie asked.

"None of us," said James, who looked to be about ten.

"Grandma Jessie always said I did," said Avery, who was maybe seven.

I figured this had to be Harry's late wife. Aunt Madge more or less settled it by saying one boy had Harry's eyes and the other his ears. That cracked them up.

We declined Harry's offer to sit with them and we went a couple hundred feet down the beach. Almost since I moved back to Ocean Alley last fall I've wondered if Aunt Madge and Harry were sweet on each other as my Grandmother Alva would say. So far I think just good friends, and I'm not crazy enough to ask.

The air was still so the mosquitoes were out in force. I had forgotten about bug spray, but Ramona had some so Scoobie and I lathered up. I don't like the smell, but I like bug bites even less.

"Jolie!"

I looked around and saw Jennifer Stenner dodging kids' Frisbees as she came toward us. She was carrying the kind of short beach chair that true sunbathers use.

"How come," Scoobie asked in a low voice, "she's known me longer and better but she calls out to you?"

"Because Jolie's better looking," Ramona said as she moved her beach towel closer to the one Scoobie and I were sitting on so Jennifer could squeeze in.

"I figured you were here. I called the B&B and nobody answered," Jennifer said.

"Glad you found us," I said. And I mostly was. I'm not sure if Jennifer is actually less pretentious than I had thought her to be or if my attitude has improved from the doldrums I was in when I got back to Ocean Alley in October. Either way, I don't mind her as much as I once did. Other than the fact that she occasionally needles me about her third-generation family firm being a bigger appraisal business than Harry's.

"So Scoobie," Jennifer asked, "have you got any more fundraising ideas for Harvest for All? Something that doesn't involve wrecking my hair?"

Scoobie turned toward her, face alight with likely some teasing response, and was about to answer when there was a loud sizzling sound, which announced the opening of the firework display. We all turned toward the parking lot in time to see the words "4th of July" light up on the ground display.

"One for all and all for one," Scoobie said, and winked at me.

I turned to get more bug spray out of Ramona's bag just as an especially bright firework burst and boomed above us. For a second I thought I saw Mystery-Writer-Marcus a few yards behind us, but the light fizzled and I didn't see him there when the sky lit up again a few second later. Probably sizing up his competition. I almost giggled at the idea. He's probably thirty or forty years younger than Aunt Madge.

Some years the fireworks seem to be over fast, but this was not one of them. By the time the lengthy final segment ended my tailbone was ready to stand. It's been sore since I fell at the end of November, and it was reminding me I should have brought a cushion.

It always takes several long seconds to adjust to the darkness again. There are lights on the edge of the boardwalk, but all they are is guides when you're on the beach. Jennifer wanted us to go to Newhart's for milkshakes — "just like old times" — but I could tell Scoobie was more than tired. He and I begged off, but Ramona said she'd go, so we split up. I could see Harry shepherding his grandsons toward the boardwalk but lost sight of Aunt Madge.

Scoobie insisted on walking to the car with me rather than being picked up. "Did you ever notice how many people there are in Ocean Alley that you don't know?" he asked.

"You might, but I hardly know anybody. Plus, aren't most of these folks tourists?"

"Probably," he said evenly. He was walking gingerly and I wished I'd thought to make him bring a cane. *As if.*

Chapter Twenty-Three

I UNLOCKED THE SIDE DOOR to the Cozy Corner just as a guest car drove into the lot. I realized I had no idea if Aunt Madge had given one of them a key and was glad I beat them home. I recognized the pair as a young couple from New York City who Aunt Madge said had come for 4th of July the past several years.

"You guys need anything?" Aunt Madge doesn't serve any food after her afternoon warm bread and tea, but since she wasn't there I thought I should be hospitable.

"We're all set," the man, whom I thought was named Jack, said.

"Weren't those the best fireworks ever?" his wife cooed.

"Terrific." I walked into the kitchen.

Mister Rogers and Miss Piggy greeted me at the kitchen doorway and ran toward the sliding glass doors. Aunt Madge never leaves them out during the fireworks, and they were ready to go. "Where's Jazz?" I asked as their tails disappeared into the dark garden.

A short mew came from below me and she stretched as she walked out from under the sofa.

"You never go under there." She ran toward her food dish and stood there expectantly. As she has trained me, I gave her a few pieces of dry food. "You've eaten already, you know." She ignored me.

I was in my shorty pajamas and about to get in bed when I realized I hadn't heard Aunt Madge downstairs. I put on a robe and walked down the back stairs into her great room. I had already let the dogs back in and slid the piece of wood into the sliding door frame, so they made no effort to get up from where they were curled next to each other on a rug by the door.

"Aunt Madge?" Her bedroom door was open so I peeked in. "Hmmm. Did she tell you guys she was going to party late?"

Mr. Rogers thumped his tail a few times, but did not respond, and Miss Piggy's yawn told me she didn't know either. I turned on the electric tea kettle and picked up one of Aunt Madge's carpentry magazines and plopped on the sofa while the water heated.

Half an hour later I needed to potty and still no Aunt Madge. It was almost eleven-thirty. *Those little boys would have to be in bed by now. Maybe Aunt Madge and Harry snuck off together.* I grinned at the idea.

At midnight I called Harry. His voice said he'd been asleep, but he perked up quickly. "What do you mean she's not home?" he asked.

"I thought maybe you guys went out to eat."

"No, that Marcus fellow talked to us for a few seconds after the fireworks, and just before I took the kids to the car she said she was going to go home with you."

"Okay, now I'm scared. I never saw her after the fireworks."

"I'm coming over," he said, and hung up.

I ran upstairs to put on jeans and got back downstairs as Harry's car lights entered the lot. I met him at the side door. "You don't think she went for coffee or something with Marcus, do you?"

"No," he said. "She doesn't especially like him." He looked as if he had dressed as hurriedly as I did, and his hair was mussed.

We walked into the kitchen and both dogs sat up straight and then came over, tails not wagging. *Funny how they sense when something's not right.*

I might have waited a little while longer to call the police, but not Harry. They put him through to Dana Johnson. "What do you mean you don't know where Madge is?" she asked.

"Just that," Harry said, impatience creeping into his voice. "This is just not like her. She said she was going to ride home from the fireworks with Jolie and Scoobie and they never saw her."

"Everybody knows her, and some of the guys just came in," Dana said. "Let me see if anyone saw her on the boardwalk or something and I'll call you right back."

But she didn't call for a few minutes, and then there was a knock on the door. Sgt. Morehouse let himself in before I got there and we met in the hallway. I put my fingers over my lips and pointed him toward the kitchen door, where Harry was standing.

He listened to Harry and me "walk through the night," as he put it, and didn't say anything for a few seconds when we were done.

"No one saw her?" I asked. Aunt Madge is better known in Ocean Alley than all the politicians combined, and a lot more popular. Surely someone has seen her.

His phone buzzed and he answered it. "So put more people on it." He looked at Harry and me. "Dana and a couple others checked the few places that would still be open near the boardwalk, and they're going to walk the beach."

A NIGHT NEVER SEEMED so long. Not the night Robby said he was going to be arrested for embezzlement or the night I told him I was leaving him. By two o'clock we knew something was very, very wrong. She was nowhere in town and not at the hospital. The police comings and goings had awakened half the guests, and though I had persuaded them that they could go back to their rooms and I was sure Aunt Madge was fine, I was very unsure.

At two-fifteen a very young officer arrived carrying what looked like a tool box. He opened it and began dusting the guests' breakfast area. *I'll never get that cleaned up by seven o'clock.*

"But it's only her guests and Aunt Madge and me who sit in there."

"Does she do background checks on her guests?" the officer asked, quietly.

I exchanged a frightened look with Harry, who asked, "When Marcus stopped by, where did he sit?"

"Kitchen table," I said, and Sgt. Morehouse nodded to the officer, who went to the kitchen next.

"Marcus?" I said.

"She says he's engaging, but she really doesn't like him, and you found him in the hallway near the room next to yours last time he was here," Harry said.

Sgt. Morehouse made me go over the day Marcus came out of Penny's room. "But, I added, Aunt Madge said his room was in about the same location on the floor above."

"We need to check everything anybody thinks of," he said, and sent me to look at Aunt Madge's B&B records to get Marcus' phone number.

HALF AN HOUR LATER Morehouse had not found Marcus at his home number and I had called Reverend Jamison and Lance Wilson to see if they knew if someone had asked Aunt Madge for help after the fireworks. Sgt. Morehouse told me to tell them not to call anyone else, and when Lance offered to come over I said no. He made me promise to call him as soon as she was home. I was trying to cajole Mister Rogers and Miss Piggy from under the large oak kitchen table when my phone chirped. I grabbed it.

"Jolie." Aunt Madge said.

"Thank God, where are…?" I began.

"Just listen, Jolie."

I felt cold all over and held the phone away from my ear so Sgt. Morehouse could hear and Harry could maybe hear.

"I am with a very angry man."

I pressed a finger over my lips to keep from crying. "What should I do?"

"There are people who know that Penny had that small suitcase with money in it. They want it."

I looked at Sgt. Morehouse but he shook his head and pointed at my phone. It was clear he didn't want whoever was with Aunt Madge to know he was there. "Okay, but you know it might take me more than a few minutes to get it."

"I'm told you'll have an hour to figure it out." In a very clipped tone, she added, "You are not to call the police. I will call you back." She hung up.

Morehouse took my phone, looked at it, and said, "Damn it." I sat on the floor.

Harry stooped next to me. "We will figure it out."

I looked up at Morehouse. "Why did you say that?"

"No name on caller ID, probably a throw-away phone." He glanced at it and back at me. "Make sure to keep your battery charged." He tossed me my phone.

He opened his phone and began to give orders.

FORTY-FIVE MINUTES LATER the kitchen was crowded with Lt. Tortino, Captain Larry Edwards, whom I'd never met, and Dana, Harry, and me. The captain had called the FBI, but they had not arrived. Sgt. Morehouse had left to work out getting Penny's bag out of evidence so it could be here when the kidnapper called back. I had no idea if the money would be in it or if giving it to someone would get Aunt Madge home.

"But what if whoever has her figures out you're all here?" I asked, for the third time.

"We'll deal with that," Captain Edwards said.

When I started to speak, Lt. Tortino interrupted me. "It will take awhile, not too long, to work with the various mobile phone companies to try to figure the tower the kidnapper's cell phone is using, but in all honesty it won't be too helpful." Lt. Tortino said this all very quickly.

"So what can we do?" Harry asked.

"First," Lt. Tortino said, "when she calls back tell her you have the money and you assume whoever has it will trade Madge for the money."

I nodded.

"As long as we are talking to Madge we know she's okay," he said.

I nodded again. I was waiting for him to say there was some kind of a plan to find Aunt Madge immediately and that she would be home to serve breakfast to her guests.

"They'll likely remind you they don't want any police involvement. You tell them you called us when you thought she was missing, but you told us you have since found out Madge is fine, and we're no longer involved."

"We are about to leave here, except for the sergeant," Captain Edwards said. "He needs to sit in an area that cannot be seen from the street. Keep the curtains closed."

"You think they're near here?" I asked.

"No idea. We don't want to give them any reasons to be angry." Lt. Tortino said.

I heard the side door to the parking lot open and there was a light tap on the kitchen door. George Winters stuck his head in. When he saw me he came in, a questioning look on his face.

"We can't have reporters in here, George," Dana said, and she walked toward him.

"And we don't want them!" I added, following Dana. "No one can know people are here."

"I'm leaving. The guys at the paper heard something on the scanner and the cop outside told me what's going on." He glanced at the other officers and back at me. "Call me if I can help." He kept staring at me.

My eyes filled with tears and I nodded, and started crying. Hard. George walked over and put his hand on my shoulder as I cried into my hands. "They'll find her. She's tough. A lot tougher than you."

I hiccupped and looked at him between my fingers. "It's not funny."

"Of course it's not," he said. "But it is true." He squeezed my shoulder, nodded at Dana and walked out.

I heard him talk to someone on the stoop and Morehouse walked back in. He was carrying Penny's suitcase.

"You have the money?" I asked, wiping my eyes with the back of my hand.

"And damn lucky we still had it." He glanced at the other officers. "Had to wait while the evidence clerk scanned some of the damn bills." He looked at his watch. "Five minutes." He sat the small suitcase on the table.

Dana pulled a tissue from her pocket and handed it to me. "Thanks, Dana."

"Everybody out," the captain stood as he said this. He nodded at Morehouse. "You clear on everything?"

"As much as I can be," Morehouse said. "I don't have a damn playbook."

And I thought I was the only one he talked to that way. "Thanks," I mumbled, as the other police left. Lt. Tortino gave me a thumbs-up sign and I tried to smile. I couldn't.

Harry and I looked at Morehouse.

"We're winging it here," he said. "If I told you I'd worked with a lot of kidnappers you know I'd be lying."

"I can drive the money somewhere," Harry began.

"We gotta hear what they say." Morehouse turned to me. "You let them know you have the money, and you want to keep talking to Madge."

My phone chirped.

"Okay, slowly," Morehouse said. "Remember, you didn't get the money from me. You had it hidden in the attic."

"Why can't you trace the call?" I asked.

"Get real. Just stay calm."

"Aunt Madge?" I asked as I pushed talk.

"Yes."

"The bag was still under the floor in the attic. I have it." It sounded as if she was talking to someone in a low tone. *Maybe she has her hand over the phone.*

"I need to tell you where to leave it. No police. I'll call back in a few minutes."

"No!" I nearly screamed. "Tell me now."

"Jolie." Her tone was sharp. "Get a grip."

"Okay, okay. Are you…?"

"I'll call again." She hung up.

BUT AN HOUR WENT BY AND she didn't. I looked at the kitchen clock. Three-forty-five in the morning. I had had two more cups of coffee and alternated between feeling alert or exhausted. Either way, my stomach was roiling with acid.

Sgt. Morehouse was sitting in the short hallway behind the kitchen area, by Aunt Madge's bedroom, where he could not be seen from the street. The small suitcase was on the hall table behind him. Harry and I were on the sofa, except that I kept getting up to walk around. Mister Rogers followed every step I took while Miss Piggy kept her head near Harry's foot. Jazz was nowhere to be found, and I'd looked.

There was a buzz and Morehouse answered his phone. "You're kidding me. Yeah. Get me all you can."

"What?" Harry and I asked together.

"Either your Marcus is Alex Masterson, the guy Penny was arrested with a few years ago, or that guy snuck into the kitchen and sat at Madge's table."

"What do you mean? Who is that?" Harry asked.

In thirty seconds I summarized the photo of the stringy-haired guy who was arrested with Penny. "But it can't be Marcus." I looked at Sgt. Morehouse. "He has short white hair, he wears glasses, and…" I stopped.

"This changes everything." Morehouse said. He started to dial his phone and I sat across from Harry.

"So," Harry said, "if it is Marcus, perhaps his earlier visit was just an attempt to find the money."

"Which is why he was outside Penny's room," I said slowly. "Even his eyebrows were white."

"Do you have the article with the photo?" Harry asked.

I went upstairs and we all studied it when I came back down.

"Well," Morehouse said, "Now we know how well the kidnapper knows this house and town. I don't like it."

Harry shook his head. "I never would have guessed. The white hair, the glasses."

"And he's a lot thinner, too," Morehouse said.

"No beard." My brain was in overdrive. Marcus Hardy. I wasn't sure whether to be more or less scared. He had always seemed to like Aunt Madge a lot. *Can a kidnapper kill someone they know? Is it easier or harder?*

The room around me intruded into my thoughts. "Yeah," Morehouse was hollering into his phone. "I'm sure." He paused. "Who the hell else would have been sitting at her table? Those weren't latent…Hey, Jolie."

I looked up.

"How often would you say your aunt wipes down the kitchen table?"

"At least once a day, if she's here." *She's not here now.* I looked toward the table. I had tried to get all the fingerprint goo off when the officer left. *Dust my ass.* It's like sticky jam from two days ago.

Harry kept telling me this would all work out, but I finally tuned in more to Morehouse. "I know Tortino, I know. Yeah, but it shouldn't be marked cars…Yes, ten years more than me. OK, call me back ASAP."

He walked toward Harry and me. "Shouldn't you stay out of sight?" I asked.

"We're dealing with a meatball here, not a professional kidnapper," Morehouse said. When I started to speak he said, "I'll go back there in a minute. The thinking is to put out Hardy's, Masterson's description, get all hands on deck and start checking motels and anyplace…"

"But they'll see you." Panic gripped me.

"He said…" Harry began.

Morehouse waved us quiet. "Tortino's organizing it so everyone is in plain clothes. The FBI just got to the station. They got a lot of ideas."

He kept talking, but all I could hear was a voice in my head saying no police, no police, no police.

I glanced toward the area where Morehouse had been sitting. "I'm hungry. Can I make you guys a sandwich?"

They both stared at me. "Come on, we ate hours ago. Unless you had donuts," I said to Morehouse.

Morehouse glared at me. "Don't be a damn smart ass."

"I could use one, thanks," Harry said. He was looking at me as if he wondered if I'd finally lost it.

I walked to the fridge. Aunt Madge doesn't keep many cold cuts but there was leftover meatloaf from yesterday. Quickly I got out the bread and made two sandwiches. "Milk or coffee?" I asked. My mind was in overdrive.

"Milk," they both said.

I started to carry the sandwiches to them and remembered one was supposed to be for me, so I separated one onto two plates.

"Come to the table. The dogs'll be all over you if you sit over there." I set the plates on the table and poured three glasses of milk.

"Thanks," Morehouse said as they sat. His phone buzzed again and he answered it as he took a bite.

I looked at Harry. "I'm going to use Aunt Madge's bathroom."

I walked through the living room into the hallway and picked up the small case and carried it into Aunt Madge's bedroom. I was out the window before any sane person would have had time to flush the toilet.

Chapter Twenty-Four

MOREHOUSE HAD SAID THE police were about to have officers everywhere. I hoped that they weren't on the way to the Cozy Corner just yet. I couldn't take my car, the keys were in the house with my purse. I had the money and my phone, and that was all I needed. There was no way I was going to let a bunch of cops get Aunt Madge killed.

I ran down Seashore away from the boardwalk. I'd gone about half a block when a car twenty or thirty feet ahead of me flashed its lights. I slowed. "Damn it all."

A low voice called out, "Yo, Jolie."

"Scoobie!" I ran toward the car. He leaned into the back seat to open that door for me.

I slid in.

"For Pete's sake, lie down." George made a U-turn and continued in the direction I'd been running. "Where are we going?"

"I don't know yet," I said.

Scoobie turned to look down at me. "Can you be a little more specific?"

The car slowed and turned a corner, and then pulled into a more well-lit area. "Where are we going?" I asked, realizing I had just repeated George's question.

"Into the *Ocean Alley Press* parking lot. That's where anyone would expect to see my car."

"Very smart," Scoobie said, as George turned off the car.

It was so quiet I could hear a mosquito buzzing against the back window.

"Now what?" George asked. "Did they find her?"

"She called."

"Thank God." Scoobie turned to look in the back seat.

"Stay facing front," George ordered.

"It's Marcus Hardy," I said.

"What? Marcus the boring writer?" Scoobie asked.

"I met him in Java Jolt," George said. "He's a cream puff."

"Except it's not Marcus. His name is Alexander Masterson."

"Have you taken some sort of tranquilizer?" Scoobie asked.

"Shit," George said. "Fun Boy."

"What are you talking about?" Scoobie asked.

George told him that Masterson had been arrested with Penny but had only done thirty days in jail. "They probably ran a bunch of scams together. Penny had the money somehow."

Silence for ten seconds. I breathed slowly, telling myself to stay calm.

"She's dead for going on two months, and my mother is still screwing up everybody's lives." Scoobie said.

"How do you know Marcus is Masterson?" George asked. "How could he alter his appearance that much?"

"He visited earlier today. Fingerprints. And short, white hair and eyebrows. Clean shaven. He's lost weight…"

"I get it, I get it," George said. "Glasses, too."

"They wanted, he wanted the case Penny left in the room." I felt myself starting to shake.

"What case?" Scoobie asked.

"Your mother asked Aunt Madge if she could leave her luggage at the B&B for a couple days, and when she didn't come back Aunt Madge packed it up. After she died, Morehouse went through it, and one suitcase had a lot of money."

"How come you never told me this?" he asked.

"Excuse me?"

"I know, I didn't want to talk about it," Scoobie said.

"Doesn't matter," George interrupted. "Focus on now."

"How do we get it to him?" Scoobie asked.

"He's supposed to call back, or have Aunt Madge call. He said no police, but when Morehouse just found out it was him they were going to put police in civvies all over the place. And Morehouse said the FBI had 'ideas.' I want to do what Marcus, Masterson, whoever says."

"We'll see what he says." George opened his car door.

"Where are you going?" I asked.

"Get a blanket out of the trunk, so nobody can see you easily."

I heard the trunk pop and he rummaged around.

"You sure about this," Scoobie asked, quietly.

"No. Yes." I paused. "When she calls I can always change my mind."

George got back in and tossed the blanket in the back seat.

My phone chirped.

"Aunt Madge?"

"Yes. Jolie, he said no police."

How could he know? Were they close? I was cold all over, and I heard Scoobie take in a breath.

"I know. I just went out your bedroom window. I'm sorry, I didn't have time to close it."

"Where are you?" Her tone was sharp.

"In a car with Scoobie." I almost said George's car. "I have the case. I, I called the police before I knew where you were. But they left when I said you called me."

There was muffled talking on her end of the line. I sat up halfway so George and Scoobie could hear everything.

"You know the roadside park, just north of town?" she asked.

As in where Penny was killed? "Yes. Can I come now?"

"Twenty minutes. Alone Jolie." She hung up.

George started the engine. "You can drop us off half a mile before the park."

"After." I slithered back down. "Less obvious."

WE ARGUED FOR several minutes as George sped down the highway en route to the park. George wanted to stay in the trunk, with Scoobie in the bushes. Scoobie wanted to drop me "anywhere" and let them "handle it," and I wanted to throw them both in the ocean by the time we were halfway to the park.

"I drive," I said. "That's all there is to it. Unless you want to drop me off and I'll walk."

A siren blared behind us.

"Crap," Scoobie said.

George pulled to the side of the road and an ambulance sped past on the opposite side of the road, likely going to the hospital.

I let out my breath. Not the police following us. "I hope we don't end up there."

"Better than the morgue," George said.

"That's just great, really great," I said.

"Sorry," he muttered. He pulled onto a side road and let the car idle. "Scoobie, can you walk from here?"

"No problem."

"My trunk has one of those safety buttons, so a person can get out from it when it's locked. I'm going in the trunk, Jolie."

"And pop out like a jack-in-the-box?" I asked.

"If needed," he said. "Me and my tire iron."

"I'll see you down there," Scoobie said, and got out of the car.

George and I watched for a few seconds as Scoobie tried to use the cane in the underbrush just off the road. He gave up and slung it over his shoulder like a soldier carried a bayonet, and walked with an awkward gait.

"He's hurting," I said. "He even brought the cane."

"He'll be all right. Come on, trade places." George popped the trunk as he got out.

I faced him for a second and looked directly in his eyes. "Thanks."

He gave a slight smile. "I like Madge."

He climbed awkwardly into the trunk and shut it. "I'm in," he said, his voice muffled.

I got in the front seat and shut the door. My hands were shaking so hard it was difficult to take the car out of park. "Calm, Jolie." I pulled down half a block until there was a driveway to turn around it, and headed back onto the highway.

I was at the small roadside area in less than a minute. I turned off the car and headlights and sat taking it in. While the mix of pine and leafy trees were not densely spaced, the undergrowth was thick. It wasn't really a park, just a place with a few parking spaces and two picnic tables. There wasn't even a trash can.

Should I stay in the car or get out? I decided to get out, so they could see the case. "Crud." I didn't even know how much cash was in the case, whether it would be what Marcus was expecting. I clicked the lock and looked in. It looked as I remembered it, lots of cash. I shut it and stood hugging myself.

My watch said it was two minutes past time, and I shivered. It was about sixty degrees, but that had little to do with my body temperature. I couldn't remember ever feeling so cold in my stomach.

What was that? There was rustling in the brush behind the trees that shaded the picnic tables. I hoped it wasn't Scoobie making noise.

"Over here, Jolie." It was Aunt Madge's voice and I turned so quickly I knocked the case off the hood of the car.

"Oh." I stooped to get it.

"Stay where I can see your hands," Marcus said.

I stood slowly and faced the two of them. Aunt Madge looked very tired, but otherwise okay. Marcus had his left hand on her elbow and a gun in his right hand. "Open the case," he said softly.

I unlatched it and opened it, tilting it so he could see what was in it.

"What's so shiny," he asked, sharply.

"Silverware. She stole it…" I began.

He chuckled. "Old Penny, she never missed a trick." He looked at me. "You two thought you'd steal my money, did you?"

I didn't like his menacing tone. "We didn't steal it, she left it. How would we know it was yours? You probably know someone killed her."

"She was supposed to meet me to give me my half. Stood me up. Tried to tell me she had to rescue her stupid son."

"Rescue?" Aunt Madge said, quickly.

"Shut up. Come over here, Jolie." He gestured with his gun.

"Let Aunt Madge go."

"Get over here!"

His fierce tone told me I didn't have a lot of wiggle room. "How about we meet halfway?" I spoke with more bravado than I felt. Heck, I felt none.

"No. You walk past me. I'll tell you where to walk to get to my car." He gestured again with the gun.

"You'll kill us at the car." My voice was unnaturally high.

"I'm going to tie you to a tree." When I didn't move he placed the gun at Aunt Madge's temple.

"Okay, okay." I know nothing about guns, but thought that on TV shows the guns with silencers had long nozzles, some sort of attachment. He didn't have that, so if he fired someone would hear him. *That won't matter if we're already dead.* I moved toward him, careful to stay more than an arm's length from him.

"That's good, very good. Just keep walking."

I passed the two of them and he pointed a bit to the left. "That direction, that's right."

I had gone about twenty feet when somebody yodeled. Marcus turned sharply in that direction and I heard the trunk pop behind us. Then everything was quiet.

"What the hell was that?" Marcus seethed, almost in a hiss.

"How would I know?" I asked.

"Sounded like a wolf," Aunt Madge said.

"There aren't any wolves here. Keep walking."

"Shows what you know," I said.

"Shut up!"

I walked slowly, still trying to stay far enough ahead of him so he couldn't grab me. I didn't see how we could foil Marcus' plan. He had a gun, and we were already pretty sure he was a murderer. He only needed two shots to kill Aunt Madge and me, and I suddenly remembered that no one would even look out a window. It was late for fireworks, but plenty of kids or stupid adults could still be using them.

I could see the end to the small woods and assumed his car was nearby. *He's not going to tie us to a tree. He's going to kill us.*

Suddenly Marcus stumbled. "What the…"

I turned quickly and Aunt Madge wrenched free and turned toward me. Marcus regained his footing, swore loudly and turned the barrel of the gun toward us.

"Duck!" came George's voice from somewhere behind us.

"Who the..." Marcus started to fall backwards.

I grabbed Aunt Madge and pulled her down. She put her arm across my head just as the gun fired. There was a thunk noise at the tree next to us. At the same time I saw George flying at Marcus, tire iron flailing toward Marcus' head.

There was the sound of scrambling and thuds. The flash of light from the gun had disoriented me for a few seconds. I couldn't see anything, but I pulled Aunt Madge's hand off my head and stood. I stumbled a few feet toward the writhing bodies on the ground, and then heard a sickening thud and a short crunching sound.

It was quiet except for very heavy breathing from two men. *Please let it be our two.*

"You okay?" George asked.

"I'm just down here taking a nap," Scoobie said.

Aunt Madge started to sob.

Chapter Twenty-Five

PURPLE. THAT WAS THE EXACT color of Sgt. Morehouse's face when he got out of his car and started screaming at me. Aunt Madge and I were sitting on the picnic table bench and Scoobie was prone on top of it, resting his dumb-ass back, as he put it. Aunt Madge was leaning on me, for a change.

George had called the police and then found the gun. He was standing near the unconscious form I still thought of as Marcus Hardy rather than Alex Masterson. George and I had dragged him from the woods back to the little park, taking no care about what branches or brambles we dragged him over.

I said nothing, but when Morehouse stopped to take a breath — Lt. Tortino and Dana Johnson running from another car toward us — Scoobie said, "It's kind of loud for dawn."

WE WERE IN AUNT MADGE'S KITCHEN because she refused — and I mean really refused, to the point that Morehouse and Tortino had backed up — to go the hospital or police station. "For most of the night I thought I'd never see my house again. That's where I'm going, and that's all there is to it."

The kitchen was crowded. It was almost six o'clock and I was on automatic pilot. I made two pots of coffee, regular and decaf, and Dana and I moved two of the breakfast room tables and some chairs into the Cozy Corner's small guest lounge. I told Aunt Madge the guests would be okay with going out to eat, but she insisted, and said the dining area had too many police walking around in it. Lt. Tortino bought the donuts. While I was getting plates and silverware from her cupboard I realized having breakfast for her guests, even if she was not the one to serve it, was Aunt Madge's way of putting order back in our lives.

Ramona showed up about six-fifteen. "George called me. He said you needed help with juice." Her eyes were wide as she took in all of us, finally resting on Harry and Aunt Madge sitting together on the couch, holding hands. She grinned at me and then opened the fridge and started to take out jam and juice. "George told me some of it. I can't believe it."

"We can talk more later." I didn't think I could string two cogent sentences together, and I was really tired of answering questions.

I carried the plates and silverware to the guest tables and leaned against the door jamb for a minute when I came back into the kitchen. Captain Edwards was in the corner by the sliding glass door talking to the two FBI agents who had shown up with their ideas a couple hours ago, and Sgt. Morehouse was on the phone with somebody. George was sitting in a chair near the couch, listening to everyone.

I walked back to Aunt Madge's bedroom and looked in at Scoobie. He looked a lot better than he had ten minutes ago when he quietly went in to lie down. "You okay?" I asked.

"Yeah. I don't think tackling was part of my physical therapy, but I'm good. Just a little sore."

I walked into Aunt Madge's bathroom and came back with a glass of water and a couple generic pain tablets. "This good enough?"

"Sure."

"That was pretty swift, tripping him with your cane." I looked at him.

"First time I've been glad to have it." He laughed and nodded toward the window. Jazz was sitting in the still-open window with a dead mouse in her mouth.

I jumped up, but she was too fast. She dove off the sill and under the bed.

I knelt to peer under the bed. I could see her green eyes. "I've been looking for you. Nuts. First chipmunks, now mice."

"At least this one's dead," Scoobie said.

George stuck his head in. "I gotta leave to write as soon as I talk to your aunt." He looked at Scoobie and me. "You sure you're okay?"

We both nodded.

"Now you really owe me a phone, Gentil." He left and I stood up.

The dogs came in and looked around, and then both heads were under the bed with their butts in the air. Jazz growled at them.

"I'm going back out."

"Damn, one of them farted. I'm coming with you." Scoobie got up slowly, avoiding the dogs.

"We're going to go through this from the top, and then let Madge get to bed," Captain Edwards said as we walked back into the great room.

Everyone stopped talking and Aunt Madge leaned against the back of the sofa. "You can guess most of it, I imagine. When we all stood after the fireworks Marcus, whoever he is, came over and stood next to me. He showed me the gun in the pocket of his windbreaker and said he would shoot one of Harry's grandsons unless I told Harry I was riding with Jolie and then came with him."

Harry winced.

"I couldn't imagine he would do that in front of everybody on the beach, but I wasn't taking any chances."

"Where did he take you, Madge?" Morehouse asked, quietly.

"That tacky Budget Inn. He already had a key to a room, facing the outside. I kept looking for anyone I knew, but it was mostly tourists." She looked at me. "I saw your friend Daphne, and a couple people from church, but they were too far away for them to notice me."

Sgt. Morehouse stepped away and opened his phone. I figured he was telling someone to hightail it to the Budget Inn.

"Why do you think he waited so long to call Jolie?" Lt. Tortino asked.

"My guess is he didn't really plan anything. He came back determined to find the money, and he obviously brought a gun, but he clearly hadn't figured out if or how he would use it. And he really had no idea what to do with me after he made me go with him." She leaned over to get her tea mug and Harry grabbed it and handed it to her.

"He was convinced Penny had the money somewhere nearby when he killed her, which he said was an 'accident.' I'm not sure how he found out Penny had stayed with us, but that's why he came in May. He left, but after Memorial Day he got it in his head that Jolie or I had found the money and we'd hidden it."

"So you were at the motel the entire time?" Sgt. Morehouse asked.

"Yes, I actually sat up against the headboard and closed my eyes a bit. A couple hours or so after we got to the motel he hit on the idea of me calling Jolie and telling her to bring the money." She drank some tea. "He's not all that bright."

"Did he really write a book?" Scoobie asked.

She shook her head.

"So you told him you had it?" George asked.

"Does this look like a press conference?" Captain Edwards asked, glaring at him. "And you watch what you write."

George nodded and when the captain looked away George gave me an eye roll. I could tell he was trying not to smirk. He was in the room because he helped catch Marcus, not because he was a reporter.

"He started waving his gun around, so I told him to put Jolie on the phone. I figured you could improvise," she said dryly, looking at me.

It didn't really register that Jazz had walked out of the bedroom, followed by the dogs. By the time I realized she still had the mouse she was at the sofa and dropped the dead mouse at Aunt Madge's feet.

"Presents," Aunt Madge said, stroking her.

Chapter Twenty-Six

AUNT MADGE AND I were in her kitchen Sunday morning. Mister Rogers and Miss Piggy would not stay more than two feet from Aunt Madge, so they were under the kitchen table, each one trying to keep their head on one of her feet. Jazz, true to her nature, was on the bookcase ignoring us.

For once George didn't get under my skin when he mentioned me in an article. The headline was in over-large letters and there was a photo of Scoobie lying on the picnic table and Aunt Madge and me on the bench. It was taken from the side and grainy, so you couldn't tell how bedraggled Aunt Madge looked. I assumed George took it with his cell phone. I had been too busy hugging Aunt Madge and watching for the police to arrive to notice.

OCEAN ALLEY KIDNAPPING HAS HAPPY ENDING

The fireworks in Ocean Alley on July 4th were literal and figurative. Local B&B owner Madge Richards was kidnapped after the fireworks display and at two-forty-five a.m. her niece, Jolie Gentil, received a phone call from a lone kidnapper demanding money for her safe return. Richards was rescued by several local residents at the small roadside park just north of Ocean Alley, at approximately five-thirty a.m. yesterday morning.

Alex "Fun Boy" Masterson was in Ocean Alley in May calling himself Marcus Hardy and claiming to be a mystery writer who wanted quiet time to finish a book. At that time he stayed at Richards' Cozy Corner B&B. He came to believe that Richards and Gentil had cash that belonged to him, and the kidnapping was designed to induce them to give him the money.

In fact, the small suitcase of cash and other items that he sought had been in the possession of Penny Pittsen (also known as Penny Marks and Penny O'Brien, among other names), with whom Masterson was arrested in New York more than three years ago on charges of receiving stolen property and identity theft. Pittsen received a three-year sentence at that time, while Masterson was jailed for 30 days.

While he held Richards against her will in Ocean Alley's Budget Inn, Masterson told her he had accidentally killed Pittsen in May, when he was encouraging Pittsen to give him his share of the ill-gotten cash. Pitssen's body was found in her car at the same roadside park north of Ocean Alley.

Although Pittsen's activities between the time of her release from Taconic Correctional Facility in New York earlier in the year and her death in May are not fully known, it appears she and Masterson had again begun stealing and reselling collectibles and other items they stole from various homes in towns throughout eastern New Jersey.

After her body was discovered, local police removed her property from the Cozy Corner, where she had stayed, and discovered she had a sum of money and other items. Captain Lawrence Edwards of the Ocean Alley Police Department said Pittsen's belongings were still in police custody, which made it possible to let Masterson believe he was being given the cash he sought. "Through a prompt investigation, police were able to locate Richards and take Masterson into custody. Masterson is recovering from injuries sustained during Richards' rescue."

Pittsen was a former Ocean Alley resident who was arrested a number of times for alcohol-related charges. Her face may be familiar because she sometimes sold ride tickets at local carnivals. She is also the mother of current resident Adam O'Brien.

"Why do you suppose George doesn't say he and Scoobie rescued you?" I asked. Aunt Madge and I had read the article together. "And he called Scoobie 'Adam.' No one will know it's him."

"Undoubtedly how Scoobie wanted it, though I'm surprised George's editor let him get away with it."

I reread the article. "Literal and figurative fireworks?"

"That's not so bad. He makes it sound like I run a half-way house," Aunt Madge said.

Our eyes met.

"Jolie, what were you thinking?"

I'd been waiting for this question. Yesterday Aunt Madge and I had gone to bed about eight in the morning and slept until mid-afternoon. My sister Renée came down from Lakewood and she and her husband sat downstairs to shoo away anyone who wanted to talk to us. And they served the afternoon snack to Aunt Madge's guests. She wouldn't hear of her guests leaving.

When we finally got up, I had to spend a half-hour on the phone with my parents assuring them that Aunt Madge and I were all right and that they should stay in Florida. Ramona and a couple of Aunt Madge's friends from church brought in supper, and we were both back in bed by nine in the evening. There was no sign of Scoobie, but I knew he would have gone over what he calls his 'people quotient' and wanted to be alone, so I wasn't worried about him.

The bottom line was that Aunt Madge and I hadn't talked much about what happened. Not to each other. So, here we were on Sunday morning, with her dressed for church and me still in my bathrobe. And I had to answer Aunt Madge's question.

"You probably think I wasn't thinking," I said, slowly. "But it seemed so clear. Marcus, Masterson, said no police. But as soon as we knew who he was Morehouse started talking about having police look for you guys in town, and I knew they'd want to be all over the place if I took him the suitcase."

"And somehow you talked Adam and George into going with you?"

I shook my head. "No, they were waiting outside the house, well, just down the street. Not waiting, kind of hiding in George's car. I guess he wanted to see what would happen. Remember, I told you I climbed out your window?"

Aunt Madge pulled me into a hug, and then stepped back to look at me. "You have to promise me you won't take a risk like that again."

"No."

"Jolie," her voice was firm.

"First, it won't happen again. And second, I won't let anyone hurt you any more than you'd let anyone hurt me."

She stared at me. I could tell by her expression that an idea was forming.

"I'll make you a deal. You stop behaving so rashly and I won't let George Winters see any of the photos of you that summer you were three and ran around in just your underwear all the time."

"You wouldn't dare!" I almost shouted.

"Try me."

Chapter Twenty-Seven

THERE WAS A LOT MORE TO learn about what Penny and Masterson had been up to, and I was convinced that she and Turk had probably worked together at least in a pickpocket scheme. Why else would she have known enough about him to make her follow Turk as Turk followed Scoobie? As the police left early yesterday morning I'd asked Sgt. Morehouse about this. His reply had to do with me minding my own business and was quite rude, but he hadn't had much sleep. I decided to wait a couple days before I asked again.

Dr. Welby arranged for the food donation day to take place at Mr. Markle's store on Sunday afternoon of 4th of July weekend. He was certain some of the many tourists in town would donate. So even though Aunt Madge had only been safe for about thirty hours, I stood in the grocery store parking lot. Lance borrowed a pick-up truck on which we hung the Harvest for All Food Pantry sign.

Scoobie had taken two pieces of poster board and strung them together so he was wearing them in the same fashion people used when they stood on the street advertising their business. On the front and back Ramona had lettered "Ask me about Talk Like a Pirate Day, September 19th."

Though I was able to agree with everyone who told me that it was wonderful that Aunt Madge was safe and to sample the baked goods that Monica had organized for the sale, I felt anything but back to normal. A couple times when people called out to me I was truly startled, and my mind kept traveling back to the walk through the woods when I had been convinced Aunt Madge and I were going to be shot.

I'm smart enough to know that it's going to take awhile to feel safe and settle back into my routine, but I had not expected to feel so rattled once it was clear Aunt Madge really was going to be okay. I accepted a sack of canned goods from a woman who works in the records room at the courthouse and barely thought to thank her. As I loaded it into the pickup truck Scoobie caught my eye. "You okay?"

"Yes, just still whipped, I guess."

By one-thirty the pickup was full and the grocery clerk Mr. Markle said could drive it to the food pantry was behind the wheel. Lance was in the passenger seat so he could tell the guy where to unload the food. The rest of us stayed to solicit more donations, and we put them in grocery carts.

Sylvia had refused to wear the pirate hat Lance bought her, so it periodically moved from my head to Ramona's to Jennifer's, depending on where Scoobie chose to put it. My grocery cart was almost full when someone said, "Smile, Jolie."

I turned, without a smile, and looked directly at George Winters as he took a photo of me in the pirate hat. "Very funny. Make sure you take one of Jennifer." I tried to be overly polite.

He gave me an odd look and then went inside the store to talk to Mr. Markle.

"Miss?"

I turned to see the taller of the two homeless men, Josh I thought his name was, looking at me. He appeared ill at ease about something. When he didn't say anything else I said, "We really appreciate your help today."

And I did. Scoobie had suggested they help, and Dr. Welby had actually tracked them down, since Scoobie was still sore. Dr. Welby told me quietly that he just followed the sound of the bongo drums, but that he didn't recognize any of the music.

"I need to tell you something." He gestured that we should walk toward the soft drink machine that sits outside the store.

When we got close to the machine I saw Max was standing next to it, seemingly trying to blend in with the store's brick walls. "What is it, you guys?" I asked.

"The lady told us not to tell," Max said quickly.

"The thing is, we didn't know she was Scoobie's mother," Josh said, and he glanced to where Scoobie was pretending his cane was a pirate's sword.

"You mean Penny?" I asked. I was trying to connect dots in my brain, but I wasn't quite getting there.

"Yeah," Max said. "The lady that got killed by the guy who took your aunt."

Slowly the dots connected. "Did you guys see something by the boardwalk in mid-May?"

Josh nodded. "It was really early. A Saturday, but I don't know the date. Joe gives us day-old muffins sometimes, so we were on the bench across from Java Jolt, waiting for him to get there."

By the steps Scoobie got pushed down.

"We saw this guy coming down the street," Josh said.

"We didn't know him," Max said, quickly.

"Anyway," Josh continued, "he walked under the boardwalk. And he said 'you aren't dead yet?'"

Max said, "Josh was a soldier, a U.S. Army soldier, so he ran over there, really fast. I kind of followed."

"I got under there in time to see him bash Scoobie in the back of the head with a beer bottle," Josh said. "It wasn't in his hand when he was walking, so I guess he picked it up under there."

"And you chased him off?" I asked, quietly.

"Me and Josh, yeah, we chased him," Max said, in an excited tone.

My eyes met Josh's. I had guessed when we spoke to them briefly Friday on the boardwalk that Max might have some sort of emotional problem. Josh almost seemed to be his caregiver. "You saved Scoobie's life." I felt myself start to tear up.

"We didn't know what to do, what to do," Max said. "But the lady came up, running up. Well, sort of running. She was kind of fat."

"And you think it was Penny Pittsen?" I asked.

Josh nodded. "We recognized her from the picture in the paper this morning." He paused. "Is she really Scoobie's mother?"

"Yes, but he hadn't seen her in a long time."

"She told us she was calling an ambulance, and to go away," Josh said. "The ambulance and police came."

"But she walked away when they came," Max said. "She could have told them who did it."

I wanted to ask why they didn't step forward, but instead drew a breath. "I really need you to talk to the police, especially if you think you know who tried to hurt Scoobie."

"He didn't just try," Max said, excited again.

A half smile formed on Josh's face, but vanished quickly. "The thing is, the police don't like us too much."

"I didn't take that apple," Max said hurriedly. "I just forgot to pay."

"I've forgotten before," I said slowly. "I know what you mean." I looked at Josh again.

"Could you maybe go with us?" Josh asked.

"Of course."

"But he's here, so it's gotta be today," Max added.

I HAD NEVER SEEN Sgt. Morehouse truly excited before. When Josh, Max, and I got to the police station about two-thirty and she heard why we were there, Dana Johnson called him to come in.

"After all this time," Morehouse said, "we're gonna get the bastard that tried to kill Scoobie."

It was indeed Turk the two men had seen. Morehouse made them describe him, and then listened while Josh explained that yesterday, when he was playing the bongos on the boardwalk near the carnival, they had seen Turk. Max had become very upset and they left

"We looked for Scoobie," Josh said. "He's pretty good at knowing what to do. But we didn't see him until today at the grocery store."

"And it was his head. His head that got busted," Max said.

"Yes, it was." Morehouse spoke quietly, apparently thinking. He turned to Dana. "I got an idea. Why don't you find Scoobie, see if he'll help."

"Don't you think I…"

"No, Jolie. This is a police matter, a very serious police matter." He looked at me with a stern expression, so I looked away.

Dana left, and Sgt. Morehouse got up and returned with two donuts and offered to get Josh and Max coffee. Both men wanted some, so he stepped out.

"I think they like us now," Max said, in a loud whisper.

I COULD TELL THAT Scoobie did not like that I had brought Josh and Max to the station without telling him why, but he didn't say anything. After a brief conversation, Sgt. Morehouse and he walked into another office and Dana came in to sit with Josh, Max, and me. She was very good at putting them at ease.

"So," Max asked after a few minutes. "You got a boyfriend?"

Dana grinned. "Even better. A husband."

After a few minutes more Sgt. Morehouse stuck his head in and asked us to join him in the small conference room down the hall. Lt. Tortino and Scoobie were already seated.

"I'm thinking that if we wire Scoobie…"

"No!" I was afraid of where this was going.

"Relax," Scoobie said, and gave me an unreadable look.

"Broad daylight," Morehouse said, "with Dana and a couple of the other young officers nearby in street clothes." He turned to Josh and Max who were sitting opposite him. "Your help has been really terrific. Later, I may need to ask you to tell some other people what you saw."

Josh nodded quietly, but Max looked fearful.

"The thing is," Morehouse said, "it would be easier for everybody if we can get Turk to talk to Scoobie about this. May not work…"

"Very well may not," said Lt. Tortino. "But worth a try."

"Will you be able to hear what they say?" I asked.

Morehouse shook his head. "Real-time listening, that's TV show stuff. We're a small department. But we will have the tape from the conversation Scoobie has with the guy."

Lt. Tortino turned to Josh and Max. "We'd like to pay for a room for you guys for a couple nights. That way you don't have to worry about running into this guy Turk while he's in town."

"And you know where to find us," Josh said, quietly.

"Nobody's going to watch you or anything," Tortino said.

"We're free citizens," Max said, talking fast again. "We have rights."

Tortino started to say something, but Scoobie interrupted him. "You do. And if you stay there I'll know where to find you, and you and Jolie and I can go to supper or breakfast or something." He looked at me. "Jolie's buying."

MY CAR WAS PARKED ON THE street closest to the carnival entrance. It was five-thirty and I had promised Sgt. Morehouse I would go home, but since I hadn't had a police escort I was sitting there burning gas by turning the air conditioner on and off.

I could see the carnival entrance, but there were too many people going in and out for me to have much chance to see Scoobie. I simply wanted to be close. I was still having an internal debate about whether to enter the carnival, but I figured the police would spot me and I wouldn't put it past Morehouse to think of some reason they should arrest me.

I kept going over what I knew and what I thought I knew. I had thought Turk might be involved in Penny's murder somehow. I couldn't figure out how, but when Aunt Madge said that Penny sometimes sold ride tickets at the carnival it seemed logical. And then we saw Penny on the tape, following Turk. Now, however, it seemed that murdering Penny was not part of his plan. Her son, yes.

In a million years I would not have suspected Marcus of anything criminal, much less violent. It wasn't just his disguise, though he had done a pretty good job with white hair dye and glasses, among other efforts to change his appearance. He fit my image of a writer, seemingly distracted at times, maybe a couple of crabs short of a bushel. And the book cover. It was awful, but just realistic enough for me to think a publisher really had given him a mock-up of his cover. Cash Out for Murder. Lame.

And Penny. Scoobie had not seen her in the Sandpiper, but it's L-shaped and always crowded. Penny saw him. I could only think of one reason for her not calling an ambulance after she followed Scoobie and Turk from the Sandpiper in the wee hours of Saturday morning. It was dark and she was just enough behind Turk after they left the Sandpiper that she missed Scoobie climbing onto the boardwalk and Turk pushing him down the steps and apparently dragging him under the boardwalk and injecting him with drugs.

But Penny must have suspected something, to have followed Turk from the Budget Inn back to the boardwalk a few hours later. She called the ambulance when she finally did find her son. Why didn't Penny want anyone to know she was the one who called? Maybe because she used a stolen mobile phone. Maybe because she hadn't checked in with her parole officer. Or maybe she thought her presence would make the police suspect her, though she knew Josh and Max and seen her rush up after they ran Turk off. From all I had heard about her and her awful behavior at the hospital, it was possible that following Turk and calling the ambulance were her only selfless acts on behalf of Scoobie. Too bad it came so late, said a small voice in my head. Better late than never.

It was hotter than blue blazes, as Aunt Madge would say. I turned on the air conditioner again, which meant I had to start the car. Somebody beeped from the street, and I rolled down the window and motioned they should pass so they'd know I was not going to leave the parking space. I was rewarded by having a man who looked older than Aunt Madge flip the bird at me. Nice.

After another twenty minutes I was thinking about driving to the police station so I'd be there when Scoobie and the officers got back there. I hadn't been given any specific orders not to do that, though I could be pretty sure Morehouse would regard "stay at Madge's until I call you," as just that.

I sighed and turned on my blinker to show I was going to leave the parking space. As I looked up and down the street for traffic I saw a familiar figure coming toward me. Turk was walking fast down the street, but not running. He hugged the parked cars and every five or ten steps he would look over his shoulder. As he got within a few car lengths I sunk low in my seat and wished I had a pimpmobile with dark windows.

I didn't even have time to consider whether it was a good idea. I probably would have done it either way. As he got to my car's front fender I swung open the door and he rammed into it and landed on his butt on the sidewalk. He jumped up, furious, and I just had time to close and lock the door before he recognized me.

"You!" His anger turned to fear and he looked back over his shoulder. It took him a few seconds to realize that the clown running toward him pointing a gun was probably a police officer. His shoulders sagged and he put his head on the hood of my car.

Chapter Twenty-Eight

PRETTY MUCH A LET DOWN, was how Scoobie characterized his short conversation with Turk. Scoobie had gotten Turk to say he hoped that there "were no hard feelings," but that was about it. Turk played dumb very well, but Scoobie was sure Turk suspected Scoobie had not just stopped by to say hello. Even so, Turk wouldn't have given the police much reason to arrest him on the spot if he hadn't left the carnival.

"Guilt by running," Morehouse said at the time.

A COUPLE DAYS AFTER 4th of July weekend Scoobie and I had again taken Josh and Max to dinner, this time at Burger King. It looked as if Max thought this should be a regular thing. I didn't know how long I could keep paying for their meals and Max's nervousness was wearing on me.

Scoobie and I had just made tea for Aunt Madge and helped ourselves to leftover muffins. We were discussing the 'carnival wiretapping' again, as Scoobie called it. "Turk didn't even turn off the Ferris Wheel when he left," Scoobie said. "About the fifteenth rotation some little kid threw up from almost the top…"

"More than we need to know, Adam," Aunt Madge said. She was on her sofa reading a book, something she doesn't often do. Usually if she's reading it's to skim a home repair magazine looking for projects. Apparently she was still healing from her ordeal, or she had decided life was too short to skip some good books.

Turk's stash of pot and miscellaneous pills was hidden in the same spot it had been when I had spotted it at the Asbury Park carnival. Police in several towns had been observing him. They hadn't arrested him yet because they were trying to catch him meeting with his supplier.

In addition to gathering evidence in Turk's attack on Scoobie, Ocean Alley and the state police thought there might be a link between Turk and the taller blonde carnival worker. The police seemed to think they worked together to do some pick pocketing during the carnivals, and that they might have committed home burglaries in several towns. I didn't care what they could charge Turk with as long as it was a lot so he'd be in prison a long time.

I still had not figured out how to "heal" completely from the tumult of the last few weeks. I could have lost Aunt Madge and Scoobie, two of the most precious people in my world. How is a person supposed to deal with that? *There must be something I could have done to keep them from getting hurt.* I kept asking Scoobie what I should have done differently, and he kept asking me why I felt guilty. It was starting to tick me off.

George was still barely talking to me. He thought I should have called him to say "what was going down at the carnival," as he put it. He also still maintained I should pay for his replacement mobile phone, and he was getting quite testy about it. He had retaliated for not being "in the loop on the carnival thing" by referring to my action with my car door as "risky behavior that should be left to law enforcement professionals or actors, neither of which is Ms. Gentil." He did this in a reflective column the editor let him write about how it felt to be part of the story instead of just writing about it. I thought it was a stretch to work me into it.

George did tell Aunt Madge and me that he had learned that Marcus/Masterson had clammed up, and maintained that he and Penny were just old friends who had reconnected. George had learned that the state police were showing their two pictures to pawnshop dealers up and down the Jersey coast, and many recognized them.

Plus, the police found Penny's purse in Masterson's trunk, so the police thought they "had him on that one," as Morehouse had said. And the room he took Aunt Madge to was not one he had registered for. It had been Penny's room during her last stay, and the key was in her purse. Apparently he was either cheap or trying not to leave a paper trail.

One way or another, Masterson was going to get what he deserved.

Ramona really wanted to go to Masterson's room at the hospital and demand to know if it was his gloved hand that had pulled her to the ground. However, as Scoobie pointed out, she had sold her drawing of a gloved hand for a pretty penny, so if he said it was his hand she might have to give him something for the inspiration. She was not amused.

Scoobie was loading a couple of Aunt Madge's extra muffins into his knapsack when the front doorbell rang. I went to answer it, assuming it was a new B&B guest, since most of them come in the side door once they check in.

"George, what are you doing here?"

"Scoobie and I are taking you somewhere," he said, and walked in.

I will always appreciate what George did for Aunt Madge, and I've come to understand some aspects of his humor. But I didn't like him just stopping by.

"Actually, we just got back…"

Scoobie stuck his head out of the kitchen. "Just be a minute, George."

"Grab your purse," George said.

"Are we talking ice cream?" I tried not to sound irritated.

"Maybe my cell phone store."

"Get a life."

I told Aunt Madge I wouldn't be long and got my purse and followed Scoobie and George out of the house. We'd driven for a couple minutes when George pulled into the parking lot at St. Anthony's.

I looked at Scoobie, and he gave me a noncommittal sort of grin. There were a couple other cars in the lot, so I guessed we were going to play bingo and wished I'd insisted on not coming.

They got out of the car and I followed, slowly. I figured I could walk back to the Cozy Corner if I needed to, though St. Anthony's is on the far end of town.

I should have brought my car. I hate depending on anyone. "What's up, guys?"

"We're giving you a helping hand," Scoobie held the door for me. George followed me in.

It took a second to get used to the dimmer light. A sign on a stand in front of us said "Twelve Step Meetings Downstairs."

I looked at both of them.

"Serenity prayer in action," Scoobie said.

"This," George said, "is where you start to learn to deal with what you can't control."

Ten thoughts went through my mind concurrently. Or maybe it was twelve. First, who did they think they were, bringing me to a twelve-step meeting? Not that there's anything wrong with them. Second, give me enough flexibility and I can control almost anything.

"I'm happy to be in charge of my life," I said, stiffly.

"You aren't in charge of any of the big things in your life, or other people's lives," Scoobie said, and started down the steps.

George gestured that I should follow Scoobie and I did so, reluctantly. I only walked downstairs to be polite. Contrary to their thinking, I managed my life pretty well. Hadn't the last few weeks shown that? Wait, they didn't.

We got to the bottom of the steps and signs pointed to Al-Anon, AA, NA, GA, and All-Anon. Scoobie was intent on where he was going, so I looked back at George. "What's All-Anon?"

"For any family member or friend of anybody with any kind of problem." He grinned. "Take your pick." More seriously he added, "I'd suggest All-Anon. We'll go to that one with you, then you're on your own if you come back."

We walked into the All-Anon room and a woman took a pillow off a shelf and put it on a seat for Scoobie. He talked to her for a moment and then walked back to me.

"Anonymous, remember?"

"I'll get you for this," I murmured, but I nodded.

He shrugged. "Take what you like and leave the rest. Or leave." He grinned.

I saw a couple of people I knew only slightly and nodded to them, but I didn't feel like talking to anyone. I'd seen Alcoholics Anonymous meetings depicted on television, but they never showed anything except somebody saying "I'm John Smith and I'm an alcoholic." I didn't know what to expect from what the sign on the wall said was a "friends and family group meeting."

George was helping himself to coffee and I studied his profile for a minute. I'd heard Scoobie say several times that he went to Narcotics Anonymous meetings, but I had no idea if George usually went with him, or to other meetings, or this one. Or if he just helped Scoobie corral me to this meeting.

I remembered George quietly putting something in a drawer in Scoobie's hospital room. It looked as if he and Scoobie knew each other better than I thought. Or differently, at least.

Chairs were set up in a large circle, and people began to sit down. I deliberately did not sit near Scoobie or George. The woman next to me handed me a small book called Courage to Change. I thumbed to the back and read the twelve steps of Al-Anon with the group. Apparently there was no book for All-Anon.

"Came to believe that a Power greater than ourselves could restore us to sanity." *Who says my sanity needs to be restored?* Besides maybe Aunt Madge. Or Harry. Or Ramona.

I was angry with Scoobie and George. How could they take me here without asking me? *Because they knew I wouldn't come if they asked.*

A woman about my age said she was struggling to come to terms with the fact that her sister, who she said drank and used pot, ran her car into a tree a couple months ago and died. "What else could I have done?" she kept asking.

Maybe stolen her keys? I noticed that while someone handed her a tissue no one really answered her question.

"For me, it's about choices," Scoobie was saying. "I'm trying really hard to choose to look ahead, not back. I'm finding it," he paused, "a lot harder right now.

Look ahead. I intended to look ahead to get people to understand why I can't leave loose ends alone, or at least get them to stop being mad at me when I try to find out something.

There was a white board at the front of the room and I read it.

Enlightening darkness unwinds
The power of light reminds
Pain offers no clear berth
Gratitude is rebirth
    Scoobie

Gratitude is rebirth. Okay, my choice was to be mad that Scoobie and George brought me here, but to be grateful they cared enough to do it. Tomorrow I'd figure how to get even. Tomorrow I'd show them I didn't need to be here.

Or maybe I'd come back.

* * * *

If you would like to read the rest of Scoobie's poem, finished as he healed, take a look.

Breakfast Table Cordial

As she undid the laces
Of her fragile mental health
Revealing to him places
Where she'd never been herself

Breakfast table cordial
Stage direction for the scene
Both being very careful
To not say what they mean

Struggling through the mourning
Of the night before
Juggling never-heeded warnings
From those who know the score

Much too close for comfort
In this game of truth or dare
A telephone-booth apartment
May be to blame, who really cares

Might as well admit it
This has been a big mistake
Fight like hell to fit it
But they knew it was a fake

Scoobie's ghost writer is real-world poet James W. Larkin.

About the Author

Elaine L. Orr writes four mystery series, including the thirteen-book Jolie Gentil cozy mystery series, set at the Jersey shore. Two of her books (including *Behind the Walls* in the Jolie series) have been finalists for the Chanticleer Mystery and Mayhem Awards.

Unscheduled Murder Trip, second in the Family History Mystery Series, received an Indie B.R.A.G Medallion. Other books are in the River's Edge Series (set in rural Iowa) and the Logland Series (set in small-town Illinois).

She also writes plays and novellas. A member of Sisters in Crime, Elaine grew up in Maryland and moved to the Midwest in 1994. She enjoys meeting readers at events throughout the country.

Authors always appreciate reviews. If you enjoyed *When the Carny Comes to Town* please post a review on your favorite web site or mention it on Instagram or Facebook, Let your local bookstore or library know that you liked a book. You can also contact Elaine to see if she would be available in person or via Zoom to talk to your community or book group.

❦

elaineorr.com

elaineorr.blogspot.com

elaineorr55@yahoo.com

Books in the
Jolie Gentil Cozy Mystery Series

Appraisal for Murder
Rekindling Motives
When the Carny Comes to Town
Any Port in a Storm
Trouble on the Doorstep
Behind the Walls
Vague Images
Ground to a Halt
Holidays in Ocean Alley
The Unexpected Resolution
The Twain Does Meet (novella)
Underground in Ocean Alley
Aunt Madge in the Civil Election (an Aunt Madge story)
Sticky Fingered Books
New Lease on Death
Jolie and Scoobie High School Misadventures (prequel)

Family History Mystery Series
Least Trodden Ground
Unscheduled Murder Trip
Mountain Rails of Old
Gilded Path to Nowhere

River's Edge Series — *set in rural Iowa*
Logland Series — *set in small-town Illinois*

*Books are at online retailers, or ask your library or
bookstore to order them — in print, large print, ebook
and audio. All books have Barnes and Noble editions,
which makes them easy to order from those stores.*

9 781948 070683